FINDING BIN LADEN

FINDING BIN LADEN

The Ultimate Reporting Assignment

a novel by Robert F. Diveley

iUniverse, Inc.
New York Lincoln Shanghai

Finding Bin Laden

The Ultimate Reporting Assignment

iUniverse books may be ordered through booksellers or by contacting:

iUniverse
2021 Pine Lake Road, Suite 100
Lincoln, NE 68512
www.iuniverse.com
1-800-Authors (1-800-288-4677)

ISBN: 0-595-33623-X

Printed in the United States of America

CHAPTER 1

▼

Four men concealed by white rags about their faces handled long knives as they appeared on the makeshift platform. Another man, blindfolded and bound, knelt before the men with his back toward them. The terrorist at the center stepped forward, raising a machete high above his head.

"Americans have been warned. The consequences of having spies disguised as reporters are upon your hands."

The speaker pulled the rag used as a blindfold away from the American reporter's eyes. A microphone was thrust under the trembling man's mouth.

"Please do as they say. Release the al-Qaeda prisoners held in Cuba. I beg you, save my life…I have children at…"

The kidnapper jumped to the reporter's side before he could finish his plea. He grabbed the shaking man's hair and with a swift motion swung the razor-sharp blade, severing the reporter's head while he was in mid-sentence. The force of the blow jerked the hair from the killer's grasp and caused the head to bounce and roll off the platform, leaving a bloody trail. The murderer retrieved it and held the wide-eyed face high above his head toward the camera while all four began to chant.

"Death to Americans. Praise to Allah."

Justin Davis, manager of the Associated Press branch in Boston, flipped on the lights. Two interns were seen scampering toward the exit of the conference room, covering their mouths as they heaved.

"Get the point? The tape is of your contemporary meeting his grotesque death televised by Al Jazeera TV last night," Justin stated seriously. The room grew silent as whispers turned to heads shaking side to side in disbelief.

"Is this really necessary, Justin?" Trish Alcort spoke up in a disgusted tone.

"I think you all need a rude awakening before I begin to hand out your assignments. That could be you. Just remember to watch yourselves over there," Justin barked back.

The competition to cover the Iraq War was intense. The war drums were beating. Every senior and junior reporter was calling in his or her favors. The war could make or break the career of a reporter. Justin Davis glanced across the eager eyes of the twenty or so seated in front of him. As he fumbled with the envelopes containing airline tickets, he knew half of them would be crushed by not getting the assignment. The others would perhaps be relieved. Because of abundant air support, the Afghan War had moved so quickly that "ground" interviews were almost nonexistent. Iraq, though, had been previewed as a long, "door-to-door" ground struggle, providing all the ingredients for the "in-the-trenches" reporting that could make one famous.

"Well there is no easy way to do this, so I'm going to handle it the way my boss did during Vietnam," Justin said while tapping the envelopes on his open hand. He began to pitch them toward the group.

"Jeff, Iraq, and take Barney with you."

"Gwen, the big show, and Dane will be your assistant."

Trish Alcort squirmed in her chair knowing she had little chance of making the A team to cover the Iraq War. Perhaps as a lowly assistant, but she had burned bridges by creating a stink after not getting the assignment to cover the Afghan War.

"Summer Tolly got hers when she and her boyfriend were given that plum. A shame about Jimmy, her beau, getting obliterated after hitting a land mine, but Summer is where she belongs, in the psych ward. It's what she deserved after gloating about the assignment," Trish thought to herself.

Trish was not interested in the Iraq job anyway. Her main goal was to convince Justin to send her to Afghanistan. She had intricate plans that depended wholly upon being located in that war-torn country.

"Sam and Trish as assistant, Pentagon background on Bin Laden and the Iraq connection."

"There must be a mistake. No way should I be relegated to digging through archives and fighting over the Freedom of Information Act. What are we going to report that has not been stated numerous times? There appears to be a connection…who cares anyway?" A million thoughts swirled through Trish's head. She needed to think fast to get what she required.

"No way, Justin," Trish said. "I want a real assignment, not some clerical research job. The real story on the connection is in Afghanistan. Finding Bin Laden is how to connect the dots. Wasting time and effort to prove that the Pentagon and president feel there is a connection is foolish. No one wants to read about their thoughts. They want to have the proof firsthand."

"Why do you have to break my balls at every turn?" Justin barked back. "Listen, we've already lost one reporter in Afghanistan. I don't want a repeat."

"There is so much to report in Afghanistan. The spin from the White House indicates a definite link between Iraq and al-Qaeda. It's my job to find the link, prove it, and report on it," Trish answered in a sarcastic voice.

"Where in the world do you start to put that together? You would need to find Bin Laden himself," Justin protested.

"Like all good reporters, you dig until you get the facts," Trish retorted. Her head was in her hands, rubbing her temples. She pulled her long brown hair over her contorted face and looked across at Sam.

Sam took pity on Trish and did agree with her stance.

"Justin, I tend to agree with Trish. The real story lies in al-Qaeda operations. Afghanistan is the epicenter of terrorism. The link to Iraq and Hussein will be found in Bin Laden's backyard," Sam stated factually.

"Okay, I'll bite. Sam, you and Trish cover the search for Bin Laden in Afghanistan."

"Thanks, Justin, but just one more little thing. I don't want Sam with me. I can do this on my own," Trish assured him.

"You have to be out of your mind if you think that after Jimmy got killed and Summer got injured I would allow you to go to Afghanistan alone," Justin stated emphatically.

"Equating my capabilities to no-talent Summer is absurd," Trish blurted. "I have more capability in my little finger than she can ever hope to have. Either I go to Afghanistan single-handedly, or I will find another news agency and report for them."

"Behind your pretty face is a callous and reckless little girl throwing fits when she doesn't get her way. No way am I giving you the assignment alone. You will assist Sam, and as soon as Summer is well enough, I will give her the same assignment. Then you two can look out for each other," Justin gibed.

"You are a prick, Justin Davis. You know little miss perfect and I will kill each other. This is not going to happen," Trish spewed.

"Oh, it will happen. Just you wait and see. Summer is getting better by the day, and she will hook up with you and Sam. Oh I would love to be there to see the fireworks," Justin said as he laughed.

"I can handle her the same way I have for years. You think she is crazy now; wait till she spends time competing with me."

"And while you're at it, miss know-it-all, find Bin Laden," Justin teased.

The whole room filled with laughter, most everyone beaming approval that Trish, the ultimate conceited bitch, had been put in her place. The reporters were expressing the same emotion some have when they see a famous person fall—not really disdain, but a reassurance that everyone is human no matter how rich, famous, or beautiful they might be. Trish held her looks above all of them, and having been Miss Rhode Island automatically set her up for the ridicule.

Trish did not wait to hear the rest of the assignments and stormed out of the meeting room, grabbing Sam by his necktie. When safely in the hallway, Trish let her feelings loose in a torrent of words.

"I am sick and tired of getting the short stick around here," Trish protested. "No matter what I do, all they think I am is a B queen, and I'm not saying the *B* stands for *beauty*. I am tempted to walk back in and tell Justin to stick this job up his ass."

"Settle down. We can dig the story out," Sam said, consoling her.

"Dig this," Trish said, "I am not going to be your assistant on anything. I guarantee I'll be working by myself, and I know just who to call to make it happen."

Trish walked away and pulled out her cell phone. Sam could see by her gestures that she was making her case to the person on the other end of the phone.

Sam knocked on the door to Justin's office and was waved in as Justin pointed to the seat in front of his overflowing desk.

"Trish is relentless," Sam said with concern. "She told me in no uncertain terms that she is going unaccompanied. She called someone, and I could tell she was pulling some strings."

"Trish Alcort has no strings to pull," Justin said. "She is a spoiled little brat and will either work with you on this or go elsewhere. I have too many issues to deal with, and babysitting is not one of them."

"What is the deal with her and Summer anyway?" Sam asked. "I thought she was going to explode when you mentioned that Summer would join her."

"It is a long story," Justin sighed. Trish and Summer are as different as two young women can be. They were both raised in New England, Trish wealthy and Summer a poor orphan. They ended up in college together and through unusual circumstances were pitted against each other at every turn. The final straw was when Trish became Miss Rhode Island and Summer won Miss Massachusetts. Both appeared in the Miss America Pageant. Trish was eliminated early on, and Summer made it to the final five. Summer was voted Miss Congeniality and beat Trish hands down in the swimsuit competition. Since then they have competed on every level. In fact, Trish applied for the job here after she found out Summer was working with AP. The competition has been ugly most of the time. Trish has such hatred for Summer that she actually laughed when I announced at our staff meeting that Summer was injured and that her boyfriend, Jimmy, was killed during the Afghan War."

"Holy crap. I knew Trish hated Summer, but I never knew why," Sam said in surprise.

"Yeah, it's a real cat fight," Justin said. "I threw out Summer's name because I know it eats at Trish something terrible. The truth is I don't know if Summer will ever be well enough to work again. The fact is you are going to be the lead on this story, and Trish will assist you or I will fire her on the spot."

The phone on Justin's desk rang, and he interrupted his conversation with Sam to take the call. Sam noticed Justin's rough demeanor change when he spoke to the unknown caller. Justin hung up with his index finger and threw the receiver across the room.

"That lousy bitch went over my head," Justin growled. "That was the CEO telling me that Trish Alcort will have the Afghanistan assignment, and she will be traveling by herself. How does a cub reporter get to the CEO? Son of a bitch."

"Does that mean I'm off the story?" Sam questioned.

"What it means is that she has me by the balls and is just starting to squeeze," Justin spewed violently. "If you haven't figured it out yet, she just chopped yours off."

Trish Alcort came from a wealthy Rhode Island family purportedly connected to the original Mayflower descendents. In some manner it helped make her father tremendously wealthy as a commodity trader. The connections gained through his lineage amassed a fortune that allowed Trish to grow up in lavish surroundings.

Her mother had died of breast cancer when she was only twelve years old. Since that time, her father had overcompensated with money to fill the void a daughter must feel after losing a mother. In reality Trish had not been very close to her mother, having been raised by servants. Her mother's time had been consumed by Junior League and yacht club functions. It wasn't until she had gone away to Wellesley College that she ever heard of anyone being brought up sans the benefit of a Nanny. She could not imagine being without a stable of horses beyond the swimming pool, and not having a winter home in Miami was just too perplexing for her young mind.

Trish had attended prep school at Stoneleigh-Burnham, the famous all-girl facility just outside Springfield, Massachusetts. Her acceptance at nearby Wellesley College was assured after her father made a gracious multimillion-dollar endowment. Her beauty was natural, except for a bit of nose tweaking done as a prep-school graduation gift and, more recently, expanding her breasts to a 34-D. Trish looked upon these as necessities and knew of no one who didn't get a little aid when it came to appearance. During her senior year, Trish had decided to go out for Miss Rhode Island. She did not need the scholarship money and did not intend to spread any type of message. She was convinced it would be an easy win. She heard Summer Tolly had won the Miss Massachusetts title and would be going to Atlantic City for Miss America. "Another chance to beat the orphan," Trish had concluded.

Trish had been in shock and could not comprehend how she did not win Miss America. She had heard all her life how beautiful she was from her mother, her father, and their servants. Trish was certain the only reason she did not win the pageant was because Summer had beaten her in the swimsuit competition. Trish, being somewhat less endowed before her surgery, knew Summer must have had breast enlargements. She would bet Summer's had not been that big at Wellesley.

Trish's love life was a complex matter. Her chestnut mane, olive-colored skin, and green eyes assured her of much attention from the opposite sex. Her perfect body molded onto her five-foot-five-inch frame always turned heads, male and female, wherever she appeared.

Trish had one convenient romance while she was at Wellesley. She had an "affair of the heart," as she described it, with her English professor. That he was in his forties and married with grown children her age did not bother Trish in the least. She had needed the stability to get her through her college days, and her daddy was not close at hand. She considered only her feelings, and if others were hurt along the way, it was their fault. Her middle-aged lover had trained her in the sophisticated arena of prose, and Trish had given an eloquent rendition of "Treatise on the Astrolabe," by Geoffrey Chaucer, in the talent portion of the pageant. Having no other ability, it had propped her beauty to the top of the heap in the state contest.

Most young women produce streams of tears having the rhinestone tiara placed upon their head. Trish had smiled confidently, having the assurance all along that the talent, swimsuit, and evening-gown competitions only filled time until they would surely crown her. The walk down the stage with her new crown would be a mere formality. Her green eyes reflected brilliantly in the lights, and the audience knew they were looking at the next Miss America.

The affair had ended abruptly when Trish refused to return the professor's phone calls after she graduated from college. He was cognizant that Trish had used him during her college years. It was also evident that she took advantage of the coaching he had given her, assuring her title. It did not matter to him, and it was a relief to end a situation he knew led nowhere, but his unlikely casting as surrogate father during this time was something he would remember the rest of his life. Although they'd had a limited physical relationship, he treasured the few times he had held her until dawn, helping her cope with the many tragedies that can befall a beautiful coed.

In a final gesture, he had sent an original poem covering the time they had spent together, reflecting on how it had changed his life. Trish had jerked the note from the envelope and scanned the first few stanzas. Without any guilt, she had thrown it in the trash. Being a grown woman and Miss Rhode Island, she had no time for any of the trivial childhood things of her past.

Trish's zest for travel was reinforced by the many appearances she made in connection with her title. Toward the end of her reign, she realized her talent for poetry reading would not take her far in this world.

Trish had no need to worry about money, due to Daddy, but she was interested in a career in journalism. This path allowed travel and sharing her unique perspective with the world. Trish was convinced she had superior qualities to the idiots who interviewed her during her tenure as Miss Rhode Island. She was positive she had the beauty and composure to be an excellent on-screen reporter, perhaps like Diane Sawyer or even Barbara Walters. It would be a blessing, she thought, for the world to wake up to her each and every morning.

The opportunity at Associated Press was ideal. She could travel and illuminate her ability to delve deep inside any topic or story. AP was a stepping-stone to big-time stardom, and she felt she owed it to the world. Just a few years of showing her serious reporting style would certainly lead to her replacing the middle-aged TV personalities, a plan devised in the heavens, she thought, and one she would pursue with passion.

Justin Davis appeared beaten. He wore the years of late nights, spiked coffee, and cigarette smoking on his weathered face. It seemed he always left a patch of scruff on his face every morning. Justin eyed the fax he had just received.

Confidential Fax Memo

To: Justin Davis

I want to confirm our earlier phone conversation. Trish Alcort is to be given the Afghan assignment without hesitation. Provide her with all requested support including financial and personnel. The matter is of a top-secret nature and is not open for discussion. The assignment is to be operated on a need-to-know basis, and this is all you need to know. I instruct you to shred this document after reading.

CEO

Justin placed the fax into the shredder next to his desk as instructed. His thoughts turned from rage to wonder as he pressed the "on" button. How in the world did this twenty-five-year-old woman get involved with something like this, he thought. As the paper was reduced to a hundred threads, he took the pint of Jack Daniels from his drawer, poured a generous amount into his coffee cup, and toasted.

"Here's to the prettiest snake I ever laid eyes on. Good luck little lady. I hope the mongoose doesn't get you."

Justin threw back the swill, knowing that Trish Alcort was on a course of her own demise. Unfortunately she is just too much in love with herself to realize it.

CHAPTER 2

▼

Summer Tolly sat motionless, staring out over the verdant lawn at Sunnyview Farms. A pretty name for a mental facility, and it would have one believe it was an agricultural operation, but the only farming was the planting of injections daily to keep the residents in tow.

Although she sat in the wheelchair, she really had no biological reason she couldn't walk. It was only her desire to walk, talk, or take any pleasure in life that held her back from being well again.

Summer had that natural, "all-American girl" look attributed to young models romping on the beach with their long blond hair wafting in the breeze while selling Coppertone. Her hair still reached down to her waist but was now pulled tightly into a ponytail. The aides would have liked nothing more than to cut it short for ease of care, but she protested so loudly when it was suggested that they just washed it and pulled it back. Summer's blue eyes were lifeless and dilated most of the time from her drug regimen. The fine features of her face accented her willowy body. Even with no exercise these last eight months, she still had a physique that most young women would kill to have.

Summer had started with AP the fall after she graduated from college. She was happy that she could stay in her hometown of Boston. More importantly, she was thrilled that her high school sweetheart was also still there. Jimmy Murphy had met Summer when the two attended Southy High School. He was a rough-and-tumble hockey player she had fallen head over heals in love with during her junior year. Jimmy seemed to have new stitches somewhere on his face every week. If it wasn't getting hit with the puck in the nose, it was some high sticking that gave him a new battle scar on his forehead. Summer looked past all the imperfections and could only see good in this red-headed, tank-built kid. She had always felt safe with him and had never given a second thought to riding the subway around Boston, any time of day or night, with him on her arm. He was her strength, and she knew she could lean on him for the rest of her life. They were going to get married once their hectic lives settled down a bit.

Summer was given an opportunity of a lifetime when she was asked by AP to cover the Afghan War. She was fairly new, but she was needed because a large geographical presence was required to cover Afghanistan. Due to the warring tribal factions in the northeast and the Taliban in the south and southwest, reporters would be spread out to get maximum exposure to where the war was happening.

Summer had only one condition: that AP hire Jimmy as her assistant. Jimmy knew nothing about reporting or about Afghanistan. In fact, he had never been much further than Cape Cod, but Summer refused anyone but him. He was the only one she felt safe with, and it was essential in order for her to comply with Justin Davis's wishes. Justin reluctantly gave his approval because he was pressed to get reporters out in the field as quickly as possible. The war developing in Afghanistan was not a real surprise, but all news agencies hate to commit resources until it is certain. Jimmy took to his new job with enthusiasm due to his desire to protect and be with Summer.

Justin Davis had regretted the decision almost immediately when other reporters started with their demands after hearing of the accommodation.

Justin had pulled everyone into the conference room and had stated clearly: "Life is not fair, war is not fair, and I am not fair. If anyone asks me for any change to their assignment, even as much as a request for a new pen, they will be fired on the spot. Understood?"

Two months had passed while Summer and Jimmy spent their time cruising the streets of Kabul, looking for someone to interview. Not only did they not understand the language, but the local interpreter assigned to them looked upon their living arrangements with disdain. It was a sin to be living together without the benefit of marriage, and he made it clear he did not approve. Summer and Jimmy were carefree, ignoring the many signals a seasoned traveler would have interpreted as crossing the line.

Summer received a report that most of the troop buildup was occurring in the northern regions, just across the border in Uzbekistan. She wanted to go, and Jimmy was all for getting out of the city. The interpreter warned them that there were many factions in that area, not all of them Afghans, and that in fact some were tribes with differing ties, some even supported by Iran.

The warning fell on deaf ears, and the three proceeded on the long trek toward the northern border. Camping at night with nomads lent a bit of a romantic aura to Summer and Jimmy's nights, neither of them realizing the disgust their seemingly innocent touching and kissing was forming within their hosts' minds and hearts.

It was early morning, just before daybreak, when the interpreter summoned Summer and Jimmy.

"Hurry, get your things. We must go now. The Taliban are less than an hour away, and we must make the border before they catch up to us."

Jimmy and Summer were confused, since the Taliban were concentrated in the southwest and in Kabul. They pulled on their clothes, gathered their belongings, and threw everything into the back of the Humvee. Jimmy was racing the engine as Summer called out her window to the interpreter.

"Come on, let's go now if you want to get going," she shouted.

"No, you two go ahead. I'll catch up later. It will be faster for you alone." The interpreter did not give her a chance to answer as he turned and ran back toward the tents.

"Hit it baby," Summer summoned Jimmy.

They had not made it four clicks when a horrendous explosion tossed the eight-thousand-pound vehicle tumbling end over end into the air. The Humvee landed top down, with the windshield cutting across Jimmy's chest. Summer was thrown free, and she scurried toward the vehicle, yelling for Jimmy. She could see he was hurt and smelled gasoline strongly. She began to pull his arms away from the windshield. Using all her might, she finally felt a sudden release and fell backward holding Jimmy's hands. She pulled herself up to see, to her horrid amazement, that she had only pulled half of Jimmy from the wreck. His bloody entrails followed along the path made by the upper half of his body. The Humvee had cut him in two, but Summer was still trying to get a response from him. She reached for the golden four-leaf clover hung around his neck, when suddenly there was a huge rush of hot air that Summer felt blow her hair backward. Jimmy's demise was not confirmed to her until almost a week later when she became conscious at the army hospital in Saudi Arabia.

Fortunately for Summer, Army Rangers patrolling the area heard the blast and came to find the disaster. An inquiry into how the accident happened reached no conclusion. The official report stated that civilians were where they shouldn't have been and had by accident run over a Taliban land mine.

The perplexing thing about the investigation was that there were no Taliban in the area and no other land mines found. The Rangers who investigated the accident suspected that the interpreter or nomads had made it look like an accident. They could not prove it and wrote it off as a casualty of war.

The streetwise Justin Davis knew he had made a mistake when he read the Western Union message from the army about Jimmy's death. Sending "green" reporters into a war zone was bad enough, but to involve innocent young people with the uncertainty that a foreign country like Afghanistan contains was irresponsible. He knew in his heart that the lovebirds had no place over there, but the pressure to cover the story had blinded his judgment.

The walk up to the ten-foot-tall doors at Sunnyview Farms was a long one. Justin had not slept in three days, worrying about what he would say to Summer. He had been warned that this once vibrant young woman would probably not even acknowledge him, but he felt compelled to see her. Justin thought talking to her could snap her out of her mental state and, more importantly, give him some peace. Seeing Summer sitting in the wheelchair, blankly staring through him, was more that he could tolerate.

Justin had this tough "newsman" image but was as gentle as a small boy inside. He could not stop the tears from streaming down his face as he knelt next to her chair. After a long struggle to get anything audible from his lips, he moaned.

"Oh Summer, why did you let me do this to you?" Justin asked. "I am so sorry."

The moment was broken when a heavyset black woman came behind the chair and, while pushing Summer away, stated, "Time for your bath, baby. We'll wash this gorgeous long blond hair of yours today."

Justin struggled to his feet and watched her disappear through his tears. "I'll be back to see you," he said quietly. "Next time we can talk."

Summer looked back at Justin and, through her drug-induced fog, felt guilty that she could not confide in him. She knew that Jimmy's death was no accident, and she could not trust anyone, especially anyone associated with AP.

Summer was slowly pulling herself from the darkness. She had started to hide the pills they were forcing on her, and the many injections had been reduced to only one a day. Summer's mind was clearing as she began to take stock of her situation and life.

She had relied so heavily upon Jimmy for everything that she found herself at a loss and empty. As her mind became lucid, the reality struck her without notice. All her life, people had viewed her as the "poor little orphan girl." She had fallen into the trap of letting Jimmy be her strength. She loved Jimmy, but now she had to acquire her own resolve. Never again would she rely on another for her own safety or happiness. The tragic event had forced Summer to become her own person. Now she was determined to control her life and never be pitied again.

Summer concluded that faking her mental illness was the best alternative for her own safety. She was confident she had the tenacity to take on the murderers, but she needed some assistance with the daunting task. The only trusted individual she could count on was Chip, Jimmy's brother. Until she could meet with him, she had to continue her ruse.

CHAPTER 3

▼

Sitting in the Sumner Tunnel to Logan Airport during rush hour is never a pleasant thing. The carbon monoxide from backed up traffic is sure to kill you if you don't die of sudden heart failure due to worry about missing the last flight out for the day.

Trish Alcort took out her cell phone to check on her flight status. Being in a tunnel underneath Boston Harbor, she had no reception. She pushed the button to lower the privacy panel between her and the limo driver.

"Get us the hell out of this tunnel," Trish yelled at the driver. "I am choking to death and can't even use my phone."

"Sorry, madam. Traffic is backed way up to ninety-three."

"If I miss my flight, I will call your boss, and you will never drive again. Get it, you pinhead?" Trish prodded.

The driver pulled around the stopped traffic and drove in the emergency lane, scraping the side of the black limo as he made his way to the end of the tunnel. He knew he would have to explain the damage to the vehicle, but it was much easier than dealing with this prima donna.

The commotion at the entrance of Logon Airport could only mean one of two things. Either the Queen of England had just arrived or Trish Alcort was making her appearance known. The ticket agent swung around to see Trish smiling and waving to groups of confused passengers as a skycap was dragging her matching ensemble of bags toward the counter. Trish was under the illusion that everyone knew her as Miss Rhode Island. The reality was that, outside of the smallest state, few people would recognize her at all. The skycap piled her bags in the cutaway at the counter and held out his hand.

"Here's all your bags, madam," the skycap said.

Trish glanced at the man's outstretched hand and turned away from him toward the ticket counter. The man, seeing he was about to be stiffed, made another attempt.

"I'm sorry, I don't think you heard me. Here are your bags," he said politely.

Trish turned to the man in anger. "You think I am blind? I see my bags are here. If you are waiting for a tip, well here it is. Go to law school. Then you won't have to beg for money."

The man felt blood rush to his head and began to speak. "Law school? I'll give you law school, you spoiled brat." The skycap had been beaten out of a tip before, but her attitude was particularly cruel. He waved his arm toward her as a sign to forget it and walked away before she could speak any further.

Trish turned her attention back to the ticket agent. "Where do you get these surly people? If he were my servant, I would have fired him on the spot."

"Sorry, miss, how can I help you?" the agent responded.

"Gee, let's see," Trish said in a smart-ass tone. "Could it be that I may want to travel? Where do you people come from, anyway?"

The ticket agent was ready to let this inconsiderate snob have it between her eyes and then took a deep breath and silently mumbled, "This takes the cake."

Trish slammed down her ticket jacket on the counter before the woman. "I need seat assignments to London and all the way through to Afghanistan. You will note that these are first class. For my flight from London, I need to sit next to my traveling companion, Mr. Harrison. Think you can handle it?"

The ticket agent began entering the information and called her supervisor over to look at her computer screen. Both women began nodding in agreement.

"I'm sorry, Miss Alcort," said the agent, "but these tickets are coach, not first class, and Mr. Harrison is in the first-class cabin." The agent seemed happy to be getting even with this pompous snob.

Trish stared at the woman, burning holes in her head with her evil eyes. She dialed her phone and covered her mouth as she spoke. The agent turned away to answer a question for another worker and then turned back to Trish.

"Check again, you inept fool," Trish said in a mean demeanor. "I am sure they are first class."

The agent looked, although certain and double-checked with her supervisor that it was a coach ticket. As she watched her screen, the seat assignments suddenly changed, as if by magic, to the first-class seats she was demanding.

"I don't know how you did it, but here are your boarding passes as requested," the ticket agent said in an apologetic voice.

"It's not what you know, but who you know," Trish spit as she grabbed the passes. "Next time be more cooperative."

"Yes, Miss, I will keep that in mind."

Trish moved toward security with her phone to her ear and again acknowledged strangers that she thought were admiring her.

The ticket agent pulled the luggage tags from two of her bags and neatly attached new ones routing the bags to Hong Kong. "You may have had the last word, you stuck up bitch, but I have the power to ruin your day," she laughed as she threw the bags on the conveyor.

Trish made certain she was the first to board the flight from London to Kabul. She wanted to make sure she had the appropriate seat next to Curtis Harrison. Once on the plane, she calmly leafed through a *Vogue* magazine as she waited. An attractive man walked toward the empty seat beside her. She made every attempt to seem engrossed in her reading as he approached.

"Miss Alcort, I am Curtis Harrison," the man stated in an English accent as he extended his hand.

Trish slowly scooted forward in her seat and limply offered him her hand, palm down. Being the proper English gentleman, he softly kissed her hand on its supple back.

"Curtis. So nice to meet you in person," Trish acknowledged.

Curtis Harrison settled into his seat, pulled down the tray table, and leaned on it as he began to speak.

"I must say, Miss Alcort, I was completely taken aback when you called me for this meeting. I have worked with your father for many years, and I am quite confused at your offer."

"There should be no confusion, Curtis. As you can see, I am a pretty young woman who is interested in the finer things in life. I do know your relationship with my father has been, let us say, less than desirable. I think we would make a better partnership, now don't you?" Trish asked as she placed her hand on his.

"Certainly a more pleasurable one, that is for sure," Curtis replied.

Curtis Harrison was a handsome, thirty-something English gentleman from London. He graduated from Oxford University and had since then owned various importing and exporting companies. Five years ago he purchased a permanent residence in Afghanistan, where he continued his business activities unaffected by the recent war. He owned a flat in London, where he visited quite often. Curtis excelled at all sports, and he maintained his six-foot-two-inch frame in perfect condition. His dark hair was set off by his tan skin, sustained by frequent trips to the islands in the Caribbean. Curtis Harrison had no problem finding suitable female companionship and surrounded himself with the best the world has to offer. Having a net worth exceeding a billion dollars did not hurt his endeavors.

Trish was excited upon seeing this attractive man. She noticed immediately the Rolex around his wrist and the custom-made suit he was wearing. She knew they would be consummating their business arrangement soon, but now it was important to sell her charms.

Trish spent most of the conversation talking about her favorite subject, herself. She would interrupt her story only by asking him rather direct questions about his money.

"Curtis, do you go to Afghanistan often for your business?" she asked. "Do you make a lot of money from this ravaged country?"

"I enjoy the culture and the people, and yes, I am able to get product in Afghanistan that is of the finest quality for the right price," he explained. •

"I have never been to Afghanistan, but I have to go where the stories are happening. My boss should have sent me to Iraq, but I am on a special assignment to explore the Iraq and al-Qaeda connection," Trish explained, sounding as though it was the most important assignment in the world.

"It can be very dangerous for a pretty young woman traveling unaccompanied in Kabul," Curtis said. "Could I offer my service?"

Trish took another look at this attractive man. He was obviously wealthy by excising goods from this poor country. His looks were that of a model, with dark black hair and a nice tan. He took his suit coat off, and she viewed his toned and solid body. His quick smile showed perfect teeth that must have been porcelain veneers. That didn't bother Trish, having had a little cosmetic help of her own. Trish was at first uneasy at the way he would lean toward her when he talked, like everything was a secret. She was impressed that he was very interested in her life and career, to the point that he did not want to talk about himself.

"I am staying at the Mustafa Hotel in Kabul," Trish said. "Call me there, and perhaps I can get loose for an evening so you can show me the nicer side of Kabul." She spoke with her head turned slightly, flirting her way along as she had become accustomed to doing.

"I have business in northern Afghanistan and will be returning in a couple of days," Curtis said. "It's a date. I will call you upon my return."

"Then we will discuss our business," Trish said, making sure to remind him of her intentions as she handed him her cell-phone number.

Once on the runway, the plane came to an abrupt halt. Trish thought something must be wrong and turned toward Curtis for reassurance.

"It's okay," Curtis said. "They don't have the full runway fixed after the bombing yet, so they have to stop quick."

Trish flashed him a smile as she had learned in her beauty-pageant days. Her eyes lit up as she realized that perhaps her idea of taking over her father's business was looking better. She made a special effort to check out his rear end while he was reaching for his jacket in the overhead compartment.

Still seated, she spoke without realizing it. "Very nice," she said softly.

"Pardon me, Trish, did you say something?" Curtis questioned.

"Oh, ah, nice to meet you. I'll expect to hear from you in a couple of days. Where is your home?" Trish asked.

"I have a home just outside Kabul. I'll call you. And be careful; there is still a lot of dissent among the people," Curtis said as he walked ahead of her off the plane.

Trish proceeded to the baggage-claim area. Along the way, she witnessed Curtis getting into a long limo with armed guards in jeeps positioned to protect the front and rear. A pretty young Afghan woman met him at the door of his Rolls Royce. He handed her his attaché case, and she moved into the driver's seat.

"No competition there," Trish said to herself.

After he shook some hands, he entered the backseat, and the convoy drove quickly off the tarmac. "Very impressive," Trish thought, wishing she could ride with him.

Trish had a feeling she really could not describe toward this man. Could she in fact like this man? It was almost too unrealistic to consider. She was looking forward to spending more time with this interesting man, and she was also extremely anxious to strike a deal guaranteed to make her independently wealthy.

The minivan that took her to the heart of Kabul and her hotel was normally used to transport six people. However, due to the amount of Trish's luggage, even having two pieces lost, it could barely accommodate her and the driver.

The first thing Trish noticed was the smell. She could not decide if it was burning garbage, some sort of native food, or the body odor of her driver, who was wrapped in sheets. She knew he had to be sweating a tremendous amount, since even she that never sweats was getting a few droplets on her forehead. "No air-conditioning in a cab? How barbaric," she thought. She glanced at the driver, and he was jabbering away on his phone in Pashto, the local language.

Every once in a while he would laugh, and Trish suspected it was about her. If she were not so tired from the fight, she definitely would have demanded better treatment.

On pulling up to the front of the Mustafa Hotel, Trish immediately noticed many armed U.S. soldiers around the premises. She had not had time to call her father before her departure, but she made a mental note to leave out the part about the armed soldiers when she did call. The hotel looked dusty and old and certainly did not deserve any rating from Formers. She only hoped the inside would be more suitable.

Trish was very hungry because the food in first class was not prepared to her taste. The filet mignon and lobster were grossly undercooked. She asked the flight attendant to cook it some more, and she had the nerve to tell Trish it was the best they could do while in flight. Trish pushed the meal back toward the attendant, ignoring the fact that it fell directly on the attendant's feet. Therefore, having had nothing since the croissant on the way to London, she was starved, which added to her foul mood.

Three bellmen dragged Trish's luggage through the revolving doors at the front of the hotel's lobby. Trish wondered how she could manage in this second-rate hotel until Curtis called her. Without warning, she heard a huge roar and the sound of glass shattering behind her. Trish turned her head in time to see parts of bodies flying from the remains of a charred bus in front of the hotel. A severed arm hit the door just behind her, and she watched as it made a streak of blood down the broken glass and landed on the marble floor next to her with a dull thud. Trish was too shocked to duck or run for cover, and she stood there in disbelief as the lobby erupted with shouts from every corner.

Two American GIs came charging toward her, each taking her under the arms and rushing her into the coffee shop just adjacent to the lobby. She was told to stay put and lie down in the booth where they had placed her. She peeked up to see the young Afghan woman who had been driving Curtis Harrison walking slowly toward the front door, stepping around legs, arms, and torsos to get out to the burning bus.

"What is she thinking," Trish wondered. "Is she crazy, or is she trying to locate me for Curtis Harrison?" Regardless, Trish was shaking so hard that there was no way she was going to try and attract her attention in this mayhem.

Trish surveyed the carnage and the frantic movement of army personnel pulling screaming bodies away from the fire. She could see the young Afghan woman looking intently over each body, trying to discern any recognizable features telling her who these unfortunates were. The woman methodically weaved her way through the bloody gore to the car that was also on fire behind the bus. Shielding her face, she quickly opened the back door and found who she was evidently trying to locate. The older Arab man seated in the back had blood gushing so hard from his jugular vein that it was spraying the front windshield. It appeared to Trish that the young woman was attempting to help this severely injured man. The girl reached over to him and, glancing about to make sure no one was observing, took a small box cutter in her hand and made another slash across his neck, assuring his death. The man slumped down as GIs rushed to the Afghan woman's back and pulled her away, not noticing what she had done. The flames hit the car's gas tank, and it exploded with a shudder.

Trish's first reaction was intrigue at what she had just witnessed. The young woman she had seen with Curtis Harrison at the airport had just now slit a man's throat. Trish huddled even further down into the booth protecting her. She was impressed that Curtis would instruct his staff to commit murder. "Curtis Harrison is a man of business," she thought to herself.

"I can use this information as an advantage, having seen firsthand his young servant's deed," Trish thought. "He will be unhinged that I personally witnessed the murderous event. He will be in debt to me for my silence, and my plan will work even smoother. Yes, things are falling into place even better than I imagined." Trish smiled.

CHAPTER 4

▼

Curtis Harrison had his TV on in the back of his limo as he sat waiting for his driver to return. A special bulletin flashed across the screen. He looked down at the *London Times* he was holding and ignored the report. Both of his bodyguards reacted and turned up the volume. The reporter for Al Jazeera Television came on in Arabic speaking in somber tones. Curtis had learned the difficult language as a necessity for doing business in this part of the world. He was not an expert, but he could easily get the gist of most conversation.

He looked up as if interested.

"There has been an explosion that has rocked a hotel in central Kabul. The Mustafa Hotel has been identified as the site where a bomb has exploded in front of the hotel. A car and a bus were involved, and police indicate that the car was the source of the bomb. The three men in the car were reported dead at the scene. At least eighteen on the bus are dead, with another twelve injured and taken to the hospital. The license plate of the car showed it to be owned by Arab business-man Abdul-Aliyy. He is well known in Afghanistan as one of the major producers of heroin. Police suspect that the bombing may have been a professional hit on this wealthy man. The hotel is the normal place where American and Western journalists reside. The damage to the front lobby area of the hotel is extensive, although no injuries were reported to its guests. Al Jazeera will bring you pictures as soon as our reporters are on site."

Curtis picked up the cell phone located in the car console next to him and dialed a number. "I see the package was delivered? Good, and how about our nemesis? Have we been successful in eradicating this problem? You have done well, my friend. I will wire the funds to your account." Curtis was beaming when he hung up the phone.

The bodyguards looked upon their boss with wonder. How could he be so happy when such a terrible thing had just occurred? They could never understand the Western mind.

Curtis again picked up the phone and told the person on the other end, "It is confirmed, wire the money, the deal is closed."

His home, as Curtis had described it to Trish Alcort, consisted of over one hundred acres close to Meydan Shar on the Derya-ye Helmand River. This lavish home had during the war received only a few small blemishes on its impressive twelve-foot-tall walls that surrounded the entire property. Most people of Afghanistan thought it to be a castle or training center for the Taliban. It was actually fully owned by Curtis Harrison and, depending upon the current political environment, was protected by the ruling army.

Curtis had been adept at assuring that his mega-investments in Afghanistan were well protected at all costs and had never been timid when paying the right people for these services. The property consisted of eight large buildings strategically placed for total enjoyment of the beautiful view of the river below. Each of the forty-eight guest suits was positioned for maximum privacy and enhancement of the relaxing scenery. The estate was without question an escape from the rigors of daily life in Afghanistan and yet was still very close to the major resources Kabul had to offer.

Curtis surrounded himself with beautiful things and stunning women. It was not unusual to have six or more beauties lounging by the half-acre pool Curtis had designed. He was a man of excess and made sure he had a constant supply of funds to support his expensive habits. The only inconvenience since the war had been restricted airspace, which did not allow him to bring his personal jet into the country. He hoped the law would be lifted soon because flying commercial was well below his standards, although he did have a pleasant time with a very pretty lady this trip, he thought to himself.

"She will be a nice addition to the surroundings, but she probably will not like being one of the playthings. I think she will have to be handled special, the way only I know how to manage," he thought to himself.

Breaking his serine thoughts, his assistant came bursting through the study doors.

"Welcome home, Mr. Harrison. I trust you were pleased with the news regarding the hotel bombing," said the young Afghan beauty.

"Yasmina, my beautiful one. Yes, I am pleased, and excellent timing as always. Now I can get down to business with him out of the way. Did you set up the meeting with the growers? I need to meet with them to talk about production, and also set up a meeting with our plant managers. I require information quickly, so see if we can't get these meetings out of the way in the next couple of days. I want my schedule clear in three days. I have a very special visitor coming, and I don't want any business to get in the way," Curtis exhorted to his assistant as she quickly made notes on her handheld PDA.

"Yes, Mr. Harrison," Yasmina replied, "I will take care of everything."

The early morning had always been the favorite time of day for Curtis Harrison. After arriving the prior evening, he had done little more than organize his agenda and treat himself to his choice of pleasures picked from the pool area. The girls knew the routine, and after he had satisfied himself, they removed themselves from his chambers to one of the other guest areas. One poor girl had made the mistake of falling asleep in his bed with him, and, well, let's just say she is no longer with us.

It seemed the servants knew every move and desire of Mr. Harrison. As soon as he was up and had his feet to the ground, his tea was served with two crumpets and a soft-boiled egg.

The balcony off his bedroom offered the best view of the river and the land beyond. Every morning when he was in residence, it was the same. After about thirty minutes, he began his shower in the marble enclave with sixteen strategically placed showerheads. He scrubbed hard to get the stink off of himself after a night with his pleasures. Not because the young women wore heavy cologne or makeup, which was forbidden, but only to wash the shame off his body. It took him several minutes to rid himself of the disgust he felt the next morning for taking tremendous advantage of these young women.

Most were still in their teens, and, as they all came from a Muslim background, their families would never accept them home again after what they had done. Retirement from these positions was literally life threatening, whether they stayed at the estate or went back to Kabul. This was baffling, since their families had gladly accepted the money when the young girls had been purchased. But once the young age, beauty, and innocence were taken away, they were of little use and were disposed of like rotting fruit.

Curtis walked from the bathroom, drying his hair as he craned his neck to view the aircraft hanger beyond the pool. He could see his Bell 407 Jet Ranger helicopter being pulled from the structure, readying it for today's adventure. The helicopter could fly at nearly 256 kilometers per hour carrying six passengers.

Curtis, an avid pilot himself, not only enjoyed the speed to cover large areas of his enterprise, but this was known as the "pilot's helicopter." He became almost giddy at the thought of taking the controls, and although today's trip was business, he was looking forward to flying his impressive machine. His thoughts were interrupted by a knock at his door, and Yasmina, his voluptuous assistant, entered.

"Mr. Harrison, I have your agenda for you today. The meeting with the producers is set for 10 AM, and at 1 PM you'll meet here with the members of the Shura Council. I understand Saleh will be here personally."

"Ah, Saleh himself. I have not seen him in ages," Curtis responded casually. "Please prepare a special present for him along with our usual contribution."

"Do you have a choice of which young girl you feel appropriate for Saleh?" Yasmina asked her boss.

"You make the choice. Just make sure she is young, the way he likes them," Curtis stated, smiling.

Yasmina laid the written agenda on the terrace table and asked, "anything else, Mr. Harrison?"

"Yasmina, I want to leave within thirty minutes to get an early start. Make sure the helicopter is fueled and serviced at once. I'll see you at the copter in a few minutes."

"Yes, I will take care of everything."

Curtis watched as Yasmina slowly backed from the room, closing the doors behind her. He was definitely attracted to this well-endowed beauty, but she was different. He had brought her to the ranch twelve years ago from the Kabul slums. Initially he considered her to be another one of his toys, but she took to him in a fatherly way. Curtis had never had any children he knew of and had decided to take a special interest in Yasmina.

The only time they were apart was when Yasmina went away to the United States to attend college. Curtis felt that her time in the States had been extremely valuable. Yasmina had returned a well-educated woman with a Bachelor of Science degree in technology. She had been essential to his operation ever since. She was now twenty-four, and her gorgeous exterior was fully complimented by her intelligence. Although Curtis had been tempted several times to "cross the line" with her, he held back and kept her pure. Curtis wanted at least one unspoiled thing in his life, and he lavished Yasmina with both material things and guidance. The other women at the ranch were green with envy because Yasmina had her own accommodations and free access to Mr. Harrison.

The trip to the northern region normally took only forty-five minutes in the Bell Jet helicopter. With Curtis behind the controls, it would take longer due to his incessant need to make low-level dives and tight turns over the vast open areas. Curtis became a boy, and the need for excitement came out as he wound his way toward the central production facility. Yasmina sat in back with the armed bodyguards and listened to her MP3 player with the most recent music that she had downloaded last night. Her taste for Western things seemed to be insatiable. Upon getting closer to the many steel buildings housing the refinery processing, Curtis flew low over the poppy fields that could be seen forever.

The Bell Jet Ranger glided onto the flat roof of one structure as the occupants began to stir and gather their belongings. The party left the flight deck and entered directly into the waiting conference room.

Seated around a U-shaped table were twenty-some robe-draped tribal leaders representing most areas of Afghanistan. Behind them were their various assistants and, although not publicly acknowledged, their well-armed body guards. Curtis Harrison moved to the podium at the center of the table, and each attendee began to pick up his earpiece to receive the speech in his own dialect.

"Today I want to thank each of you for traveling here so that we can meet and discuss our combined future. You can see we have many new tribes represented here today. The untimely death of our friend Abdul-Aliyy at the Mustafa Hotel has brought us closer. Many of the new tribes here today worked with him. We welcome them and assure all our longtime allies that their addition to our consortium will only be of benefit and will not detract from any single tribe's profitability.

"Later today, I am meeting with an al-Qaeda commander posing as the Afghan council member appointed by the Americans. As you all know, since the American invasion, poppy, and therefore heroin, production is up over twenty percent. I have promised the American-appointed council that we will encourage our local farmers to move some of their poppy crops into wheat production. We all know that our business is thriving, and we can make small gestures to appease the Americans. If it were not for them, we would still be under Taliban rule and would be forced to eliminate poppy farming. The political change has allowed our average farmer to increase his annual income from about $170 U.S. to almost $3,000. This increase has raised the standard of living for the people of Afghanistan. Therefore we all have to encourage the farmers to at least give the appearance that we are trying to satisfy the Americans. I would strongly suggest that each farmer put in at least five percent of his crop into wheat. This will be enough to keep the Americans out of our business, and we can still thrive. I ask now that you signify your agreement by raising your hand."

All within the room gladly raised their hand. They were very happy that the Americans had removed the Taliban, allowing them to produce as much poppy as they desired.

"Thank you all for your support on this issue," Curtis said to the consortium of growers. "I will relay our support to Saleh, the al-Qaeda representative on the American-appointed council. He will smooth the way for our success."

The room erupted in cheers. The growers were thrilled with the prospect of even higher returns but were also joyous that they were beating the Americans.

"One other positive note is that with our new agreement we will be allowed to again transport our finished product throughout the world using our own aircraft. With this new commitment, I am sure the private-aircraft restrictions on international flight will be lifted. This will help alleviate the backup we are currently experiencing due to transporting our goods over land and sea."

Another raucous cheer filled the room.

"Please enjoy the hospitality we are offering you today. A sumptuous buffet will be served, and entertainment will be provided for your pleasure. Blessing to you all until we meet again."

Curtis Harrison was cheered as he moved toward the tribe leaders. They surrounded him as a team would their pitcher during a World Series win. To them, he was a savior. The Americans had made it possible by eradicating the strict rules of the Taliban. Now they could enjoy the many benefits that being in the heroin trade offered. Perplexed by the Americans' assistance in getting rid of the Taliban and essentially condoning the sale of their product all over the United States, they could rejoice at the peculiar situation they now found themselves enjoying.

Curtis Harrison controlled the production and distribution of the product and therefore really controlled all aspects of the growing trade. His job had become much more profitable due largely to not paying huge graft to the Taliban. Today, not only was production drastically up, but profit was up even more. Curtis Harrison was quickly moving from being a billionaire to being a multibillionaire. This business would indeed keep him in the style to which he had become accustomed.

The Bell Jet Ranger lifted off, and Curtis's many supporters raised their weapons in cheers. Curtis waved back to the crowd as a king would to his subjects, the difference being that Curtis Harrison was much wealthier than most any king.

Saleh was patiently waiting for Mr. Harrison's arrival, with his entourage filling the great hall of Mr. Harrison's ranch. The servants were waiting on him and the others hand and foot. All servants were dressed in the traditional garb, and the normal cast of nubile beauties by the pool was not present today. Curtis Harrison had strict orders to assure that the al-Qaeda were not offended by any Western trappings of greed. Curtis always made them wait for his arrival because he felt that coming in on his private helicopter set the tone for their meetings. Curtis was the one in power, and they were only puppets to him financially and to the United States politically.

The black Bell Jet helicopter could be seen hovering for a smooth landing just beyond the pool area. Curtis Harrison was first off and was followed closely by four other men and a woman wearing the traditional burka.

After exchanging pleasantries, Curtis Harrison raised his coffee cup to his guests and spoke in Arabic. "May all of you be successful in life, have many wives, and be blessed with a multitude of children. Praise Allah."

Curtis then settled directly across from Saleh and spoke directly into his eyes, using his best Arab tongue. "Mr. Saleh, today I am happy to report that I have met with the farmers in the North and, as per your request, have agreed to move their production from poppy to wheat."

"How much in wheat as a percentage of their total crops?" Saleh asked.

"They have agreed to five percent, a major move that should make all very happy," Curtis replied.

"Yes, that makes me very satisfied and will also assist me with the Americans. I do appreciate, as always, your cooperation. In this way, we can assure everyone's success, in particular ours," Saleh explained.

The occupants of the room looked toward Saleh and Curtis to see what response they should make. Curtis Harrison was first to begin a strained laugh, followed by Saleh. Then the whole room erupted as if a funny joke had just been told.

"Saleh, I insist, as do the farmers, that we give you a token of our appreciation for your support, to take home with you," Curtis proclaimed.

The door opened, and a young girl in a burka appeared carrying an aluminum briefcase. She knelt before Saleh and proceeded to open the container. The case was stuffed full of American currency. Saleh took one of the wrapped packs and fanned it across his face.

"Ah, the fresh air of American freedom," Saleh said sarcastically.

The room immediately broke into laughter as if the big joke was on the Americans that provided the opportunity for these men to become wealthy and wage their war. Saleh closed the case and handed it back to the young girl. Carrying the case, she followed him with the others and entered the limo with him.

Curtis stood at the door, waving to his guests as they were leaving. Curtis thought to himself that the only thing Saleh and al-Qaeda loved more than killing Americans was money and young girls. Curtis knew he had to keep al-Qaeda supplied with both if he was to continue his profitable operation in Afghanistan. Curtis knew that in this part of the world all business was transacted in this manner. The only change had to do with who the current winner was of the never-ending power struggle. The comedy of the entire situation was that it was always a foreign power, be it government, business, or drugs that was really in control.

Yasmina walked up to her benefactor and began to speak. "Mr. Harrison, we will miss the young girl known here as Yanna. She will provide good service to Saleh."

"Yes, Yasmina, that she will do, and more," Curtis Harrison said as he walked away laughing.

CHAPTER 5

▼

Three days had passed since the bombing outside the Mustafa Hotel. Trish had remained in her room and had only opened the door for her substandard room-service meals. She had kept herself busy watching the progression of the Iraq War on TV. She did not speak the language but was fortunate that the hotel received the BBC via satellite. She decided it was best to stay put until the violence subsided.

In the meantime, she only sat and worried. Trish was anxiously awaiting a call from Curtis Harrison. He had said he would call, and she was sure he was so taken with her that he would contact her without question. Trish felt that this attractive young man was in her control. The plans she had made would come together as intended. Also, she wanted him to take her away from this dreary existence.

She had neglected to call her father as of yet because she did not want to alarm him. She knew if her daddy heard the truth about this horrible place, he would be on the first plane to retrieve her.

Trish heard someone at her doorway. It was not time for room service, so she hid next to her bed. She could see an envelope being pushed under her door. When she felt it was safe, she crawled over and retrieved it. She tore it open as if receiving a reprieve from the governor. The envelope was sealed with wax, as in the old days, with the initials "CH."

She mumbled the words to herself: "Miss Rhode Island, Trish, I am sorry I could not call you directly, but I have been away on business. I would be most honored if you could visit me at my home in the morning. I suggest you bring clothing appropriate for casual horseback riding and a swimsuit to relax by the pool. My car will be at the hotel entrance at 9 AM. I am anxious to see you again. Curtis."

Her heart raced, not because she had a crush on him, but because she wanted to get away from this hotel room in the worst way. "It is so sweet he remembered I was Miss Rode Island," she thought to herself. Trish ran to her closet and began to throw things on the bed after holding them to her body and admiring herself in the mirror. "He does desire me. I knew he could not resist," she thought as she packed her necessities for the trip. Trish decided to call her father. She thought he should know where she was so he would not worry and "call out the army."

"Alcort residence, how may I help you?"

"Jasmine, it's me, Trish. Is Daddy there?"

"Miss Trish, yes, he is in his study," the servant replied. "I will get him at once."

"My baby, how are you doing?" Mr. Alcort answered in a concerned tone. "I haven't heard from you in days."

"Daddy, it's so good to hear your voice. I'm on an important assignment in Afghanistan. AP asked me to research the al-Qaeda connection to Iraq," Trish explained.

"Afghanistan," he replied forcefully with concern. "You have no business being there. I know these people and they would just as soon kill you as give you the time of day. I will call and get you on a flight home this moment. Have you lost all common sense?"

"Daddy, wait. I'm okay and well protected," Trish said. "You worry way too much. I am a big girl now, and this is my job."

"You don't need a job," he exhorted, "not if it means jeopardizing your life. Don't argue with me, baby. I know what's best."

Trish cut him off in mid sentence, "I'll call you in a few days. Love ya, daddy." She ended the conversation abruptly. She knew from past experience that it was better to not argue with her father. He would always win those battles.

James Alcort hung up the phone and, putting his head in his hands, began to cry. This was the first tear he had shed since the death of his wife many years ago. Softly under his tears he mumbled, "What have I done, my baby, what have I done?"

The sudden reality hit him that he had told her he "knew these people." He wondered if she had caught that. She should never know his connection to that country. His sadness turned to fear, and a tight knot was created in the pit of his stomach. "I have to do something," he thought. "I'll call my connections first thing in the morning."

Trish brushed off the incident and calmly continued her packing. She had much to look forward to, and her father was not going to ruin it for her. After packing, she lay down to get a good night's rest for the activities Curtis had in store for her in the morning.

She turned the page in her notebook and made the following notes to herself: convince Curtis Harrison to do my deal, enjoy company of this attractive young man, and get even with daddy.

A knock on the door interrupted her thoughts. A voice from the other side said, "Your laundry, Miss Alcort."

Trish peeked out, and she recognized the bellman. He was holding what looked like numerous shopping bags. She opened the door and accepted the bundles from him.

She ripped through the packages from Harrods. The assortment of casual wear included a complete English riding ensemble. All the swimsuits were thongs, and the evening gowns were cut quite deep and slit very high.

The card attached said simply, "I thought you might enjoy some things, so I had these flown in from London. I can't wait to see you in them. As always, Curtis."

She wondered how he knew she had lost two suitcases on her trip to Kabul by Inept Airlines, as she now called them. Trish was impressed by the sophistication of her new acquaintance. "I guess I made an even bigger impression on him than I thought," she mused. "He should be an easier mark than I realized."

Trish changed into her negligee and pulled the sheets up around her neck. While cuddling her pillow, she watched BBC News and drifted off to sleep.

The TV continued to broadcast the news. "U.S. Army Rangers are searching the many tunnels in the mountainous regions. An army spokesman said a capture of Bin Laden is eminent. A statement from Saleh of the American-appointed council was released in response to the Army's claim. 'Stupid people running stupid people. Osama would never be so dumb as to hide out in the very tunnels the U.S. helped build so many years ago. A dog chasing it's tail, nothing more.'"

Yasmina, while seated in the coffee shop of the Mustafa Hotel, gave the bellhop a wad of U.S. currency for delivering the packages of clothing to Trish Alcort. She had sewn small radio transmitters into several of the garments, and she placed the headset to her ears. She could hear the faint sound of the TV in the background of Trish's room. She was pleased her ingenuity was working well. Her attention was diverted by the sound of a chair being pulled away from her table. She looked up and saw her handler as she took the earplugs away from her head.

"Did you get the bugs planted in the clothing?" the Arab man asked.

"Yes, and I have tested the connection. It is working very well. I should be able to hear any conversation she has with Mr. Harrison."

"It is very clever the way you placed the receiver and recorder into an MP3 player. You will be able to listen without any suspicion."

"I am wondering why the CIA is so interested in what this woman has to say to Mr. Harrison. My assignment is to report on his activities with al-Qaeda. How does she fit into the equation?" she asked.

"All in good time. Now just listen and record all conversations between the two. Perhaps it is nothing, but we think Miss Alcort may be trying to infiltrate Harrison's operation for her own gain. It could be nothing."

"I will report back to you in a week unless an emergency situation precipitates an earlier communication," Yasmina concluded.

Yasmina had been sold to Curtis Harrison by her poor parents from the slums of Kabul when she was twelve years old. She immediately saw that the housekeeping position promised to her parents was nothing more than a ploy to have young girls for sex. Yasmina was smart and watched as the other girls succumbed to Curtis Harrison's requests. She decided early on that her best defense against becoming another sexual toy was to manipulate him. She decided that if she called him daddy he might feel compelled to treat her in a different way. Her plan worked, and he began to treat her as a daughter.

Yasmina was a beautiful child and had grown into a strikingly attractive young woman. Now at the age of twenty-four, she could easily attract any man she desired. When she was in the United States, she had been stopped several times a week by people telling her she looked exactly like the young woman who appeared on the cover of *National Geographic*. In reality it was her mother who was shown nearly twenty years previously. Yasmina had acquired the same flawless tanned skin, dark flowing hair, and her mother's trademark pure green eyes. She was blessed with a perfect body that she dressed conservatively.

For reasons only known to Curtis Harrison, he had provided Yasmina with the finest American education money could buy. In exchange, Yasmina had become his most trusted employee and assistant. Yasmina took care of the daily business and only bothered him with major decisions.

The CIA had recruited Yasmina while she was attending MIT. At the time, it was thought she would be placed in the technology arena of the intelligence agency. That was until her handler found out she was connected to one of the largest suspected heroin dealers in Afghanistan. When Yasmina was first approached about the idea of going undercover against Curtis Harrison, she had balked at the idea. Then a female agent had spent many conversations with her and had illuminated the tragedy he was forcing on the lives of the young girls, their families, and people throughout the world addicted to his drugs.

Yasmina had a difficult decision. In her own way, she loved Curtis Harrison. He had become her surrogate father. Finally she had agreed after reading classified reports of how he retired his young girls when he grew tired of them. Yasmina had returned to the estate and had worked gathering information against him ever since that time. Her ability to speak Pashto and Dari, the official languages, was a valuable thing during those trying days.

Curtis had challenged her loyalty upon her return from MIT. He had explained that he expected her to do his bidding without hesitation. She had also sensed that he was concerned he had lost his grip on her while she was away. In order to prove her position to him, she had been ordered to shoot a young girl of only thirteen. Curtis had called it a necessity because the young girl was rallying the others to not do their work. In reality, this poor unfortunate had only refused to allow Curtis to take her virginity. It was excruciatingly painful for Yasmina, but she had pulled the trigger. She had collapsed on the floor and had awakened to find that the gun was not loaded and that the young girl was fine. Curtis had laughed at her, but he was satisfied that he had her under his thumb.

Since that horrible day when Curtis had challenged Yasmina, the trust he had in her was unbreakable. The most difficult part for Yasmina was the waiting, waiting to either put the monster away for good in an American prison or kill him like the dog he was. Yasmina's handler constantly preached patience to her, but it was wearing thin. Yasmina dreamed of the day she could take him by the neck and choke the life from him while plucking out his eyes, eyes that had seen too much.

CHAPTER 6

▼

Justin Davis turned on the light in his office, revealing the piles of clutter that never seemed to be altered. The Mr. Coffee was still on from the night before and filled the room with a burnt aroma. Justin gathered the day's newspapers piled by his door and threw them at the top of his desk. Falling into his chair, he abruptly jerked forward, catching his balance after leaning back too hard. With his hands laced behind his head, he continued his morning routine of worrying about Summer.

Since he saw Summer at the "funny farm" two months ago, the same darkness had befallen him daily. Justin had to find some way to get to Summer and make her well again. The guilt he felt for putting her in that strange country and losing Jimmy was unbearable. Justin had many ideas running through his mind, many logical, but without the emotional jolt he thought was needed to bring Summer out of her trance.

Summer had no family, having been raised in an orphanage in South Boston. Her mother had died of a drug overdose when Summer was five. Justin could still remember seeing the headlines in the *Boston Globe* when he was a young reporter.

"FIVE YEAR OLD GIRL FOUND IN SOUTH BOSTON APARTMENT LYING NEXT TO DEAD MOTHER."

It was a horrible story in which Summer, as a young girl, had watched her mother overdose on heroin. Summer, not understanding that her mother had died, had stayed curled up with her until a neighbor had smelled the stench of a decomposing body. Summer never knew who her father was, since her mother had become pregnant while trading her body for drugs. This beautiful, precious child was never adopted, perhaps due to the stigma her mother had placed on this innocent. The only real family she had ever felt she had was Jimmy Murphy, her boyfriend, who had been so tragically killed. Summer referred to Jimmy's parents as "Mom and Dad," but they had both passed away several years ago. There was only a brother that had attended Jimmy's funeral.

"That's it," Justin shouted as he jumped up from his chair. Justin began thinking his new angle through.

"The brother had to be close to Summer," Justin thought to himself. "Hell, she almost lived with the Murphys. I wonder if he has seen her. She was too distraught to attend the funeral service for Jimmy, so maybe she hasn't seen him. Maybe seeing him, someone she was close to, could snap her out of it. Damn, what was his name? There have to be thousands of Murphys in the Boston phone book."

Justin fell back into his chair, again losing his balance, trying to make his memory come to him about this young man. "I remember he was very good-looking. A model, I think. Blond and tall, and he had on a dark pinstriped suit. I remember shaking his hand and introducing myself as Summer's boss. He said his name…Damn, what was the name? Bill, Steve, Bob, or Mark. Oh shit, I'll never remember. Wait,…shit,…no, not shit…Chip."

Justin pushed the heaps of paper to the floor, exposing a two-inch-thick Boston telephone directory. It was a year out of date, but he began looking through the many Murphy listings. He was not sure that Chip still lived in the Boston area, but something told him that a South Boston boy would not wander too far.

Line after line, Justin checked the many listings for Murphy. Fortunately there were only twenty or so for anything with a "C."

"Here it is. This must be him listed as a South Boston address."

Justin scribbled the number on the palm of his hand. It was a bad habit he had learned as a cub reporter. Two-one-seven-O-five-six-nine. Chip Murphy.

Justin instinctively looked at his old Timex, absentmindedly forgetting he was in the same time zone, let alone the same city. Being 6:45 AM, he convinced himself that it was not too early to place the call. He pulled the black phone toward him, knocking papers to the floor. Justin held the phone and dialed with the same hand while looking at the ink-smudged number in his other palm.

"Hello," A tired, weak voice answered.

"Good morning, is this Chip Murphy?" Justin asked anxiously.

"Yes it is," Chip replied. "Who is this?"

"This is Justin Davis from AP. Summer Tolly worked for me, and of course your brother. I am so happy I was able to track you down. Remember? We met at the funeral."

"Ah yes, I do remember you now. How can I help you Mr. Davis?"

"I went to Sunnyview Farms to see Summer several months ago, and she is not doing too good. Have you seen her?"

"Well, no, I haven't been out to see her. I was told she doesn't recognize anyone, and I still am not prepared to be reminded of my brother's death."

"I can certainly understand that, but I'm hoping that by seeing a familiar face Summer may snap out of her trance," Justin said. "Were you two close?"

"Like best friends. I'm a couple years older than my brother and her, but we were all real close. I was away attending college at Notre Dame, but I spent every holiday with her and Jimmy, especially after Mom and Dad died."

"Could we get together and talk about Summer?" Justin begged. "I would really like to see how we can possibly help her."

"Oh boy, I don't know, Mr. Davis," Chip whined. "I'm not doing well, and I'm only now getting out a bit to go to work. Jimmy's death has been real hard on me, and he was the only family I had left."

"That is my point exactly, Chip," Justin explained. "You do have family. Summer. And she needs you very badly, as I think you need her."

There was silence on the other end of the phone. Finally Chip said, "I can be at your office at noon during my lunch break. I think what you are saying is true, and I do sincerely want to see Summer again."

"Noon it is, at the Prudential Suite, nineteen-twelve…"

Chip interrupted Justin's desire to give explicit directions. "I know where it is. See you then."

Chip Murphy worked for the Gillette Company, a giant in the health-and-beauty-aid industry. He had been working at their South Boston headquarters for almost five years. Chip had begun in the sales-planning area, but after getting his MBA from Boston College at nights, he was promoted to brand management in the safety-razor division.

Chip had spent his youth involved with every kind of sport, but baseball was his favorite. He would play baseball every morning and then catch the subway to Fenway Park to watch his favorite team, the Red Sox. Gillette had always been involved with sports, from All-Star game voting to the World Series. Growing up, Chip had thought he would like to work for Gillette, after his professional baseball career was over, of course.

Unfortunately, his baseball career was over before it really got started. After he tore his rotator cuff three times in college, his doctor gave him the bad news that he would never pitch again.

Chip accepted the news badly but eventually regained the positive attitude he tried to carry into any situation. He changed his college major to marketing and set his sights on working for the company that in his mind meant sports. Chip was hired immediately from college. His graduation from Notre Dame with honors did not hurt at all. Being a local star athlete had also helped because most of the workers at Gillette were from the South Boston area and knew of Chip's athletic accomplishments.

Chip was over six feet tall and had blond hair and aquamarine-colored eyes. He kept his strong physique in shape by running three miles five times a week and lifting weights every other day. He had a strong-structured face and seemed to always have glowing skin even during the harsh Boston winters.

As the brand manager for the popular Excel Shaving product, he worked closely with the advertising agency that produced the many ads seen in *Sports Illustrated* and TV sports programming. Early on in the product launch, the search for a young male model for product ads turned out to be frustrating. The agency suggested that Chip become the "Excel Man," and he had fulfilled this duty ever since. He got ribbing from his counterparts, but he found the modeling to be fun and exciting. There were few singles bars he entered where someone didn't shout out, "there's the Excel Man." Chip would blush and keep his modest behavior intact. He never had felt himself to be good-looking and saw his own faults clearly.

Chip jumped on the subway in South Boston for the short ride to the Prudential Building, or the "Pru" as the locals call it. He proceeded to the nineteenth floor where he used to pick up his brother on occasion after Jimmy started with AP. Chip knocked on the half-open glass door leading to Justin Davis's office. Justin looked up and stood while removing his reading glasses. Justin extended his hand.

"Chip, so good to see you again under better circumstances," Justin said pleasantly. "Thanks so much for coming to see me."

Chip suddenly got a twinge in his chest as his eyes wandered over to see where Jimmy used to have his desk. He caught his breath and said, "Mr. Davis, I am still perplexed as to how you think I can help Summer when even the doctors have had no success."

"Summer knows you as family," Justin said. Think about this poor girl's past. Her mother died at a young age, she never knew her father, and of course now losing Jimmy. You might be the only one who can save her. Just seeing you may bring her back to reality."

"I have thought about it all morning, and I don't know if what you say is true or not, but I do know that if I can help her in any way, well, that is what Jimmy would want," Chip said with tears welling up in his blue eyes.

"I am so relieved to hear you will try. I have been sick with worry that she will never get better. I will take you whenever you want to go."

"No, I think it's best I go alone. If she wants to open up at all, she'll probably only do it with just me there. I've put in to take off all day on Thursday. I will go see her then," Chip promised.

"Great, please let me know what happens, if you would. Any type of acknowledgment will put my mind at ease. Call if I can do anything to help her, or you for that matter."

Chip had said what he came to say, and he did not want to make any further promises. Chip would have to dig deep in his emotional reserves to be able to see Summer. The complexity of her problem, the reminder of his brother, and the heavy burden he felt to help her was overbearing.

Chip told himself it was the bottom of the ninth, tied game, runner on third with three balls and two strikes. He had to throw a strike, and everyone on the team and in the stands depended on him. Suck it up and throw the ball. "Yes, I will be fine," he convinced himself.

Chip did not sleep or eat for two days after agreeing to visit Summer. His nerves were still frayed from the loss of his brother. He knew seeing Summer would cause all the bad feelings about his brother's death to come flooding back.

Chip had to try to help Summer, and he knew he must put his feelings aside. He had always felt a little guilty about his secret crush on Summer. He had kept his feelings in check, and he would never go after his brother's girl. Even now, he would never cross that line.

Chip drove the forty-five minutes to Sunnyview Farms in a daze. He had thought so much about what he would say to Summer that his mind was like mush. What words could sooth the pain she must be feeling? Chip knew himself that the agony of losing his brother would take a long time to heal. Upon entering the lobby area, he dragged himself to the nurse sitting behind the reception desk.

"Hello, I am here to see Summer Tolly," Chip said.

The nurse looked at the attractive young man before her and asked, "Are you related to her?"

"Yes,…well, not exactly, but she is…I mean she was my brother's girlfriend," Chip explained. Uncomfortable with the long pause from the nurse, he asked, "How is she doing?"

"Better, I would say. I'm not her doctor, but she has been writing notes in her journal. It's the first sign we've seen that she is communicating in any fashion."

"What is she writing? Do you know?"

"She is very protective of her journal," the nurse said, "but after she is asleep, we review it with the doctor. Most of the initial writing had to do with her life as a child. Now it has progressed to her time with your brother Jimmy. As of last night, she was up to the time frame of when she was in Afghanistan. The doctor thinks she is very close to a breakthrough. He feels that if she can confront what happened in Afghanistan she will be able to grieve your brother's death. That is the only way she will come back to the present and address her problems."

"Maybe it's not a good time for me to see her, then," Chip offered. "Perhaps once she gets through this process, it would be better."

"No, I think your being here now may be just the thing needed," the nurse said. "Just keep our conversation secret, because if she knows we are reading her journal, she may lose the trust she has in the staff. I could get fired for what I'm about to do, but I think you should read her journal before you see her. That way you'll understand better where this poor girl's mind is focused," the nurse said as she slid the document toward him.

"I don't know if I should," Chip said in a concerned way. "It seems like an invasion of her privacy."

"You may be her only chance. Please take it, I implore you, and read it. Then comfort this lost soul. She is in room 204."

Chip looked into the nurse's eyes and could see the concern she expressed. He took the copies and proceeded to a bench outside under a large oak tree where he began to read her innermost thoughts from the beginning of her young life.

"I remember things from when I was three or four years old. My mommy would hold me, and I knew I was safe. Sometimes men would come to our tiny one-room apartment, and mommy would tell me to sleep. I could not sleep because the bad men would hurt mommy. She made painful sounds, and I could see tears running down her cheeks. The men would jump up and pull on their pants while walking out the door. Mommy would take the stuff the men would leave and heat it in a spoon. Then mommy would give herself a shot like I got at the doctor's. I knew mommy was sick because she gave herself shots.

"Mommy loves me because she tells me so, and I feel it when she holds me. I don't know why she lets the bad men into our home. The men sometimes hit mommy, but she tells me not to worry, that she is okay. I want to play like the other kids I see out my window. Mommy got real tired, and she fell asleep on the floor. She won't wake up, and she is cold. I snuggle up to her to keep her warm, but she gets even colder. I smell something bad. The neighbor pulled me away from mommy. The police came, and they took mommy away. I hope she will be okay and come home soon.

"I hate this place. It is full of kids and noisy. Other kids take my food and stuff. The nun says mommy is not coming home and went to stay with God. She can't be right. Mommy would not leave me with these mean kids.

"My best friend has gone. She got what Sister Michael calls adopted. I think it means, like mommy, she won't be back. Why does everyone I love leave me? I try to be nice.

"Girls in high school make fun of my clothes. They have pretty things with name brands. The boys call me stick girl. I am happy I have long hair to hide behind. Jimmy Murphy hit one of the boys, and they stopped picking on me. I love Jimmy. I feel so safe with him. Please don't let him leave me.

"My body is changing. I am growing boobs. Sister Michael says I need to wear a bra. Jimmy says I am beautiful. I love Jimmy so much.

"Sister Michael told me I have a scholarship to go to Wellesley College. I'm not that smart. Jimmy can visit me. It is not far away. I met Jimmy's family. His mom and dad are so nice. I will adopt them. Jimmy's older brother Chip is so handsome. I bet he has a lot of girlfriends.

"My friends sent in an application for me to be in the Miss Massachusetts Pageant. I think it was a joke, but I need the scholarship money for grad school. I have no chance. I am too tall and gawky. I do have boobs that I don't know where they came from. I can sing. Some say pretty good. I will do my best.

"I can't believe I won the pageant. The other girls were so much prettier. I don't understand, but I did get scholarship money I need.

"Trish Alcort will be in the Miss America Pageant with me. She never spoke to me at Wellesley, and every time I passed her and her friends they would laugh. She is so pretty. I have no chance against her.

"Associated Press agreed to send Jimmy with me to Afghanistan. Now I feel safe."

Chip put the pages in his lap. He unconsciously wadded them as the pain and anger welled up from the pit of his stomach. This young beautiful girl had been exposed to so much tragedy. One could not imagine the horrible pain she must feel after losing Jimmy.

Chip wiped the tears away and pulled himself together. He walked determinedly with the nurse toward Summer's room. Chip could smell the antiseptic aroma of freshly cleaned tile floors. There were halfhearted souls sitting on benches in the hallway, talking to their "invisible friends" seated next to them.

Glimpses into partially open doors showed hollow beings staring into space while lying on their beds. Some were tied to the rails of the hospital beds. The commitment to get Summer out of this place grew ever stronger.

The nurse escorted Chip into Summer's room. Summer was sitting in a chair, gazing out the window. In her lap was a spiral notebook that appeared to be about to fall onto the floor.

"Here she is. Good luck," the nurse said as she departed the room.

Chip took a few steps forward and positioned himself directly in front of Summer. He knelt down to get at her eye level and saw tears forming in her blue eyes. Chip began to reach toward her hand, and Summer put her finger to her lips to make certain he did not say anything. To Chip's shock, she walked over to the door, looked up and down the hallway, and softly closed the door to her room. Suddenly in full stride, she threw herself into Chip's arms.

"God, it is great to see you. I have been praying you would come for me," she choked out with tears now streaming down her face.

Confused, Chip squeezed her and whispered in her ear, "What is going on? I heard you were not well at all and were not speaking to anyone."

"I have to pretend I am sick, for my own safety. If they knew I was in my right mind, they would kill me, too."

"I don't understand. Who would want to kill you? What are you trying to tell me?"

Summer pulled back, took his hand, and led him to her bed. She sat on the edge, and he joined her. She began the long explanation of her dilemma.

"I am certain that Jimmy was murdered. The explosion in Afghanistan that blew up our Humvee was meant to get both of us. I now believe that the interpreter was part of the plan all along. When he told us to go quickly, I did not think, and I encouraged Jimmy to get going. Now I realize that the last thing I saw was the interpreter running away from us toward the tents. He knew we were going to hit the land mine because he or the others were the ones who planted it."

"I'm confused. Why would some interpreter want you and Jimmy dead? It makes no sense to me."

"I've gone through it a hundred times in my head. It always comes back to the fact that when we insisted on going north through Afghanistan, they must have been afraid we were getting too close to someone or something they didn't want us to know about.

"It's the only explanation. The Taliban were not anywhere close to where we were located. I suspect it could have been in relation to the poppies and heroin trade, since that was the area we were traveling through. Perhaps knowing we were reporters, they feared we would uncover something to do with the drugs."

Chip reached over to her and hugged her even tighter. "I am so sorry. I would have come if I had known the truth. Are you really okay?"

Summer lifted the corner of her mattress, exposing a pile of pills. "Now every time they give me medication, I hide it under here. I am clear and alert. If you mean mentally, then yes, I am better than ever. If you mean am I worried, you cannot believe how concerned I am about my safety. The only way I know to save myself is to find out who is responsible for this whole thing and expose them as the murderer."

"The way Justin described your condition, you were drugged and barely existing. Why would you not ask for his help?"

"I cannot trust anyone with AP. Someone made the arrangements for Jimmy and me and set us up with the interpreter. I doubt it was Justin, but I just can't take any chances. I went through a long period of fear and anger. I found that I relied on Jimmy way too much, and with him gone I now realize I must depend upon myself."

"Where do you start?" Chip asked. "How could you possibly find this interpreter in Afghanistan and then connect him with someone here at AP?"

"AP has their own internal support staff that organizes all arrangements for reporters when going on assignment. I am sure the person who arranged for the interpreter who lead us through Afghanistan knows what really happened."

"Who could this person be who arranged to put you and my brother in the hands of the killer?"

"I suspect Trish Alcort has a hand in this in some way. She hates me and was super pissed when I got the Afghan assignment. She really came unglued when she found out Jimmy was going with me," Summer said with an intensity that filled the room.

"I know Trish has an evil side. I remember when you beat her in the Miss America Pageant. I'll never forget the look in her eyes as she told you she would settle the score with you."

"The part you are leaving out is when she said she will kill me like a slum rat. It still gives me shudders when I think of her vile words."

"When you are up to it, we will confront her, and I swear on my brother's grave, we will get to the truth."

"I am fine now, stronger than I have ever been, and I have planned the whole scenario of how to proceed. I only need for you to assist me with executing my strategy. I have recently checked up on Trish by calling AP and disguising my voice. I found out she is on assignment in Afghanistan. Now isn't that a coincidence? Afghanistan is where we must go."

"Wait, are you seriously thinking that we go over to Afghanistan to find her? You must still be sick. There is no way I can drop everything and go there."

"Jimmy was your only brother and he was my only love. We must avenge his murder. We can't let them get away with it. Please, Chip, please help me. You are the only one I can trust."

Chip stood up and walked to the window. Summer stood behind him rubbing his back, sensing he needed comforting. Looking out, he could see huge trees creating darkened shadows over the ball field. He thought of the tough life this young woman had faced and her resolve to find Jimmy's murderer. Summer's new tenacity inspired him to follow her. He could see in her eyes that she had the determination and confidence he lacked himself. Chip knew he could rely on this strong young woman. He reflected about his brother and the many times they had played baseball under the trees in his neighborhood. He began to choke and cleared his throat as he felt Summer come behind him now and hug his back. He wiped away his tears and turned to her.

"Tell me what you need," Chip said. "We will get Trish Alcort and everyone linked to the killing of my brother, no matter how long it takes or how far we have to travel. I make this promise to you, Summer. I will follow your lead and work every waking moment to see justice for Jimmy. I will make plans and go at once, if that is your intent. We will find Trish and force her to divulge the truth about Jimmy."

Summer rolled around to his front as he was speaking. She tilted her head back to look up at her tall handsome accomplice and spoke. "I knew I could count on you, Chip. Jimmy loved and respected you so much. I believe in you, and I firmly agree this is now my life's work. I am ready to do anything necessary and will check myself out of this godforsaken place in an hour."

CHAPTER 7

▼

Trish awoke and spent considerable time primping for her adventure. This was truly the most exciting thing that had happened for her in quite some time. Curtis was even wealthier than her father. She dreamed of the many benefits a life with greater wealth than her father's could offer. Her father was wealthy, but not in the realm of super rich or like what the casinos in Atlantic City called "a whale." She could be so much happier having more, and this just may have been the connection she deserved.

She called down to the front desk for assistance with her bags. It looked as though she was going on a weeklong cruise from what she had packed. The new clothes Curtis had sent over were obviously taken as well. Trish did not want to have less than three or four outfits with her for any occasion, in case she changed her mind once there or, if lucky, would be asked to stay longer. The bellhop announced his presence at her door.

The black Mercedes limo was waiting at the lobby entrance. Trish was relieved that she did not see army personnel anywhere when she followed the bellhop to the waiting conveyance. The driver wore a white tux shirt, a bow tie, and black trousers. Trish was relieved to finally see the elegant class she had become accustomed to.

After arranging her bags in the trunk, the driver returned to his seat and lowered the tinted window between him and this beauty. "Miss Alcort," the diver said, "our drive will be about forty-five minutes to Mr. Harrison's ranch. There is spring water, champagne, and soft drinks. A phone is provided for your use, and a TV if you are so inclined. Please let me know if I can be of any further assistance."

"Thank you, I am fine," Trish replied.

Trish poured herself some spring water and busied herself by reading the *Mademoiselle* fashion magazine she carried with her. Several times she looked out the window and wondered why the driver was speeding up and then quickly turning into a small side street. She was not concerned, since he probably knew a shortcut to avoid the morning traffic.

The driver noticed someone on a scooter as they pulled away from the Mustafa Hotel. He was trained to take the entire area into his mind as he scanned around him. The scooter rider seemed to fall back and then speed up as the limo would make turns. The trained driver knew this as the hallmark of someone tailing him. His training kicked into his instincts as he quickly put an evasive plan into action. Within three miles, the scooter was nowhere to be seen, and the driver began to relax and proceed to the ranch.

The car slowed, and Trish looked out her darkly tinted window. A huge gate in front of them began to open slowly. Two armed men came from the small guardhouse and exchanged pleasantries with the driver. Starting up again, they passed along the winding roadway until Trish could see the most magnificent structure of her life. There, sitting on top of a gentle slope, was what looked to be an exclusive resort. The neatly fenced pastures contained frolicking Arabian horses running with small colts in tow. The circle at the entrance contained a huge fountain cascading down into a pond that seemed to be fed by the stream they were now passing over on a small bridge.

Trish could see men in white shirts stationed strategically about the property. Once she got closer, she could see that they were adjusting an earpiece and speaking into something concealed in their hand. She was impressed that Curtis was having his servants announce her arrival.

The limo stopped in front of two hand-carved front doors that must have been fifteen feet tall. Two men dressed as the others stood close by the doors. The driver opened her door and offered his hand to help her out of the car. She took advantage in order to appear as "royal" as she thought Curtis would expect. One of the men from the doorway came to greet her and guided her through the massive doors that were now open. Inside, Trish could see a an impressive entry that extended twenty feet high to a dome that was obviously hand painted in a Michaelangelo style. The solid marble beneath her high-heeled feet clicked her along her way.

The doorman showed her into the study directly off the entryway. The marble of the floors coordinated perfectly with the mahogany precisely carved into loaded bookshelves. The furniture, in contrast to the hard marble, was soft leather and was filled with inviting pillows.

The doorman asked her to take a seat. "Mr. Harrison will be with you in a minute," he said. "Please, can I offer you a beverage?"

"No thank you, I am fine," she replied.

The doorman departed the room, closing the doors behind him. Trish was a bit upset that Curtis was not waiting at the curb, anxious to see her, as she had become accustomed to with other suitors. She stood up, tired of sitting from the long ride, and adjusted her outfit, pulling at the bottom of her tight dress. She was concerned that she might have overdressed. Perhaps this was a more casual encounter than she had anticipated. Her white linen suit showed her ample breasts perfectly and enhanced her stately long neck, her hair tied back in a pony-tail. Since Curtis was not there waiting for her with "bated breath," perhaps she should have just worn pants and a sweater. Maybe she should have dressed in blue jeans, but highly unlikely since she never wore those common things. This was perhaps only business to him, and she was embarrassed that she had dressed so provocatively.

Trish heard a noise from across the room, and the large wooden bookcase began to open on a swivel. Curtis appeared in khaki-colored shirt and pants with riding boots.

"Welcome, my beauty queen," Curtis gushed. "You are stunning in your out-fit. I trust my people have taken good care of you."

Trish looked at him and immediately felt a spark of desire. This handsome young man before her, with his strong build and dark hair, looked remarkable in his casual clothing. "Yes, everything has been fine," she said. "You have a very nice home." She tried to control her enthusiasm.

"Well, you have seen hardly any of it as yet. That is why I thought we could start with a horseback ride of the property. In that way we can talk, and you can see why I love my home so much. Sound okay to you?"

"Yes, fine, except I must change into my riding clothes."

"Of course you will need to change. I have had your bags taken to a guest suite. I will call and have one of my servants help you find everything so that you may get ready. Then we will meet at the stables in about twenty minutes, if appropriate."

"That sounds perfect," she said, relaxed.

Yasmina pulled the scooter into the servants' entrance at the side of the estate. She could easily have kept up with the limo carrying Trish Alcort if she had intended. But she had only remained in close enough proximity to hear any conversation Trish had with the driver. It was a good test of the MP3 player she had modified to eavesdrop on her new target.

Normally a following scooter would not be noticed or considered a threat in any way. This driver, taking all precautions, had done his best to lose the intruder, but of course this was of no consequence to Yasmina. She had only needed to look at the tracking screen receiving signals from the GPS devices she had planted in Trish's gifts of clothing. It also seemed she was getting multiple signals, meaning Trish had done as expected and had brought all of the bugged clothing items with her. Now all Yasmina had to do was wait to see if she could get within range to monitor her conversation. In addition, she was ever vigilant to avoid the abundant security personnel. Yasmina cowered into the shrubbery, hid the scooter, and provided herself with a good vantage point to begin her observations near the stables.

Trish was led down a cobblestone pathway just past the largest pool area she had ever seen. The waterfalls flowing from every direction into the pool created an atmosphere of being in the South Pacific. She noticed that there were many people using the pool area, most of whom were attractive young women. She thought it very strange that in this retreat these young beauties were wearing bikini thong swimming suits when the female servants were restricted to wearing burkas. The contrast between the Western way of thinking and the conservative theology of Afghanistan was dramatically shown.

Trish carefully checked the burka-wearing female who was leading her to the stables. Although she was covered from head to toe in her garb, Trish could see through the netting over her face that she was a beautiful young woman. Trish determined that it was not the same young woman she had seen commit the assassination at the hotel. How odd she must feel around the girls at the pool who were showing off their curvaceous bodies.

The girl spoke clear and concise English, which Trish thought unusual for a native. She was impressed at how well this Englishman attended to every detail. They arrived at the stables and entered through the main gate. The appearance inside the stables was as fine as any luxury hotel lobby, in fact better than the Mustafa Hotel where she is staying. Each enclosed corral area sported a gold plaque with the name and lineage of the horse to which it belonged. At the center of the stable were two white gray Arabians pulling on their leads, nervously waiting to be on their way. Just beyond, Trish caught a glimpse of Curtis talking to what appeared to be a stable boy. The young woman escorting her interrupted him.

"Mr. Harrison, your guest is here for you."

Curtis dismissed the young boy and turned his attention to Trish. While patting the larger of the two animals, he said to her, "This is Abi Da, one of the best Arabians ever bred. The other one here is his son Abi Di, also a very fine animal. Have you ridden Arabians before?"

"No, but I have jumped Thoroughbreds."

"Arabians are more spirited, I think. They love to run, and you will notice that even at a full gallop their heads remain upright and noble."

Suddenly the young Afghan girl appeared again and whispered something to Curtis.

"I am terribly sorry Trish," Curtis said. "I have a call that I desperately need to take. It will only take a moment, and then we will be on our way."

Curtis took the satellite phone from his servant and walked a few steps away, turning his back to Trish. Trish strained to hear what was so important, but only hearing one side of the conversation made no sense to her. She gave up and began to get acquainted with her stallion by stroking his strong face. Curtis occasionally turned back toward Trish and smiled as if to say that everything was all right and that the person on the other end was annoying him. Finally Curtis's voice rose to mark the ending of the call. She heard him say, "Yes, my trusted partner, I will indeed satisfy your request. I will have my people on this as soon as I hang up the phone."

Curtis handed the phone back to the girl and proceeded to mount his handsome steed. Trish followed suit, with a leg up from the stable boy, and the horse's hooves' made a clopping sound on the stone floor as they left the barn.

"That sounded important," Trish said. "Do you have to get someone to take care of it?"

"No, just a concerned business associate, nothing unusual," Curtis replied tartly.

Yasmina could not believe her good fortune. After only about an hour, she had already received some important information. The voice transmitter in Trish's riding jacket was not only picking up her conversation with Curtis Harrison but was powerful enough to hear even the other end of a phone conversation within one hundred yards. This was a tremendous advantage because trying to tap these secure phone calls was almost impossible with modern encryption methods. The tape recorder automatically stopped when the conversation ended to conserve recording tape. Yasmina was anxious to send the results to her superior to show that the CIA theory about Trish Alcort seemed to be correct.

Yasmina decided to get on her scooter and move further away so she could make her report. She went just a mile away, far enough that she could speak openly with her superior. Yasmina dialed the number for a secure line. Once she gave the operator the correct code, she heard the familiar voice.

"Yasmina, do you have something to report?" the voice asked.

"Something really huge that proves our thesis about Trish Alcort and her family's connection to Curtis Harrison," Yasmina began to detail.

"To the point, no fluff," the voice demanded.

"I have tracked Trish Alcort to Curtis Harrison's ranch. As you know, I have planted a listening device in her clothing, and I have just received both sides of a phone conversation I think you should hear." Yasmina moved the small recording device to the phone mouthpiece and pressed the play button.

"Hello, this is Curtis Harrison," the tape began.

"Curtis, I have a very big problem that I hope you can help me with. This is James Alcort."

"Of course, how can assist you?"

"My daughter works for Associated Press. I got a call from her last night that she is on assignment in Afghanistan. I know how dangerous it can be now over there, and I was wondering if you could have some of your people keep an eye on her. I would appreciate it, if you do see any danger coming her way, that you inform me at once."

"Yes, my trusted partner, I will indeed satisfy your request. I will have my people on this as soon as I hang up the phone."

Yasmina turned off the recorder and listened for her superior's reaction.

"My God, Yasmina," the voice on the phone said. "We were right all along. James Alcort is a distributor of heroin for Curtis Harrison in the States. For years we have been trying to determine how this wealthy man acquires his funds for his extravagant lifestyle. His money is drug money, dirty money. But I am confused. How does his daughter, Trish, fit into this situation? Is she an accomplice?"

"No, I wouldn't go there right now. I think it is more probable that she has designs on taking over her father's business. I can assume this because of the drug-business connection between Curtis Harrison and James Alcort. I am certain she is trying to pull a power play or gain leverage."

"You are walking a very fine line between success and failure. We need the info to connect Curtis Harrison to al-Qaeda and Osama Bin Laden. It is still our belief that the drug business and the money supporting al-Qaeda are intricately wound together. The job of infiltrating Curtis Harrison to gain this information can become complicated if she derails our mission."

"Trish Alcort is too conceited and naive to put anything together other than that Curtis Harrison is enthralled with her, and she is convinced in her own mind that she can control him. Curtis Harrison is a very smart man, but Trish Alcort is a vexing beauty who plays to Curtis's major weakness. Both of these egomaniacs will make their play, and the whole thing should work right into our hands."

"Be careful, Yasmina. Even the best of us get blindsided every now and then. Just make sure this complicated assignment does not translate into your end. Upload the tape to us at once, and don't let Trish Alcort out of your sight."

"Yes sir, I will be cautious as you suggest."

Yasmina knew Curtis had arranged that a lunch to entertain his guest be set up by the river farther away on his property. Yasmina jumped on her scooter and proceeded to a concealed location across the river, off the property. She was hoping she would have a good vantage point to view and record Curtis and Trish's meeting.

James Alcort hung up the phone and stared at the picture of his daughter on his desk. He loved his daughter more than life itself. He prayed he had made the right choice in calling Curtis Harrison. He was left with few options and felt he had to use the only contact he had in Afghanistan to help his strong-willed daughter. Trish's success in winning the Miss Rhode Island Pageant had given her even more confidence, and he knew she now felt she could accomplish almost anything. If he had known she would become so headstrong, he would have forbidden her from ever entering. Now he was put in the position of begging the one man he despised for a favor.

The partnership between James Alcort and Curtis Harrison was a love-hate relationship at best. The supply of illegal drugs assured that Alcort could provide his daughter with all the finest things in life. Over the years, though, the business between the two men had been strained. When the United States had invaded Afghanistan, he had begun purchasing South American heroin to fulfill his customers' demands. Addiction does not understand the effects war has on supply, and he was required to have product. The decision to buy elsewhere was looked upon by Curtis Harrison as a betrayal of their unwritten business arrangement. The men had since mended their disagreement because the U.S. occupation made the supply even more readily available.

James Alcort wondered if there is not some residual resentment on the part of Curtis Harrison. He would certainly find out posthaste due to the request he had made that day. If Curtis Harrison could not find and protect his daughter in Afghanistan, nobody could.

CHAPTER 8

▼

The hour drive back to Boston from Sunnyview Farms gave Summer time to review her plan with Chip. Both agreed that if she was accurate about Trish Alcort's involvement in Jimmy's murder, they would have to be extremely cautious talking to anyone working at Associated Press. There was no definitive evidence with which they could establish a link between Trish and Jimmy's death, but Trish certainly could have been the instigator by setting them up with the interpreter. Summer discussed the possible connections that could be made between Trish and Afghanistan. None seemed to make any sense. Trish would not be linked to the Taliban, because, being American, why would she care about the group controlling Afghanistan? Certainly Trish could not be connected in any way to the U.S. military, and even if so, how could she and Jimmy have been any threat to a U.S. operation?

Summer filled in the gaps for Chip regarding her long, adverse relationship with Trish. She explained that they often ended up in competition with each other and that she fortunately came out on top in most instances. Suspecting Trish of being involved with Jimmy's death, it must have more to do with her envy of Summer. There did not seem to be many possible connections between Trish and Afghanistan.

The recurring thought was the al-Qaeda connection to money and Trish's obvious greed. Summer was convinced she and Jimmy had been getting too close to the heroin production facilities, which had made the interpreter nervous. Al-Qaeda relied on the drug money to fund its war of terror. Hence, an innocent request to go where the fighting was happening translated to the paranoid conspirators as an attempt to expose the drug connection. Summer concluded that it was most likely Trish was involved in this for the money.

Chip and Summer agreed that the best way to find out exactly where Trish Alcort was staying in Kabul was to ask Justin Davis. But they felt they couldn't trust him or anyone else with AP at this point. After all, Justin was in charge of handing out jobs, and he supervised people's duties. If Trish was getting money through al-Qaeda, then perhaps Justin was as well. An implausible idea, but, being a reporter, Summer had learned to think outside the box. They decided it was best for Chip to call Justin, under the pretense of reporting on Summer, and attempt to get the needed information. If Justin became suspicious and called Sunnyview Farms, it would be too late, since their flight out was in an hour and a half. It was a risk, but a small one they needed to take. Chip picked up the phone and dialed the AP office number.

"Associated Press. How may I direct your call?"

"Justin Davis, please," Chip said.

"I will connect you."

"Hello, Justin Davis here."

"Justin, this is Chip Murphy. I wanted to call you and update you on Summer's progress. I saw her today and…"

Justin cut off Chip's statement. "Did she know you? How is she?"

"Wait a minute, and I will tell you as best I can. She seemed to recognize me a bit. The doctor thought it to be a positive. She has been writing in her journal, which again is a good sign from the doctor's perspective. I think we can help her, but I need some information from you."

"Anything at all. How can I help?"

"Summer wrote in her journal about Trish. Do you know anything about her relationship with Summer?"

"Well, yes, they both worked for me. I don't know what connection she could possibly have with Summer's problem. Trish is just one of a hundred I have in my department."

"Please be patient with me, Mr. Davis. I don't know either, but the doctor said perhaps talking to her might give us some insight. Would it be possible to meet with her?"

"Yes, normally it would be no problem, but she is on assignment and cannot be reached. Perhaps I can get a message to her, and she could call in a couple of days."

"Boy, I was hoping we could find out something sooner. I hate to wait, with Summer in this state of mind."

"I'm sorry, that is the best I can do. I have your number, and I will call you as soon as I find out something. Oh, I have to go. Someone is waiting for an appointment to see me." Justin hung up the phone.

Chip turned to Summer and said sadly, "A no go. He either would not or could not tell me where she is on assignment."

"That is utter baloney. Justin knows where everyone is when on assignment, where you eat, where you sleep, or where you go to the bathroom. This is strange. I've got an idea. Call back and tell the receptionist answering the phone that you just talked with Justin and he said she should give you the phone number of the hotel where Trish Alcort is staying."

Chip called Associated Press back.

"Associated Press."

"Yes, you just connected me to Justin Davis. He indicated that you could give me the phone number for the hotel that Trish Alcort is staying at while on assignment." Chip was using his best persuasive voice.

"One moment, please. I will check."

Chip turned to Summer and said, "Keep your fingers crossed. She said she would check. I don't know if that means with Justin or if she is looking up the information."

The receptionist came back on the line, and Chip repeated the information so Summer could write it down.

"Mustafa Hotel. Kabul, Afghanistan. Got it, and have a nice day."

Chip and Summer screamed at the top of their lungs like they had just won the lottery. In fact, this was a minor detail compared to what they were ultimately trying to accomplish.

Justin Davis decided to leave the office early. He hated to lie to Chip, but it was all he could do under the circumstances. He wanted to help Summer in the worst way, but he could not give out any of Trish Alcort's details to this innocent kid. Justin decided, as he had many times before, that a stiff drink was in order. Justin gathered his coat and hat and walked past the reception area. He stopped momentarily to tell the receptionist that he would be out of the office for the rest of the day.

"See ya in the morning. I have some business on the way home tonight," Justin announced.

"Yes, Mr. Davis. Have a nice evening," she replied.

"Oh, by the way, Mr. Davis, I was able to give the young man on the phone the information about Trish Alcort that you wanted me to relay."

"Wait, what in the hell are you talking about?"

"I told the nice young man the hotel where she is staying in Kabul. He said you told him I would give it to him. Any problem?"

"Problem? You bet your ass there's a problem. Never give out information. My God, I've got to stop this thing before it gets out of hand."

Justin ran back into his office and threw his hat and coat across the room. He began talking to himself. "Settle down, now. It means nothing. Chip just wants to try and help Summer. That's it. The best thing to do is check with Sunnyview Farms. They will tell me if something is going on other than just a call to Trish to help Summer." Justin dug through his wallet until he found the phone number for the mental facility. He nervously dialed the number.

"Sunnyview Farms"

"Yes, this is Justin Davis, and one of my employees is under your care. I was wondering if I could get an update on her condition."

"Normally, Mr. Davis, I could not give that type of information over the phone, but I remember you. We met when you visited here several months ago. I have some really good news. Summer had a visit by her former boyfriend's brother, a very nice young man, and Summer snapped out of her condition and checked herself out this afternoon. The young man promised to take care of her and inform us if she has any setbacks…Hello are you still there?"

Justin slowly moved the phone from his ear as if he were melting. Once down to the base, he slammed the phone over and over until it broke in two.

Justin Davis knew that when the CEO of Associated Press had told him it was a security issue and that information would be provided on a need-to-know basis, it was quite possible that it was being controlled on a higher level. The leak made inadvertently by the receptionist could have severe ramifications. Justin could lose his job, or even, though a remote possibility, his life. He never knew when these things identified as "top secret" were part of a bigger picture. He had learned long ago to go with the flow, not ask any questions, and keep information close to his vest.

Justin would handle this problem as he had the many others that had come his way over the years. He sat back, took the bottle from his desk drawer, and poured a healthy serving into his coffee mug. Yes, he and his friend Jack Daniels would have to think on this one.

CHAPTER 9

▼

Trish and Curtis were riding along the riverfront when they came upon a white canopy set up next to the banks. Curtis tied his horse to a low branch hanging from an indigenous neem tree and walked over to assist Trish.

"You ride pretty well for a city girl. I am indeed impressed," Curtis said.

Trish dismounted her horse and brushed off her rear end. "I had my own horses when I was growing up," she said. "I learned to ride almost before I could walk. My father made sure that I loved horses as much as he does."

Curtis took her hand after giving her horse's reins to a servant and guided Trish toward the canopy where she saw that a romantic table was set with two waiters hovering nearby. Trish and Curtis were seated with the assistance of the staff. Wine was poured, and Curtis raised his crystal glass toward his guest to make a toast.

"May we always be able to enjoy the finer things in life, even during impossible circumstances."

Trish clicked her glass to his but did not really understand what he meant by "impossible circumstances." How could he think living on this lavish estate could be impossible circumstances, she wondered.

"Can I ask you some questions about yourself?" Trish inquired.

"Yes, ask away. I always tell my associates I will answer any question, but that they should not be surprised if the answer is no or not what they expect to hear." Curtis sat back in his seat, waiting for the normal deluge of questions about his wealth, business, and relationships he normally had to endure.

"Obviously you are a man of means and great taste. It is surprising to me that you would invest so heavily in an estate that resides in such a volatile area of the world."

Curtis was flattered by her intelligent question and duly impressed at how she was able to massage the same worn-out questions other women plied on him into something that accomplished the exact same result but was far less controversial. Curtis considered that this beauty was more intelligent than he had anticipated.

"Miss Rhode Island," he said, "are you asking me this question as a friend or as a reporter?"

"As a potential friend and business associate, I would better describe it. You know I am only here under the guise of a reporter. I convinced AP I was here for a story about al-Qaeda to protect my real motives."

"I conclude you are withholding your true intentions until you know me better. I like a cautious woman."

Curtis reached across the table, and she allowed him to hold her hand. The delicate breeze off the river stirred the small wisps of hair not confined by her ponytail. She shook her head and exposed her emerald-green eyes. For a brief moment their eyes met, and both felt a warm surge funneling through their fingers.

Trish pulled her hand back abruptly and said, "Is this how you avoid difficult questions, Mr. Harrison?"

Curtis laughed. He took his left hand and shook his napkin open, placing it on his lap. "Well, let's just say that I am hoping we can have fun and enjoy each other's company. I would rather not dwell on such mundane topics as myself."

Trish reluctantly pulled her napkin into her lap as she stared through him as a subtle warning. Trish abhorred not getting her way. This was true even if it were as simple as not receiving answers to her questions. Trish decided to delve directly into her purpose for the visit.

"Curtis, I expressed to you my desire to take over my father's operation in America. Have you given serious thought to my proposal?"

"My dear Trish, you need to be patient. I am a simple man who has acquired wealth through hard work. I am careful of whom I do business with and need to know my associates intimately before I am willing to take any permanent steps. I have just met you. However, I have known your father for many years."

Trish took her napkin and delicately blotted her pouting lips. "Now Mr. Harrison, I would be surprised if we could not become much closer than you are with my father," Trish said in a teasing way.

"Oh my goodness. Are you trying to seduce me to close this deal, Miss Alcort?" Curtis asked playfully.

"Let's just say that I am prepared to do anything required to make this happen. I can be very persuasive."

"I can assure you that romance has its place, and business quite another. My father had a saying he preached to me: never dip your pen in company ink."

"You should not misunderstand my intention. My purpose is strictly business, and I can assist you with information that may protect you," she said in a forceful way.

"What can you tell me? You have only been in Afghanistan for four days."

"I can tell you that I saw your young female driver slit a man's throat at my hotel. Now, isn't that interesting information?" she asked temptingly.

Curtis Harrison did not like surprises, and he was astounded that Trish had witnessed the assassination of his business rival at the Mustafa Hotel. He had specifically told his envoy to wear a burka to conceal her identity. He did not want any problems with the local police, as it would just end up costing him more money in payoffs.

"You must be mistaken. I believe the incident you describe was during the time I was being driven home from the airport. Many Afghan women have a similar appearance. Please rid your mind of any such horrid thoughts," Curtis recommended sternly.

Trish leaned back in her seat and eyed her opposition. She really preferred to challenge him on this issue, but she could tell he was getting perturbed. She felt it best for her overall plan to not push the issue at this time.

"Of course it may not have been her," Trish said politely. "I could be mistaken."

Curtis Harrison could read people better than most. He had to in order to survive in his wicked business. Curtis realized he had just been given a "mulligan," as they do in golf when a bad shot is given over without charge. Curtis knew nothing in life was free, and this streetwise young woman would demand payment someday in the future.

Yasmina was coming up to the far side of the river across from where the two were located. With her binoculars, she could see them under the canopy, eating lunch and conversing. She was too far out of range, and to her dismay the voice transmitter did not work. After her earlier success gaining valuable information about James Alcort and Curtis Harrison, she was now frustrated with the capability of the device. Yasmina knew she would have to either get an enhanced device or take the precarious option of recording inside the property perimeter to capture these conversations. She imagined it possible that they were at this very moment discussing the intimate details of their connection. She could not afford to miss such valuable information in the future.

Yasmina was not seen, but one of Curtis's bodyguards saw a flash of light from across the river. The guard was not certain if it was binoculars or possibly the lens of a scope on a high-powered rifle. Regardless, it was his job to get Mr. Harrison to safety. The man came to the side of the table where Curtis was seated and bent toward his ear. Curtis did not hesitate and immediately stood up.

"We must go back to the house now," he said. "I have some important business that I must attend to."

"But I am enjoying your company, and we have barley started to eat."

"There is plenty of food at the house. Come, we must leave now."

Trish stood up, shaking her head in disbelief. By the time she was handed the reins to her horse, Curtis was in a full gallop, with three of his men surrounding him along his way. Something horrible must have happened to cause such uproar. Even so, a gentleman would have waited for her to come along. "This man is a mystery I am not sure I want to read," she thought to herself.

Yasmina could see the chaos on the other side of the river. She knew instinctively they must have spotted her. She pulled herself along the grass and brush on her belly until she made it to the clearing where her scooter was hidden. She jumped aboard and proceeded to get far away in case they began searching for the intruder. Yasmina decided to go directly back to the ranch and behave as if nothing had happened. She concluded this type of surveillance was not going to work. The receiver in Trish Alcort's clothing worked well, but only if she could get within transmission range of the device. Mr. Harrison's ranch was far too large for her to be in range at all times while hiding beyond the exterior wall. She must have a higher frequency connection to achieve the type of coverage this operation required.

Yasmina entered her room and threw her canvas satchel on the bed. She pulled her cell phone from her pocket and dialed the number of her handler. She typed a text message, as was her usual way of communicating with her handler. "Need help with operation. Must meet with you."

A message flashed across her cell-phone window. "I can meet you this evening at eleven thirty at the regular place."

"See you then," she replied.

Trish was escorted back to the guest room at the main house. Curtis had obviously returned ahead of her but was nowhere to be seen. She was confused as to what had just happened. She wondered if he had taken offense at what she had said to him regarding his young staff member. Regardless of the circumstances, a servant began to place Trish's belongings back in the bags she had brought with her. She assumed this could only mean the date has now ended.

"The car will be at the front door in five minutes, Ms. Alcort," the servant said. "I will take your bags."

Trish looked around the room and out the window over the luscious pool area. She was despondent at how she was being treated, but to whom could she complain? Curtis was in control whether she liked it or not. She would have to play by his rules even though she did not like any rules at all.

Trish settled back into her dingy hotel room. She was very confused by how the day had ended, and she sought answers. She knew men well and was positive she had him under her control. All the things that normally worked with men, her flirting, playing hard to get, and challenging their intelligence, seemed to fail at every turn with this complicated man. The "important business" had just been his excuse to get away from her, she figured.

Trish turned on the TV to move her mind off of Curtis Harrison. The feed from the BBC satellite to the hotel was much-appreciated company. She began to get caught up in the events of the day.

"Coalition forces have begun the bombing of Baghdad," the BBC reporter said. "Led mostly by the technically advanced American B-2 stealth bomber, there are many scenes of fire, explosions, and destruction. English aircraft are involved, and it is reported that the antiaircraft from the Iraqi ground forces is useless against the high-flying bombers. If the beginning phase of this battle is any indication, Iraq has little chance to defend against the coalition."

Watching the reports from the war in Iraq only made Trish more miserable. She could be the one covering Iraq, but she was in this awful place trying to force her relationship on Curtis Harrison and get him to cancel the agreement he had made with her father many years ago.

Trish resented how she had found out how her father really made his fortune. She had spent time on an AP assignment and by using her connections had shifted through DEA reports about Afghan heroin trafficking in the United States. She felt that her father's days were numbered by the government's knowledge of his complicity in the business. The DEA would pursue and indict him at any time. Trish had decided to not warn him and proceed to protect her own interests. She now had to protect her own supply of money or, God forbid, be poor.

It was imperative to do the deal with Harrison before her father was charged and sentenced to do hard time. Her father's money would be seized, and she would be left broke, something she was sure she could not handle. If Curtis Harrison knew the truth, Trish was sure she would lose all bargaining position with him. She must proceed quickly and not create any suspicion with this cautious man.

She finally dozed off and was awakened by a knock at her door. "Miss Alcort, I have a delivery for you," the voice from the other side of the door beckoned.

Trish got up and while rubbing her eyes awake looked out the peephole. It was one of the bellhops holding a bouquet of flowers. She quickly threw open the door. The bellhop was followed by three more, each carrying a bouquet of flowers more beautiful than the first. They were set about the room, and when the bellhops were gone, she pulled the card open that she had been handed.

"Miss Rhode Island, I am so sorry that our date ended so suddenly. I can only beg your forgiveness and assure you it was indeed an emergency. Could we please resume our date tonight at eight? I will have a limo waiting. Certainly call me if your plans will not allow you to come. Thanks for your understanding. Curtis Harrison. PS: Please bring enough clothing to stay a few days as my guest."

Trish waved the card toward her face and placed one corner of it between her front teeth. She slowly removed it and said aloud, "Well, Mr. Harrison, I did get to you. You complicated little rascal. Next time you will learn not to treat Trish Alcort in that fashion, or I may not give you another chance." Trish fell back onto her bed, hugging the card as some schoolgirl might.

Curtis Harrison gathered with his security chief and Yasmina in his study. Curtis was seated behind his hand-carved desk while the others were seated in chairs to the front.

"What happened out there today?" Curtis exploded.

"My man saw a flash from across the river," the security chief explained. "It could have been a mirror, lens from a binocular, or anything. Under the protocol, they must take anything of this type seriously and move you to safety."

"I was having an important meeting, and I don't know if it can be repaired. You may think it was just another beautiful woman, but this is not pleasure; it is business. Do you understand?" Curtis yelled.

"I do Mr. Harrison, and I would never presume the importance of any visitor. We only reacted according to protocol." The Security Chief said apologetically.

"Now for damage control. Yasmina, I need to send flowers to Trish Alcort at the Mustafa Hotel with a note of apology. Something to the effect…"

Yasmina interrupted. "They have already been sent, with the appropriate apology card. She should have them by now. I asked her to return this evening and plan to stay a few days."

"I don't know what I would do without you, Yasmina," Curtis gushed. "You always know what I am thinking and take care of things before I have to ask. It might be good if the security chief took some lessons from you. Perhaps then I would not be caught in these awkward situations."

"Yes sir, I agree wholeheartedly," the security chief said apologetically. "I will make the security staff aware of the difficulties."

"That is all. You can go now," Curtis stated flatly, dismissing the chief from his office.

Yasmina stayed, knowing Curtis would want her opinion on this tragedy, as he did on so many things, and for her to listen to his constant insecurities about his safety. She always knew the correct thing to say, and Curtis felt much better after these little sessions with her. She was particularly anxious to cast dispersions on others so she could protect her own schemes.

"Mr. Harrison," she said, "before I go, I wish a favor of you."

"Certainly, Yasmina. You have earned it," Curtis responded.

"I worry for your safety, and I am always concerned, no matter how good your security may be, that someone may penetrate and get to you. Today was just another example of the possibilities. If the person across the river had a high-powered rifle, they could have killed you with one shot."

"You need not worry about these things."

"No, please let me finish, Mr. Harrison. I know you trust me more than anyone. Is that an accurate statement?"

"Yes, of course it is, Yasmina. Today was a perfect example of how you know me so well that you thought to send the note and flowers."

"Well, then provide me with a weapon so in case someone gets too close to you, I can defend and protect you," Yasmina pleaded.

Curtis Harrison was taken aback by this request. He had never had anyone really care about him other than superficially by those who relied on him for money. He was very impressed with the way this young woman thought and had matured under his guidance. He walked to the back of his desk and swung open the original Matisse painting above his credenza to reveal a wall safe. He opened it and produced a wooden box. He placed the box on the desk, turning it toward Yasmina as he opened it to reveal a chrome handgun with a white pearled handle.

"This is a Walther P99 given to me by a business associate of mine in the United States," Curtis explained. "He gave it to me as an apology for a misunderstanding in our business dealings. This is the same gun used by James Bond, the fictitious British agent. I want you to have it as a gift."

"Thank you, Mr. Harrison. I will treasure it not only for the peace of mind it will bring to me, but also because it is a special gift from you," Yasmina said.

Curtis stood behind his desk as he watched Yasmina pull up the bottom of her burka and place the gun in her waistband. He was proud of his accomplishments regarding her, and he felt an overwhelming desire to hug her and hold her. He always resisted crossing the line because she was his only connection to civility. His molding of her made him feel as if he was a good human being.

"Yes, you are my trusted one, Yasmina. I respect you for what you have become," Curtis said as she left the office.

Yasmina's handler sat sipping his hot tea, waiting for his Curtis Harrison connection. He knew it would be difficult to convince this young woman to personally carry a wire inside the compound. Based on her description, he knew this was possibly the only way to tape the conversations between Trish Alcort and Curtis Harrison. He did not know her thinking on the subject, but he had to convince her any way he could. Curtis Harrison had devised better security than most foreign presidents, he concluded. In order to infiltrate his operation, the CIA had to rely on this young Afghan woman.

The handler recognized the woman in the dark burka entering the lobby of the hotel. She had her head down and proceeded directly to his table without looking up.

"I appreciate your meeting me again so soon," Yasmina said.

"Unquestionably, not a problem when we are working on such an important assignment," the handler said calmly. "I know it must be difficult for you to sneak out of the ranch."

"I need your help," Yasmina said. "The conversations between Mr. Harrison and Trish Alcort cannot always be recorded, due to the long distances that tax the transmitter. I need to place a device powerful enough to pick up conversations throughout the ranch and perimeter."

"Yasmina, you should know firsthand that it would not be possible to permanently place anything inside the compound walls. Security is excellent, and they have sophisticated devices used to sweep the entire estate daily. The reason the transmitter planted in Ms. Alcort's clothing works so well is because she is not subject to a physical check by security."

"I have an idea of how to proceed," Yasmina stated confidently.

"Please tell me."

"I have several, but you will need to supply the items based on my design. Now listen closely. The compound has a wireless network that connects all of the buildings together. This network is also used for security-camera uploads to the main file server. The main connection to the outside world is by satellite, and the compound has a multitude of dish antennas that are strategically located to match the western movement of satellites in orbit. The way for us to monitor the conversations would be to tap into the uplink. The only thing needed is to install a super strong transmitter in the computer center covering the entire acreage. The device can be powered by the file server itself."

The handler looked confused. "Why wouldn't security find the transmitter you would install in the file server?"

"Very simple. Mr. Harrison has given strict orders that I, as network administrator, am the only one to have access to the computer center. Even the head of security cannot enter the room without me accompanying him. Mr. Harrison has full trust in me and my technical capabilities."

"Wonderful. How are you going to get me the design to build the device for you?"

"I will make a CAD drawing of it and send it in a PDF file to this Web address." Yasmina pulled a small spiral notebook from under her burka and wrote down the information for her handler. "I can have it completed by morning. Check to see if the file is on the Web site by 10 AM. The file name will be 'chrome9.pdf.'"

The handler admired Yasmina as she walked confidently from the coffee shop to the hotel lobby and entered the black Mercedes limo. He felt fortunate he had made this contact. She seemed to be a tremendous source for not only getting information about Curtis Harrison, but also as a superior intellect. He sipped down the last drop of his tea, rewarding himself for putting the entire operation together.

CHAPTER 10

▼

Chip Murphy stretched his tiny airline blanket up to his neck as he tried unsuccessfully to get comfortable. The flight from London to Kabul was much more sedate than the Boston-to-London flight had been hours earlier. It seemed that during the seven-hour flight Summer had never stopped talking. She discussed the past, Jimmy, how to find Trish, and even what supplies they should acquire when they landed. Summer sketched out a plan for when they hit the ground in Kabul. Part of the plan was for both of them to get plenty of sleep on this leg of the fight so they could begin looking immediately for Trish in Kabul. Summer was following the plan perfectly as she was curled up next to the window with her head propped against a pillow.

"She looks so calm and peaceful," Chip thought to himself. "The determination and confidence she has gained is so attractive."

An announcement on the PA from the captain startled Summer.

"This is your captain speaking. We will be altering our course to Kabul slightly, taking a much further southern direction than normal. This is due to the report of restricted airspace around military operations commencing in Iraq. The change in flight plan will delay our arrival about thirty minutes."

Summer looked toward Chip with squinted eyes and asked, "What was that about Iraq?"

"It sounds like they have started the war in Iraq," Chip said. "The captain said something about military restrictions on airspace, which may delay our flight. No big deal."

Summer rolled back over and fell off to sleep without hesitation. Chip continued to fluff the small airline pillow, wondering if he would ever get any rest. He was not certain if it was his nerves about going to Afghanistan, his concern over how to best assist Summer, or the unprofessional way he had broken ties with Gillette by informing them he was not coming back that bothered him the most. Chip had a lot to think about, and as soon as he exhausted one subject in his mind, another problem replaced it immediately. He was committed to avenging his brother's murder and was convinced he might not sleep until he had acquired that satisfaction.

Justin Davis knew the leak of Trish Alcort's location was a major security breach. He should have known better than to feel forced to put up with Trish's crap in the first place. The innocent disclosure by the receptionist to Chip and Summer of where Trish was staying in Afghanistan could blow sky high. Justin debated whether he should inform Trish ahead of time or just play dumb. Justin did not have any desire to get involved in this thing any further. After all, he had not been told anything about the real purpose of her trip. The insistence by his superiors to give Trish the assignment had never made any sense.

Justin questioned whether Trish had a connection with the CIA. If so, she would be more a liability than an asset. The assignment was purportedly a story about the al-Qaeda and Iraq connection. Justin knew better. Something else was behind this plan. It was just too clandestine to be a regular article. Justin had run across these "spooks" before in his many years of reporting. If you talked to one of them long enough, they could convince you that you didn't even know your own name.

The beleaguered manager decided a quick phone call to Trish in Kabul would at least warn her that Summer and Chip were on their way. What harm could it cause? he thought. Then he could stay clear of the real plan they were hatching. Justin carefully dialed the number of the Mustafa Hotel.

The hotel phone was answered by an automated voice. Justin listened until he heard the menu option to use English. He pushed number three on the phone, and the language was now English.

"If you know your party's extension, dial it at any time, followed by the pound sign. If you wish to connect using the party's last name, please enter the number eleven, followed by the pound sign."

Justin followed the directions.

"Please spell the last name using the telephone keypad," said the voice on the phone.

Justin dialed carefully.

The mechanical voice came back and said, "Connecting you to Trish Alcort. Please hold."

Justin began shouting obscenities into the phone regarding his displeasure and hatred of these automated devices. Then he heard a familiar voice.

"Hello, how may I help you?" Trish answered.

"Trish, this is Justin. I need to tell you that I think Summer Tolly and Jimmy Murphy's brother Chip are on their way to Kabul. I found out when I called the mental institution where Summer was staying, and they said she had checked out with Chip."

"Wait a minute, Justin. I am very confused. How would they even think to come to Kabul, and why would they be looking for me?" Trish sounded exasperated.

"Well, I'm not sure why they would want to talk to you, but they called our office and unfortunately the receptionist let it slip where you are staying," Justin said sheepishly.

"You were told, in no uncertain terms, that my destination was on a need-to-know basis," Trish raved violently. "You are a stupid son of a bitch. You broke security protocol by letting a receptionist know my location? Obviously you don't understand the importance of this operation."

"Trish, I would never do anything to put you in jeopardy," Justin said. "You have to understand it was a…" The phone went dead in his hand.

Trish began to plot how she would "welcome" Summer and Chip to Afghanistan. She decided to put her plan together later when she was not as furious as she was now feeling. She could not control her shaking, she was so upset. She walked over to the desk and snatched up her cell phone to dial the secret number.

"Clear line 0-9-7-8-9-3, please," she said into the phone.

"Security line established," the mechanical voice said. "Hold for your party or leave a text message."

Trish began the tedious task of entering the text message. The agency felt it was a more secure and reliable way to transmit important messages, thereby leaving no room for human interpretation. The message read, "Problem with cover. OO7 Justin Davis."

Trish flipped the phone closed and was gratified at how simple it was to kill a man by dialing a few digits. Trish thought it childish to use the James Bond 007 number to signify a hit on someone, but it was precise. A license to kill with those three digits meant the person would be extinguished.

A bad day for her, she thought, having to deal with incompetents. In her own way, she tolerated Justin Davis. A likeable enough guy, but his excessive drinking caused him to say things that should not be said and impeded his judgment. Justin Davis was just another casualty of war that could not be avoided, she thought.

Trish's cell phone rang, and a text message displayed in the phone's window. "Message received OO7 Justin Davis. Call secure line conference. Call fifteen minutes."

Trish looked at the message and wondered why headquarters requested a conference call. Perhaps they desired a better explanation of the problem with the cover. It might be that they didn't want to put the hit on Justin Davis. This would be a surprise, since Trish normally had full operation authority in the field, and her motives and requests had never been questioned in the past. This was a very unusual demand.

The fifteen minutes seemed more like an hour. Finally Trish called the secure line, and it was answered by a mechanical voice. "You are connecting to voice conference 1-Z-3-8-8-3-2-H-2. The other participants are already on the line."

"This is Trish Alcort calling as per request."

"Trish, this is the agent operations director. I have three other superiors on the line with me. As is normal procedure, no names will be used. I received your 007, and we feel it is time to discuss how the plan is evolving. Bring us up to date on your progress."

Trish was taken aback by the request and wondered if her handler had been sending her reports up the chain of command.

"I am in country, have established communication with Curtis Harrison, and have been invited to stay at his compound. I have not established any links to drug trafficking or al-Qaeda as per assignment. I have reported that a female staff member of Mr. Harrison's was seen killing a man at site of Mustafa Hotel bombing. Connection vague, but possible business deal gone bad. My cover working as AP reporter is functioning as anticipated and has opened necessary channels. AP bean-town manager has overtly jeopardized my cover. Subject reports two individuals en route and due in country within six hours. They are Summer Tolly and Chip Murphy. Justin Davis gave them my location. I fear my cover will be compromised on this important mission. I am moving my location to Harrison's estate to avoid possible contact with Tolly and Murphy. The 007 on AP manager is to assure no further connection between the company and myself after infiltrating Harrison compound." Trish said this all in a monotone voice.

"Message understood and confirmed," the operations director stated. "Handler will contact if any change to plans required by HQ. Next report due on normal schedule. Out."

The three men seated in the Langley, Virginia, CIA headquarters rubbed their foreheads in unison. Each thumbed through the reports received before speaking. After a ten-minute silence, the field director spoke.

"We have two operatives within the Harrison compound," he said. "The first one is a young Afghan girl who has been with the target for many years. The second one is a young American beauty queen posing as an AP reporter. Neither one knows of the other's identity or connection to the CIA."

"The concern for both agents is their possible association to the target," the assistant director spoke up. "The Afghan girl was raised by the target and may have some remorse over his capture or demise. She may be working both sides of the track. Trish Alcort was placed into the mission due to our highly placed intelligence that her father is the U.S. distributor for the target's drugs. She may have other motives, and we have reports indicating she may be in this for personal financial gain. Gentlemen and ladies, I hope we have not created a kludge here. Now we have two agents we think are keeping an eye on each other for the safety of the assignment, when in actuality we now are confused as to which agent to believe."

"If we look at the intelligence we have received thus far," said the handler, "the Afghan girl has provided us with much more. Trish Alcort is only making promises. I trust the Afghan girl, Yasmina."

"Keep close track of each of them," the assistant director said. "I want reports daily till this thing breaks open. Now, does everyone agree to the 007 on Justin Davis?"

The people in the room were quick to raise their hands. To them it was just another lost pawn in the big game of international espionage chess.

"What I see from these reports does not provide the connections between al-Qaeda, the heroin trade, and Iraq we are seeking," the handler said. "It appears what we have discovered so far is that James Alcort and Curtis Harrison have a relationship confined to the processing of poppies into heroin. James Alcort is distributing the finished product in the U.S. It seems to me this is a DEA problem. I conclude we should just turn the whole thing over to them. It is nothing more than a drug deal, in my estimation."

"I concur with you that it seems straightforward at the current time," the assistant director said. "Trish has only been in country for ten days. What we do believe is that Curtis Harrison is the largest producer of heroin in Afghanistan. The hit made on his rival last week at the Mustafa Hotel assured his continued prominence. I have seen many briefs tying the ill-gotten drug money to support al-Qaeda operations. The reports preceding 9/11 specifically showed a money trail back to Afghanistan. This money could come from no other viable source than drugs. I suggest we continue to follow the money and see where it takes us."

The field director sat back and looked to the other men in the room for any sign of disagreement. Finding none, he said, "I agree there probably is a connection between the heroin trade and al-Qaeda. This alone means nothing unless we can tie it to Iraq. I know you gentlemen understand that the intense pressure to find Bin Laden and tie him to Iraq is huge. We need the connection to al-Qaeda and weapons of mass destruction so we don't lose face with the American people or our allies. We need to be cautious with our limited resources so we don't fish in this pond too long. Understood?"

"I do, sir, and I assure you I will pull the plug if nothing happens soon," The handler reassured.

CHAPTER 11

▼

Trish Alcort heard a knock on her door, and by looking out the peephole, she was able to see it was the bellhop. She quickly moved to the side so he would not be able to discern that she was looking out at him. She hesitated for a minute, holding her breath, and heard his footsteps getting fainter as he walked down the hallway. She looked down to the floor and noticed an envelope just under her door. She read the note.

"Miss Alcort, I have confirmed that Miss Summer Tolly has reserved a room beginning this evening. According to her reservation, she should be landing at Kabul International Airport in about one hour. She is traveling with a Mr. Chip Murphy. Thanks. Guest Services."

The plane landed with a thud, waking both Summer and Chip. They pulled themselves up in their seats and craned their necks to get their first glimpse of Kabul. Summer remembered the airport well, but this was the first time for Chip. The plane came to an abrupt stop, and people filled the aisles, pulling items from the above compartments.

Summer turned to Chip and said, "Well, we are here. Now let's find Trish."

The cabs out front of the airport were plentiful, with each driver bantering in has native tongue to acquire passengers. Summer grabbed Chip by the arm and jumped into the first taxi they saw. Summer leaned forward and told the driver, "Mustafa Hotel."

Although the ride from the airport to the Mustafa Hotel was uneventful, Summer grew increasingly solemn. The reminder of this strange land brought back the horrific memory of when Jimmy was killed. Chip attempted to talk to her during the ride, but she responded in short yes-or-no answers. Summer told herself to get a grip and be strong, or her plan would not be successful. She was concerned how she would react to Trish's seeing her for the first time, convinced she had been involved in Jimmy's death. She had to remain in control and not be confrontational with Trish, even though her inclination was to scratch her eyes out. If she attacked directly, Trish would most certainly deny any connection and would surely avoid any further contact.

Summer determined that her best alternative was to manipulate Trish into revealing her complicity. In that way, Trish would divulge additional information that Summer could use to find all of the murderers and avenge her lost lover. By the time they arrived at the front entrance to the hotel, she had rallied herself to be strong and, more importantly, smart.

Checking into the hotel was difficult until the front-desk clerk produced an English-speaking associate. They were informed that their rooms were ready. Summer started firing her questions at once.

"I just remembered something," she said. "Could you check to see if a Trish Alcort, my business associate, is checked in at this time?"

"I will check my records," the clerk said. "Yes, Ms. Alcort did check in several days ago. She is in room 204."

Summer and Chip smacked hands with each other as if celebrating a home run. The clerk looked at them askance, wondering why Americans acted so strangely.

The two made plans to meet in thirty minutes, after getting settled, to fine-tune her plan for confronting Trish. They decided to meet in the coffee shop just off the lobby. Both went to their rooms to shower and unpack before they started their search.

Trish Alcort called the front desk for a bellhop to carry her bags down to meet Curtis Harrison's limo. She was extremely upset over Summer's unexpected arrival, but the thought of staying at Curtis's estate for several days was comforting. Perhaps this wealthy man had learned his lesson and was ready to treat her as expected. Regardless, she had a very good reason to disappear, since Summer and Chip would arrive at any moment. Trish had no intention of dealing with Summer directly. She needed time to devise the appropriate scheme, and for now she certainly did not want Summer to know where she was headed. Trish felt she deserved a couple days of rest. She knew Summer was intelligent and would attempt to follow her. Summer had the ability to figure out that this wealthy man doing business in Afghanistan was connected to the drug trade. Trish would have to devise a plan to throw Summer way off her trail, or she could once again use the magic 007.

The limo was waiting when she walked into the lobby, and the familiar driver was standing by the door with his hat in his hand. Trish Alcort was once again off to see the finer side of Afghan living.

Yasmina's handler entered the safe house on the west side of Kabul. The winding back stairs to the entrance made a surprise visit virtually impossible, he thought to himself. An old woman who escorted him to his room greeted him coldly. Once inside, he opened the parcel his contact had handed him on the street. It was carefully packaged in bubble wrap to protect its delicate circuitry. Looking at the device meant nothing to him. He only wanted to be sure that the new transmitter would indeed work. His agent at the Harrison Estate had designed the new electronics, and the CIA had sent it to him within twelve hours of receiving the drawings. He would contact Yasmina and get the device delivered to her so that surveillance could resume in the morning.

Yasmina's phone rang. She looked at the caller ID and recognized it as being from her handler.

"How can I assist you?" Yasmina calmly asked.

The handler recognized her voice and immediately began to detail his plan. "I have the electronics ready that you designed. I need to meet with you to deliver them."

"I can meet you at the coffee shop at the Mustafa Hotel in an hour."

"No, that will not work. I have moved to a new location. The safe house."

"This concerns me. How did this happen?"

"I have been informed that an employee of Associated Press, Summer Tolly, is on her way to Kabul. I met her when I traveled with her party during the war, disguised as a nomad. It is only a precaution, but I do not want to talk with her."

"Where do we meet?"

"I will bring the package to the western edge of the river, across from the Harrison Estate. Can you meet me there in one hour?"

"I will be there," Yasmina confirmed.

Yasmina flipped her phone closed and thought to herself, "I don't like surprises. First I find that this reporter is coming to snoop around, and then that my handler knows her? Just what I need, another reporter I will have to track and control. I wonder sometimes if my decision to join the CIA was very smart. Either these people are the most brilliant in the world, or they have no idea what their missions may or may not accomplish. I hate to not trust these people, but they make me nervous for my own safety."

Summer saw Chip sitting on the far side in the coffee shop. She was tempted to stop by room 204 on her way down, but since this could be a serious confrontation, she decided it best to wait. Summer knew she must be patient and consider alternatives for how best to handle the situation. She caught Chip's eye, and he stood as she approached the table.

"I ordered you a latte," Chip said. "I hope that is what you like."

"That's great," she replied. "I appreciate it. Now, we need to rethink our plan. We know Trish Alcort is here, but I question how much information we can get from this viper."

"Summer, it sounds like you don't care much for her. I know you filled me in with some details, but there must be more to the story."

"As I told you, Trish is a very pretty girl in her mid twenties and is the ex-Miss Rhode Island. Trish is similar to some of the other girls I met in the pageant. They think that because they are blessed with beauty, the whole world should bow to their wishes. Trish seems to stop at nothing to get her way. We had a major run-in when I was assigned to Afghanistan during the war. She made a huge stink with Justin Davis when he gave me the assignment. I am sure she is here now because Justin wanted to get her out of the office for a while."

"So Justin doesn't get along with her either?"

"I'm sure Justin would fire her in a minute if he could."

"Well, the obvious question is, why hasn't he?"

"Trish uses her wiles to get her way with men. I have always suspected she is doing someone at the top. My assignment to Afghanistan was the first time she was not able to pull some strings to get her way."

"It sounds like you two have had many run-ins. I guess I don't understand her motivation."

"If you look up the word *snob* in the dictionary, you would see a picture of Trish Alcort next to it. The fact that I was an orphan on scholarship to Wellesley rankled her to no end. Then we were pitted against each other at the Miss America Pageant. I was fortunate enough to come in ahead of her, and she has never been able to deal with what she considered a put-down and a blow to her ego."

"The important thing is your precise understanding of the relationship. We cannot be too overt in questioning her, or I agree with you that she will clam up if we push too hard."

"Exactly. That is what I mulled over on our way here. Trish will divulge nothing to me voluntarily, so our only chance is to come up with a scheme that tricks her into giving us information. I have been thinking that you are better suited to deal with her."

"Like the male spider in a black widow's web. Thanks, Summer. I appreciate your mercy," Chip teased.

"I hear a black widow makes love to her mate just before she kills him," Summer quipped.

"What a way to go. Now, back to reality."

"The first thing is that I know her much better than you do. Therefore you must follow my instincts regarding Trish. The second thing is that I have been thinking about shortcutting our search. We know the interpreter is the one who knows the most. I suggest we find him and not waste our time trying to pry information from Trish, when I know she will not give us what we want. I have the name of the interpreter on my PDA. Here, let me look. I know his first name is Abdul."

She clicked through the pages, touching the screen with her plastic pointer.

"Here it is. Abdul-Hakim, which is an Arab name. He is actually from Saudi Arabia. I have a local contact number, but we need to have someone call who speaks Arabic, in case someone other than him answers. At least it would be a start."

"The front-desk clerk we spoke with may help us out. We need to come up with a story so no one gets wise to our real intent."

"I have an idea. We can tell the desk clerk we are doing a follow-up story about Abdul. I can convince the clerk that Abdul helped me during the war. At least it might get him to make the call and give us a lead," Summer said happily.

"Super, but if Abdul becomes suspicious, he may contact Trish or God knows who. Since we are convinced Trish was behind Jimmy's death, it could put us in danger," Chip said haltingly.

"I can assure you that most anything we do in this country will put us in danger. The people here don't trust any foreigners, particularly Westerners. We need to take risks, or we will never be able to find out who killed Jimmy and why."

"I know you are right, Summer, but I think we need to check and double-check the risks we take. I can't help it, but I'm afraid. If something happens to us, Jimmy's death will never be avenged. That said, let's go forward with the plan and see if we can get the front-desk clerk to make the call."

Summer leaned across the table and took his hand while looking into his eyes. "Chip, you have to trust my instincts," she said. "I will not put you in any danger knowingly."

Yasmina could hear a car approaching from the distance. She stood up and could see headlights dim about a hundred yards away. She knelt back down until she could see a man approaching. Yasmina could not be certain it was her handler, because from a distance all men looked the same in the native garb. The figure was moving his head from side to side, scanning to locate his contact. When he was within ten yards, Yasmina revealed her location, frightening the handler.

"There you are," Yasmina declared. "I have trouble seeing in the dark night."

"Allah save me. What is wrong with you? I could have shot you for less," the handler screamed.

"I'm sorry. I am being cautious."

"I have the package here," the handler said as he moved toward her with the object. The handler began to unwrap the device, but Yasmina stopped him.

"No need to do that here. I am sure it is okay, and I will inspect it once I am back at the compound. Can you tell me more about this Summer and why she is here in Afghanistan?"

"I will tell you this to ease your mind. I know you are taking great risks to carry out your assignment, and I want you to know that you are safe. Summer's boyfriend was killed when they were on assignment during the war. I suspect she thinks it was no accident. There was a contact within the Associated Press operation who made the travel arrangements for them. Subsequently, they hit a land mine while being guided by these people. The same person arranged for the interpreter and the guides who were with the reporters. I was planted as one of the nomads. You know that during the war anything could happen, and the risks were great. It was most unfortunate that the accident happened. They were just a casualty of war."

"Who was the person in AP responsible for the setup?"

"I was not told. But the rumor was that a young woman made the arrangements and that she was CIA. I checked with my superior to see if she was indeed an agent, and I was assured there was no connection."

"My concern is that this Summer may interfere with our assignment by digging up information related to the accident."

"I can assure you she will not be a problem, and if I see it developing into one, I will have her taken care of."

Yasmina listened to the words carefully, and she clearly understood that her handler would have this woman disposed of if she interfered. She began to relax her nerves and proceeded with the issues at hand.

"I will be able to install this device during the night," she said. "I will test it first thing in the morning. If my design was followed properly, I should be able to pick up the voice transmission from any location inside or outside the compound."

"Yes, I want to test at once, but Trish needs to be on the property."

"I took care of that. Trish is on her way now to stay at the compound for several days. It will be ready for testing first thing in the morning."

"Well, you are resourceful. I will expect an update after you have put the transmitter through its paces at sunrise."

The mystifying agent walked away toward his waiting car. Yasmina did not know his name, only his voice and eyes. She felt uncomfortable with this arrangement, but she knew he was her only contact to the outside world. She felt fortunate she had someone she could rely on to assist with the dangerous situation within the walls of Curtis Harrison's estate.

When Yasmina arrived back at the compound, she could see Trish Alcort walking toward the front entrance. The driver was struggling with the many bags accompanying her. Yasmina was proud she was in control of this complex situation. The young Afghan woman was very adept at developing a plan and letting the males in her life think it was their idea. Yasmina had survived by being smarter and staying at least three steps ahead of these arrogant men. Her implementation was perfect, and all was going according to her secret plan.

The only possible complication disrupting her intentions was this beauty, Trish Alcort, with whom Curtis had now become enamored.

CHAPTER 12

▼

Trish settled into her guest suite and decided to use the whirlpool tub in her bathroom to relax before dinner. She was looking forward to the evening, in particular to seeing Curtis stammer and beg forgiveness. She thought she would begin with a bit of a cold shoulder and warm up gradually. Trish had found with men that it was best to train them from the beginning.

She remembered how well she had handled her professor in college. She would give him just enough attention to get what she wanted and then constantly pull the rug out from under him. By the time she graduated, he was so well trained he did not make a fuss at all when she had dumped him. "I will have to put Curtis Harrison through obedience training in the same way," she thought.

Dinner was served in a covered gazebo in the pool area. Torches lit the pathways, candles were everywhere you looked around the pool, and palm fronds cushioned the ground. Trish felt like it was a dream as she walked toward the table. Curtis stood at the entrance to the gazebo and escorted her to her seat. Waiters quickly placed her napkin in her lap, and a fine bottle of wine was opened.

"Well, Mr. Harrison, what do you have to say for yourself?" Trish asked sarcastically.

"Trish, I am so sorry that our lunch ended so abruptly. I had an emergency that needed attention," Curtis said, begging forgiveness.

Trish Alcort had a profound sense of when to go in for a kill, much like the initial hesitation of a tigress before unrepentantly lunging at her prey and killing it with one bite.

"Curtis, I have never been treated so shabbily. I am a fair woman, and perhaps I can give you another chance. I must tell you I hesitated coming tonight."

"Trish, I promise it will never happen again, and I do appreciate your coming. I will make it worth your while."

Trish sat back in her seat, giving space between them to assure he had understood her message. She then cocked her head and said, "Well, I forgive you, conditioned on your promise to not let it ever happen again. I suggest we consummate our business deal. That will help make it up to me."

"I have decided to seriously consider your offer to take over for your father. But I am interested in how you intend to accomplish this task. I don't suppose James Alcort will just hand over the keys to you."

"No, he is an Alcort. None of us give up too easily. I will take the responsibility for getting my father out of the way. I just need your commitment that we have a deal," Trish said, batting her eyes.

The dinner continued for several hours. The seven-course meal contained the finest continental cuisine she had ever tasted. Trish was duly impressed but did not want to let her host have that satisfaction. After finishing a port wine, Trish announced, "Well, Mr. Harrison, I believe it is time for me to retire to my suite. I enjoyed your company, and I expect you have planned something exceptional to entertain me in the morning."

Trish rose from her seat, and Curtis walked toward the vixen, bending to give her a kiss. She abruptly turned her head in a teasing way, allowing him to only kiss her cheek. Curtis was so surprised by this refusal that he had a difficult time speaking.

"Yes, I do have an interesting activity planned for us in the morning. I will have a servant advise you. Good night, Trish," Curtis stammered.

"I hope the activity includes a letter of intent spelling out the details of our arrangement," Trish gibed.

"Miss Alcort, we are not in bed together yet," Curtis reminded her.

"That, Mr. Harrison, is an understatement."

Trish smiled and walked away toward her room. She knew the tide had now turned in her favor. She had used this ploy often before, and it worked on men famously. Initially let them think they are in control, and once you have them hooked, you then push them away a bit. Every spoiled little boy then learns to become obedient. Trish liked her men to be well behaved and in her control.

Curtis Harrison wished he had not used the cliché "getting in bed" with her. This was a common term he had used often in business dealings as slang for finalizing a deal. Obviously she had grabbed onto the snafu and had stuck it to him.

He did not understand why he was putting up with this insolent young woman. It was true she was breathtakingly beautiful, but he had plenty of those tucked away on his estate. Perhaps, he thought, she intrigued him because she was so different from the others bowing to his every desire.

Yasmina heard Trish returning to the suite next to hers. Now she could accomplish the installation of the new transmitter device. Yasmina wore her burka to conceal her identity as she carefully found her way to the third building from the pool. Access to the communications center was restricted to only her and Curtis. Yasmina entered #-3-3-8-2-3 onto the keypad lock, and the lock clicked open.

The burka was the perfect cover to move around the property without creating any suspicion. All of the female servants wore them, and if seen she would just appear as any one of them. She opened the door to a modern suite of rooms. All glass enclosed, she could readily see large banks of computers placed neatly into racks. Without hesitation, she walked quickly to the server console and began her work. Yasmina installed the transmitter and checked to make sure the satellite uplink was working. Now all she would need for a final test was for Trish to wear one of the articles of clothing she had outfitted with a bugging device. At this point in time, with the use of the satellite, she should be able to hear any conversation of Trish's.

Curtis Harrison returned to the study adjacent to his room. He poured a healthy snifter of Carte Noir brandy and fell into his overstuffed leather chair. Normally at this time of the evening, he would have selected several of the young women for his pleasure. Tonight, though, he wanted to sit and think about this alluring woman so interested in being his partner. He tossed the partnership idea around many times in his head. He was not particularly fond of James Alcort, but getting into business with his young daughter could be more complicated than Curtis preferred.

Soon Curtis had consumed almost half of the expensive brandy. His mind was not working as well as his libido. He had a choice to make. Either summon one of his regular dalliances or go to Trish. With his logic dulled by the drink, he decided upon the latter. Curtis grabbed a bottle of Dom Perignon and two glass flutes and strolled toward Trish's room. At the door, he hesitated, having just a bit of doubt, and then in a soft murmur he said to himself, "What the hell. You only live once."

Curtis knocked lightly on the door and was covert enough to make sure Yasmina in the next room would be none the wiser. Suddenly the door swung open,

and standing before him was Trish, wearing a see-through negligee. It was obvious she had not been to bed, as her hair was perfectly in place.

"Well, Mr. Harrison, I have been waiting for you. What took you so long?"
Trish said curtly.

To say Trish was ready for him would be an understatement. She had lit candles about the suite, and the bed was turned down, revealing satin sheets. Of
course she had the letter of intent placed neatly on the table by the veranda, with
a pen lying on it ready for use. Curtis immediately went to caress this beauty, and
she resisted his pass by grabbing him by the hand and guiding him directly to the
table.

"As we discussed at dinner, we desire to form a relationship," Trish said. "I
hope it can be both personal and business. I think you put it aptly when you said
we are going to get in bed together. Before we proceed with our personal relationship, it is essential that you sign this letter of intent and agreement." She handed
him the pen.

Curtis Harrison was under the influence of the liquor but not sufficiently so to
be forced into any arrangement he might regret later. He read the document and
slammed the pen on the table without signing. He began to get up from the chair
to leave the room, and Trish grabbed his shoulder and pushed him back into the
seat. Seeing his reluctance, she slowly untied the delicate satin ribbons holding
the negligee in place. Adeptly, she exposed her perfectly pert breasts and then
expertly revealed the soft fold between her thighs. Curtis lunged forward, and she
met his advance with the unsigned form. He grabbed it out of her hand and
quickly signed the document, sealing the deal.

The two lovers fell onto the bed and let their passion flow.

Yasmina awoke early the next morning and was excited to test her new listening device. She went about her normal routine with her modified MP3-player
earplugs in place. She could see one of the servant girls taking the usual breakfast
tray to Curtis's room. She did not know when Trish would awaken, but expected
she was a late sleeper. The transmitter would not function until Trish was dressed
with one of the bugging devices.

The young girl came scurrying back into the kitchen with Mr. Harrison's tray
still in hand. Yasmina was close by, preparing her latte she had become accustomed to having each morning when she had attended college in the United
States. The child was babbling in Pashto, attempting to explain the problem to
the cook.

"Child, what is the problem?" Yasmina questioned.

"It is Mr. Harrison. He is not in his room, and his bed has not been slept in. Where could he be?" the child cried.

Yasmina strode rapidly toward Curtis's suite and told the cook to call security. Yasmina cautiously entered his room and shouted out for him. She also observed that his bed was perfectly made.

Yasmina was alarmed and began walking back toward the front of the house, where she could hear the chief of security entering. As she was about to talk, she heard something over her MP3 headphones. At first it sounded like static. Then she realized it was running water. She must be picking up the sound of Trish in her shower. Yasmina was pleased the new device was working so effectively. The chief of security walked directly to Yasmina for direction.

"Mr. Harrison is missing?" he asked, stunned.

"He is not in his room, and we determined he did not sleep in his bed," Yasmina explained.

The earphone of her MP3 started to pick up voices. She could hear Trish's voice and a male voice in the distance. She held her finger to her lips in order to halt the security chief's questions. Then she heard the voices much more clearly.

"Trish, you look as stunning this morning as you did last night."

"Thank you, Curtis, or should I say partner?"

"You may say anything you like, but I want to have more of you."

The transmission went silent, with the exception of low moaning sounds emitted from the sexual beings. Yasmina realized at once that Curtis had spent the night with Trish. She was very shaken by two things. First, he had stayed in her room, rather than his own, which was unheard of, and second, he had obviously spent the whole night with her. The last time a girl spent the entire night with him was entirely by accident when she made the unfortunate mistake of falling asleep. She was permanently terminated the very next day.

Yasmina wondered why Trish would call him partner. This certainly was a major red flag to her, and all the sirens were screaming.

"Yasmina, please instruct me as to what to do," the security chief begged.

"Begin by searching all the rooms, starting with mine, and leave nothing to chance. Open all doors and closets. Look everywhere. We must find him at once," Yasmina ordered.

Yasmina had been plotting a way to get rid of the security chief and fortunately may have just found it by pure luck. She concluded that Curtis was with Trish in her room, and when the chief opened that door, surprising Curtis, the chief would likely be taking a long leave of absence.

Yasmina positioned herself down the hallway and could hear the entire episode unfolding on her MP3 player. She heard the door open to Trish's suite. Curtis began cursing profusely at the chief. Without warning came the sound of two quick gunshots. Yasmina ran toward the sound to observe the carnage. She could see the chief staggering backward, falling out the open door while holding his chest. Blood was erupting through his fingers from the obvious hole in his beating heart. The blood stopped spurting as the chief fell and hit the marble floor with a thud, his head bouncing twice. Curtis was standing stark naked in front of the dying man, holding a gun. Yasmina averted her eyes and promptly retreated to the pool area. She listened intently on her MP3 player as Curtis justified his theory of why this man deserved to die.

Yasmina pulled out her cell phone and, due to the confusion regarding the shooting, felt comfortable calling her handler.

"Yes, how may I serve you?" the handler answered.

"The test of the new transmitter worked well," Trish said. "In fact I picked up a conversation between Curtis Harrison and Trish Alcort. It seems they have made some type of partnership. I will keep you posted."

"Good work, agent."

The line went dead, and Yasmina had time to piece some things together. She remembered that the handler had told her it was a woman at AP who had set up Summer Tolly with the interpreter during the war. Could it be that this young woman, Trish Alcort, was the same one who had arranged Summer's boyfriend's demise and had attempted to murder Summer as well? The coincidences were simply too astounding to not research fully.

CHAPTER 13

▼

Summer and Chip were driving their rental car to Pul-e-Charki prison in Kabul first thing the next morning. Summer had been successful at using the front-desk clerk at the hotel to call the number she had for Abdul-Hakim, the interpreter. The woman answering the phone indicated that her husband had been arrested and taken to the prison over three months ago. His wife had seen him only once since the time his formal charges were read in open court. He was accused of being a traitor to the new Afghan government. A charge of this type always meant, at minimum, life without parole.

Pul-e-Charki prison had a notorious past. It was known for many atrocities committed during the Soviet occupation. The prison consisted of eighteen blocks, each block having 116 rooms. It was reported that when the Soviets ran the prison it had a population of over 117,000. The Soviets' normal practice was to kill off dozens every night just to make more room in the sardine-packed facility. The prison was now run by the United States with the assistance of the new Afghan government. The situation was still deplorable, having ten people incarcerated in each three-by-five-meter cell.

Summer was convinced the U.S. guards would allow her access to Abdul so she could pry out some answers about Jimmy's death. She realized that the man who had been her interpreter could not have planned the assassination attempt alone. Summer carefully considered the entire situation, and though she would have liked nothing more than to kill the man on the spot, the bigger picture was to discover who had ordered the bombing of their vehicle. Summer needed to establish what involvement Trish had partaken in Jimmy's death.

"Okay, let's cover our plan again," Summer said. "We need to keep our cool when we approach Abdul-Hakim, and show no emotion. I will ask the questions, and you run the video camera."

"That's fine, Summer, but we first have to determine how we can get access to him. I don't think the guards will let just anyone walk in and talk to the prisoners."

"I have considered the problem, and we will use my AP press pass. I think the best way to soften the guards up is to convince them we are doing a story on how efficiently they handle these dangerous prisoners. I can throw in a bunch of hype about how brave they are and how very proud their families will be when they read about them back in the U.S."

"How do we get to Abdul-Hakim, then?"

"We tell them word on the street has it he is one of the most dangerous and has many connections we hope to expose. We can entice the guards by inflating their egos regarding how well they manage the worst of the prisoners. In fact, we will offer to take pictures with Abdul, much the same as a hunter poses with dead prey. These macho GIs will eat this stuff up."

Gaining access to the prison was a simple matter. Summer's plan to entice the U.S. GIs by inflating their egos worked perfectly. Summer made certain she photographed all the GIs, carefully took their names, and promised to highlight them prominently in her article. Summer and Chip were led into a stark room used by intelligence officers to question the prisoners. The guard indicated that one of the duty officers would join them in a minute.

The door opened, and to Summer's surprise a rather petit woman officer entered the room. Summer could ascertain from the markings on her uniform that she was a captain. The rough-looking lady began to speak.

"I understand you are here to do a story about our prison and the fine men and women managing the quarters," the captain stated.

"Yes, we are reporters with Associated Press, and we would like to interview one of your prisoners and also do a complete background story about you fine Americans," Summer lied.

"Well, I think the story would be superb for morale. Which animal is it you have taken an interest toward to do the interview?" the captain asked.

"Abdul-Hakim is his name," Summer said. "He was acting as an interpreter during the war, and we have been told he has been arrested for treason."

"Yes, I know who you are talking about. Abdul-Hakim is the lowest slime. He was able to infiltrate our intelligence community during the war, pretending to be assisting the U.S. effort. In reality we found he was al-Qaeda and had provided all the information he had garnered directly to Osama Bin Laden. We have him under special wraps because we believe he knows significantly more than he has shared with us. I will go and get him so you can have a little talk with him," The captain said hoarsely as she left the room.

The sounds echoed in the hallways of Pul-e-Charki prison. The mixed tongues blended with the never-ending screams and moans. There was a stench in the air of a mixture of body odor, urine, and feces. Summer and Chip sat nervously looking at each other as they felt the pain of the environment around them. Abruptly they could hear a struggle just outside the door. With a crash, the door flew open to expose the female captain prodding Abdul into the room. The filthy man dragged his shackled legs under him, and his hands were bound tightly. It was shocking to see Abdul with a leather lead choker about his neck, like one used to walk a dog.

"Here is your prisoner, Abdul-Hakim," the captain announced.

The petit female captain tied the man's leash around a steel loop permanently attached to the wall. She made Abdul-Hakim crouch on the floor directly below the apparatus.

"He can't reach you, so you'll be safe. When you are done with this dog, just holler out the door, and a guard will come to drag him back to his cell," the captain stated as she slammed the door behind her.

Abdul-Hakim seemed disoriented. He kept his head bowed toward the ground and would not look up to see who was here to visit him. It was clear the abuse had caused this lowlife to become a very meek man.

"Look up at me," Summer barked.

Abdul-Hakim slowly jerked his jittery head up until he could determine who was speaking. He did not recognize the young man, but he defiantly recognized Summer. It was a tremendous shock to him, and he thought he was hallucinating for a moment. The last time he had seen her, he was certain she was dead.

Chip grudgingly kept his word to Summer and did not speak. He busied himself taking pictures and running the camcorder. Chip wished he had not made the promise to keep quiet, because he had plenty to say to this vile man. Chip agreed that Summer was correct in her warning about attacking Abdul. It would cause him to be defensive and not cooperative. Summer began her questioning.

"I am sure you remember me today. I am convinced my boyfriend was killed, and it was no accident. You gave us the warning to evacuate, and within seconds our Humvee hit a land mine and was obliterated. I have two simple questions. First, who hired you as the interpreter, and second, who ordered the killing?"

Abdul-Hakim was a significantly different man since the time he had worked with Summer and Jimmy. At that time, he had been robust and overweight. Today he was a very thin and frail man reacting in a timid way. He had aged ten years in a few months while doing time in the prison. Life was harshly cruel in this godforsaken place, and death would be preferable for its inhabitants. He struggled to talk.

"I will tell you anything you wish. Just one condition is all I demand. Get me out of here. Otherwise I tell you nothing," Abdul said.

"You are in here on a life sentence, and you think we can get you out? You cannot be serious," Summer said decisively.

"I will tell you this much. I was hired by someone claiming to be working with the American military. I now realize what she ordered us to do was not in the interest of the Americans. Her intentions ended up being more of a personal vendetta against you," Abdul spit out.

"Tell us who this American woman is that you are referring to so we can bring her to justice," Summer demanded.

"There is no justice," Abdul stated in a matter-of-fact way, looking directly into Summer's eyes. "Look around, and you can clearly see we are treated more lowly than animals. You Americans speak of justice. You cannot comprehend what justice is, since you are so spoiled. Real justice would be my release from this awful place. This is my offer to you. If released, I will personally deliver you to the people responsible for the attack. Otherwise I will stay within these walls and pray for death."

Abdul struggled to stand to his feet and pounded against the door. The female captain came, untied his leash from the wall, and literally dragged him out of the room. Summer and Chip followed their prey into the hallway, finding heaps of naked prisoners piled on top of each other. A dozen guards were laughing and provoking the unfortunates by kicking them and spitting on them. Abdul was dragged in a circle around the pile of flesh while the female captain lit a cigarette and joked about the naked forms before her with the other military guards.

Either by instinct or insanity, Summer encouraged Chip to videotape the entire scene. Summer also used the digital camera she had attached to her belt. The guards, noticing the cameras, began posing and posturing next to the disgusting piles of humanity. Summer and Chip were appalled by the display, but the guards continued to ask them to take pictures of these revolting scenes.

Finally the female Captain announced, "The fun is over, boys. Put these monkeys back in their cages."

Summer and Chip were still in disbelief when they began the drive back to the hotel. Chip clicked through the pictures on the digital camera while Summer viewed the sickening images displayed on the small screen attached to the video camera.

"I can't believe what we just witnessed. That type of abuse has to be a violation of the Geneva Convention rules for prisoner handling. The woman captain was really getting off on it, and she was in command. It makes me sick," Chip choked.

"You know, the sad part of the whole thing is that they were actually proud of what they were doing to those poor people. I assume the prisoners have done horrible things, but Americans should be above these gutter tactics. I have never had connection with the military, but if that is what it is like, I never want to be associated with it," Summer said.

Few other words were spoken on the way to the hotel. Every once in awhile, Chip would quickly cover his mouth and choke. Summer sat motionless in a daze, concentrating on the dirt road she was driving. Both agreed upon returning to the hotel that they must shower to cleanse the rancid smell of the prison from their bodies. Summer, in her disgust, planned to throw away the clothing she had worn into the prison. Chip proclaimed that he would attempt any means to get the vile images out of his brain. They decided to meet in the lobby and proceed to the bar in one hour in an effort to erase the images from their minds.

Summer sat patiently sipping her martini. She could not get the pictures of what she had seen at the prison out of her head. She made a few phone calls and found that the captain they had met reported directly to a Colonel Mathew Hadley. Summer wondered if the colonel was part of the seemingly abusive situation at the prison. She thought the man probably seldom visited the facility, since he was responsible for the entire prison system in Afghanistan. Summer could see Chip walking toward her table. She was relieved at how well Chip supported her and followed her instructions. Summer adjusted the low-cut black dress she was wearing, reflecting her modesty.

"Hello," Chip said. "Boy, I feel better. I let the shower flow over me, and I just soaked to make sure the scum was washed away."

"I ordered you a martini, okay with you?" Summer asked.

"Anything to calm my nerves, and it sounds like what the doctor ordered." After a pause, he said, "You know, with everything that happened, we never talked about Abdul's demand. Do you think it is possible at all to get him released?"

"No, not in the normal fashion. He is looked upon as a spy, and considering the treatment of the prisoners, they won't likely be open to a request of that type."

"I feel so helpless. I am certain Abdul will not give us the information we need unless we get him released. I think he was serious when he said he would pray for death."

"I did some checking, and I have a crazy idea," Summer said. "A lot depends on whether the abuse we witnessed and photographed is standard operating procedure. If it is, we are sunk, but if it is an abnormality, then perhaps we can apply pressure up the chain of command. Even if it is common, the higher-ups definitely would not want it shown on American TV news."

"I agree, but are you suggesting we somehow blackmail the U.S. Army?" Chip asked in surprise.

"I am suggesting we go to the head of prisons, Colonel Mathew Hadley. We make our best case for Abdul's release, and if not agreed, we show him the pictures and videotapes. If he is worried about the exposure, one more al-Qaeda prisoner missing may be worth it to him."

"So we are going to blackmail the most powerful force in the world?" Chip asked in disbelief.

"Yes, we are, and I bet it works better than you could ever imagine."

CHAPTER 14

▼

Yasmina once again tested the new electronics during breakfast, when Curtis and Trish sat by the pool enjoying eggs benedict and mimosas. Perhaps it would seem strange to some, but the killing of the security chief earlier in the morning did not ruffle any of the day's activities. It was merely an inconvenience for the housekeeping staff, who had to dispose of the body and clean the blood off the walls, floors, and furniture.

Yasmina was taken aback that the conversation between Curtis and Trish was upbeat, flirty, and mostly sexual. Yasmina knew this budding romance was a problem; she just was not sure how to handle the situation. She was amazed that the visitor showed no real emotion upon seeing a man killed for no apparent reason other than seeing his boss's "ding dong" being pumped into his new toy. Trish Alcort must have a heart of steel, she thought to herself.

When Yasmina could hear that the brunch had ended, she went to ask Curtis if she could review some things with him. Yasmina found him sitting alone by the pool, smoking a cigarette. She looked around to see if Trish was anywhere close by in the pool area. Once she was confident that Trish was gone, she sat in the chair opposite her target.

"I am sorry to interrupt your thoughts, Mr. Harrison," Yasmina stated politely. "I have some business I think we need to discuss."

"Yasmina, I am always available to you for counsel," Curtis said. "I was just thinking about this young woman, the American, Trish. She perplexes me. I show her the most respect possible, and she acts as though I am the lucky one. Can you believe the nerve of this woman?"

"Mr. Harrison, I know from when I was in America for study that American women are very different in their beliefs. They are looked upon as cherished items by their suitors and treated like princesses by their fathers. It is much different than what I have seen here in Afghanistan."

"Yasmina, I am insulted that you don't think I treat you like a princess. How many American girls live with the luxury I provide for you?"

"You misunderstand me, Mr. Harrison. I am very satisfied with my life and all you have done for me. I was relating the story of the common Afghan woman."

"That's better. Well, anyway, I don't understand this Trish Alcort very well. I need to gain confidence and comfort with her capabilities. Yasmina, I tell you this as my confidant. I plan to use this woman as my envoy for the American distribution system for our products. Her father is currently in control of the eastern part of the U.S., but I think I can use his daughter to grab the whole pie for myself."

"How do you see this working, Mr. Harrison? Is the young woman going to help you with getting her father out of the way?"

"All in good time, Yasmina. I will keep you up to date on the highlights along the way. I need for you to help me keep this woman interested. Send her an invitation to stay here on a permanent basis. Then I can control her every move. The rest is already in motion and will fall into place nicely," Curtis said with determination.

"I understand and can appreciate your motives. I am also concerned that we need to replace the security chief," Yasmina stated, still not comprehending this man.

"You have an excellent point, Yasmina, and I have decided to make you the new chief of security due to your loyal service," Curtis said emotionally.

"Thank you, sir. You will not be disappointed."

Curtis waited until Yasmina had walked to the main house and entered. His conversation with her caused him concern. He was stymied over how much he could trust this young Afghan woman. Part of him desperately wanted someone he could plan and connive with who was unquestionably trusted. He had brought her along well. She knew his business almost as well as he did, but she had been protected from most of the dark side.

There were times when people, either purposely or not, got in the way of the operation. Some you could buy, some you could influence, and others you simply must kill. Yasmina had seemed shocked when she saw him shoot the intruding security chief earlier. He took notice that she had run out to the pool area. Curtis concluded Yasmina needed more exposure to the seedier side of the business if she was to be of value.

Curtis picked up his satellite phone and dialed the number of James Alcort.

"Good afternoon. Alcort residence," an older female answered.

"Yes, may I speak with Mr. Alcort? This is Curtis Harrison, and I know he is expecting my call," Curtis explained.

"I will transfer your call to him."

"James Alcort," a male voice on the other end of the line said.

"James, my friend, this is Curtis Harrison."

"Curtis, I am so happy you called. I have been so upset about Trish and have not heard a word from her since she called last time from Afghanistan. I have called the AP office in Boston, and they will not even acknowledge that she is over there. Please tell me you have found her," James pleaded.

"I wish I had better news for you, my friend. I have used all my contacts, and I am quite fearful that she may have fallen into the hands of undesirables."

"You don't mean she has been kidnapped," James said in a plaintive voice.

"Well, I am not certain, but as you know, money loosens lips here in Afghanistan. I would be happy to front you the money, but we are talking about a substantial sum."

"What amount are we talking about?" James asked carefully.

"I am in contact with people having information, and they indicate that a sum of ten million U.S. dollars would be the minimum before they would risk talking to us."

"Ten million, just for some information?" James exploded.

"Please consider that these people are risking their lives, and information about lost Americans is expensive. All people are very fearful of al-Qaeda."

"I am sorry I reacted so strongly. I will do anything necessary to get my daughter back safely. I just don't know if I can get my hands on that much money very quickly." James sounded defeated.

"That's what friends are for, James. I told you I will front the money, and you can repay me later," Curtis stated in a friendly tone.

"It may take me a while, Curtis, to get you repaid. Please do everything you need to do, and I assure you I can get the money."

"Consider it done, my friend. I will keep you informed." Curtis ended the call.

Curtis Harrison sat back in his chair, watching the pool begin to fill with the pretty young women for his afternoon entertainment. He was proud he could pick up the phone and offer to lend this man ten million dollars to get information about his daughter who not only was not kidnapped, but was sleeping in his bed. To top it all off, he now had this poor schmuck indebted to him, financially and emotionally, forever.

"Life is good," Curtis confirmed to himself.

James Alcort put his head in his open hands as tears streamed down his face. Could it be that his beautiful young daughter was in the hands of the most feared al-Qaeda? How could he ever repay Curtis Harrison the money and the favor? How much could he trust this man? he wondered. In order to raise the money, he would have to sell everything. He would be a ruined and broken man.

James Alcort mulled over the idea that he should make a trip to Boston and force Justin Davis to divulge any information he had about Trish's whereabouts. If he could find her before Curtis Harrison paid the money, then maybe he had some hope of saving his fortune.

Yasmina sat at her desk, thinking about what Curtis had just told her and how it could affect her assignment. She knew Curtis well enough and was convinced he intended to take James Alcort out of the heroin distribution business. How could she work this to her own advantage in order to get additional information to give to the CIA and punish this horrible man? He was able, without any emotion, to sit there worrying about his love life and business just after killing a man who had been his chief security guard for ten years. He was even more evil than she had ever imagined. The good news now was that being chief of security should make her mission simpler, giving her ever-broadening access.

Yasmina realized she needed to be flexible and fluid considering the constantly changing environment. She had to look at all the possibilities and have contingency plans in place. If Curtis took over control of distribution on the East Coast of America, it could be beneficial if she were able to connect him directly to al-Qaeda. Then, not only could they take Curtis Harrison out of the picture, but they could shut down all of the illicit drug trade in the eastern United States. This of course meant Trish would have to be either implicated or eliminated.

Yasmina was not clear whether Curtis truly was using Trish for his business purposes as he had indicated. It was more likely that she had taken Curtis in with her female charm and attributes. Trish was disposable. Yasmina really was in desperate need of positive proof about the al-Qaeda connection. Now, with the Iraq War in full swing, the CIA was committed to making the connection between al-Qaeda and Iraq. Her employer, the CIA, was never satisfied and was determined to connect al-Qaeda to Iraq and the weapons of mass destruction. On the other hand, al-Qaeda fed like a hungry pig at the trough of human suffering and relished the confusion it had created for the United States.

She was relieved that Curtis wanted Trish to be permanently relocated to the compound. It would make it easier for her to keep an eye on both of them. Also, it was a good indication that Curtis indeed cared for Trish and might confide with her about his plans. Yasmina placed the earplugs back in her ears. This was the best way to hear his most intimate thoughts and plans. She hoped the information came soon.

Yasmina saw Trish going out the front door of the estate. As expected, she was returning to the Mustafa Hotel to get her remaining belongings and check out. Trish Alcort was on her way and soon would be a permanent fixture around the Harrison Estate.

Trish returned to the hotel, proud of her accomplishments. She had played Curtis Harrison perfectly and had reeled him in like a big fish. Her plan was working great. She soon would be in control of the largest heroin distribution system in the world. Trish would be able to enjoy the necessities of life she had come to rely upon.

She regretted that her father would have to succumb to her wishes and step aside. Trish told herself it really was his fault for not being honest with her about the source of his money. She had found out quite accidentally when she was doing research for a story about Afghanistan during the war. It was a background "fluff piece" about the drug trade. Every government document and source seemed to lead to her father. Since that time, she had lost all respect for him and had only superficially put up with him for short-term financial needs.

Trish stopped by the front desk and handed the clerk a hefty sum of money. The instruction attached to the bribe was to call her as soon as Summer reappeared at the hotel. Trish knew she had to come up with a scheme to get Summer and Chip to follow false leads and stay out of her way.

She devised a plan that, in her mind, was perfect. She decided to fill some notes with false information and accidentally drop them for Summer to discover. Trish was sure that Summer would take advantage of the information in an attempt to track down Jimmy's killer. Trish prepared the notes carefully. She used different pens and wrote somewhat cryptic notes that appeared to be authentic. Now she needed to get them into Summer's hands. Trish was confident she could entice Chip Murphy by using her wiles and disable him from helping Summer. Trish was satisfied that Summer was just a temporary nuisance that would go away soon. If not, she had no problem having the duo eliminated. Only this time she would use a more reliable assassin to assure that Summer didn't survive as she mistakenly had before. "Boy, I regret not handling Summer's killing myself. If I had, then I would not be having these problems now," she thought to herself.

CHAPTER 15

▼

Summer and Chip met at the coffee shop in the hotel. Both had gone their separate ways the morning after their visit to the prison. Following the plan they had made the previous night, Chip went to the army command post to set up an interview with Colonel Mathew Hadley, the commander of the Afghan prison system. At first he thought it to be a bust, but he told the corporal that he was an AP reporter, and suddenly the colonel's schedule became very flexible. He was proud to say they had a meeting set for eight in the morning.

Summer's duties had been to take the digital pictures and print them on the color printer she had in her room. She wanted to download all the evidence and transfer it to SD memory cards so they would have multiple copies. Summer decided it was smart to send the pictures to the United States with instructions as to what to do with them if their plan did not work. She sent the copies of the pictures and video to Mary Wallace, her attorney in the United States. This was the only person she knew who could be trusted except for Chip. Mary and Summer had been roommates in college, and Mary had a successful law practice in Boston. Summer attached a note with specific instructions as insurance for her safety.

The note read: "Mary, I am sorry I could not see you after I got out of Sunnyview Farms and before I traveled to Afghanistan. I made the decision in a hurry because Chip, Jimmy's brother, offered to go with me to Afghanistan and find out how Jimmy was killed.

"Contained on these SD memory cards and this videotape is substantial evidence that atrocities are being committed at Pul-e-Charki prison in Kabul, Afghanistan. I am attempting to use this evidence to free a man I think can lead me to Jimmy's murderers. Please hold these in strict confidence. In fact, forget you have even seen them until one of two things happens: I return home and ask for them, or I am killed. If I am killed, please give these directly to Paula Zahn at CNN News to be broadcast.

"We are using this evidence to guarantee our safety. Please tell no one about them. Our lives are in your hands. Love, Summer."

Summer and Chip updated each other on their accomplishments of the morning. The meeting with Colonel Mathew Hadley the next day was particularly important. Summer agreed she would see that the package containing the photos was sent off before the day was done. During their conversation, Summer could see the front-desk clerk watching them and suddenly pick up the phone. She was certain he was telling someone about her, because his eyes concentrated on her as he talked. It did not take more than five minutes to understand what he was doing.

Trish Alcort entered the coffee shop and abruptly stopped in her tracks when she saw Summer. She grabbed her knees with both hands, bending over far enough to give Chip a good view of her ample breasts bouncing fully under her low-cut top.

"Summer, my goodness, what are you doing here?" Trish asked in a fake surprised tone.

Summer stood up and walked toward Trish.

"You know me, Summer. I'm a hugger." At that, Trish grabbed Summer and pulled her close. Trish gave "air kisses" to each side of Summer's face. Summer stood there stiff as a board, putting up with the nonsense while gritting her teeth.

"Trish, I heard you might be in this neck of the woods. It's been a long time. The grapevine still has you as a real man killer," Summer choked out the obvious.

Trish pulled back and looked into Summer's eyes, wondering about the offbeat comment. She finished with the formality and walked directly to where Chip was seated. "And who is this handsome gentleman you are with today?" Trish asked curtly.

Summer turned to notice that Chip was intrigued by the show Trish was putting on for him. Trish had extended her hand to Chip's face, waiting for him to kiss it.

"This is Jimmy's brother, Chip," Summer said. "You remember Jimmy, I am sure."

"I am delighted to meet you, Chip. I am sorry about your brother. He was so dear to all of us at AP. I don't think you recall, but I did give you my condolences at Jimmy's funeral," Trish said in a soft tone.

Chip stood up and grabbed a chair from the next table. Trish was already beginning to sit as he quickly put the chair under her. Trish went to set her open purse on the table, and it fell to the floor. Chip quickly gathered the various pieces of notes she had dropped and handed them back to her. Summer shook her head and sat back down with the two. She could taste the blood in her mouth from biting her lip.

"So tell me, Summer, why are you two here in Kabul? Justin have you on another assignment?" Trish demanded.

"No, this is a personal trip," Summer said. "We are checking into some things surrounding Jimmy's death. Maybe you can help us with some local knowledge?"

"Of course I will help you," Trish said. "You have been through so much that I will help in any way possible."

Chip glanced over at Summer, wondering where she was going with this. They had not talked about having Trish help.

"I understand you are here doing a follow-up report on the al-Qaeda and Iraq connection," Summer said, seeming innocent.

"Yes, I have been given the assignment for the story. Justin wants me to investigate the Iraq and al-Qaeda connection. He also would be pleased if I found Bin Laden, like that will happen. I am covering some leads in the city. I have some good leads, but nothing real solid as of yet."

"Well, that sounds exciting," Summer said pleasantly, gritting her teeth.

"I am here alone, and I get very lonely at night," Trish said. "Chip, perhaps I could show you around Kabul a little bit?"

Summer looked over at Chip and noticed he was not giving Trish an immediate "no" answer. In fact, it looked as though he was in a trance, just glaring down Trish's cleavage. Summer kicked him under the table and gave him a knowing look.

"Oh, how nice of you to offer, Trish," Chip said. "Right now is not a good time, though, because we are so busy, but maybe in a day or two?"

Summer gave him another quick kick under the table, and he looked at her as if asking "what?"

Trish rose and grabbed her bag to leave. Some additional notes fell to the floor without her noticing. "Good luck to you, Summer and Chip. I do hope we can see each other soon," she said as she left the coffee shop.

"I hope to see you again too," Chip stammered.

Summer looked at Chip after Trish was gone and tried to stare straight through him with her ocean-blue eyes.

Chip uncomfortably adjusted in his seat. "What did I do? Every time I said something to her, you kicked me. What was that all about?"

"Can't you see what she is trying to do? She jiggles her boobs, and you start panting like a hound dog in heat. God, men disgust me," Summer chastised.

"Well, for one thing, I did not act like that. I was being polite to her. The second thing is, if I want to flirt a little with her, it is none of your business," Chip protested.

"This is the woman who probably had something to do with Jimmy's death, and you flirt with her? What kind of man are you?" Summer questioned furiously.

"The kind of man who is passionate about finding his brother's killer," Chip snapped back.

"The only thing you are passionate about is satisfying your lust for that artificial bitch," Summer barked.

Summer was so mad at him she could spit nails. It had nothing to do with the fact that Chip was very good-looking. After all, she would never get involved with Jimmy's brother. It was only because Trish was one of those women who always got what they wanted by using their bodies. It frustrated Summer that men were so weak and stupid to be taken in by her. To think he would fall for such an obvious ploy sickened her.

Summer looked into Chip's eyes as he moved in close to her face. A shot of adrenaline filled her stomach. "My God, he is going to kiss me," she thought. Suddenly Chip took his tanned hand to her chin and turned her head to the side. He began to whisper in her ear. Summer had not been this excited since being with Jimmy. The words came out of his mouth soft and quiet.

"Trish dropped these notes, and I grabbed them. I don't know if they are of any value, but let's take a look," Chip informed her.

Summer took a deep breath and sat back in her seat, trying to regain her composure. The feelings were a big surprise to her, and the larger revelation was that Chip only wanted to tell her about swiping some of Trish's notes.

They began to look through the notes and saw several references to OBL. The notes referred to a GPS location within Kabul. It also discussed seeing OBL making a video.

"OBL must be code for Osama Bin Laden. I wonder if Trish has a source that really is providing information on Bin Laden's hiding place," Summer said.

"This note gives GPS coordinates for where a drop of additional information is to take place. I wonder if Trish has informed the military," Chip mused to his partner.

"Don't be ridiculous. Trish would not give the military the time of day unless there was some advantage for her to do so. This might be another thing we can use in our meeting with the colonel in the morning. I am sure they would like any leads we can give them," Summer rationalized.

"Good idea. It is one more trick to put in our bag to pull out if the time is right."

"Chip, I am sorry I snapped at you, but we have to be cautious with anything Trish says or does. She is a snake, and it is possible she could be intentionally misleading us and that dropping the notes was not an accident," Summer warned.

"I think she is a very clever young lady. You are right to be careful, and you have a very good point. The best thing I can do is to take her up on seeing her again to keep a close eye on her," Chip volunteered.

Summer thought to herself she had really blown it and was mad at herself that she had told Chip about her suspicions, because now he would go out with her. Summer knew that with Trish's good looks and equal body, she could persuade any man to do her bidding. Summer thought that if she protested too much, Chip might take it as jealousy. She had to be careful, and the best tactic now was to cut her losses.

"I think it's time to take a little expedition. I have a portable GPS in my rental car that we can use to track down the coordinates in the notes. I assume it has probably been picked up, but it is worth checking it out," Summer suggested.

Summer and Chip used the portable Garmin GPS to find the location. The coordinates took them to the Kabul Museum. It had once had a collection of over thirty thousand Asian antiquities, being the largest collection in the world. During the war, however, most had been looted.

The GPS took them to a metal electrical service box located just behind one of the massive pillars at the entrance. Chip took out a Leather Master multitool and snipped the wires holding the lid in place.

"Be careful, Chip. It could be a bomb," Summer warned.

"You should have told me before I cut the wires," Chip said in a sarcastic tone.

Chip, now more careful, eased the lid open. The first thing Summer noticed was red LED numbers flashing by sequentially in a blur. Instinctively she threw her body across the five feet to where Chip was hunched over, and knocked him to the ground. Summer covered his body by lying on top, and she shielded her face, waiting for the explosion.

"What the hell are you doing?" Chip shouted.

"I thought it was a bomb," Summer answered as she crawled over to inspect the device more closely. She glanced at the digital display, seeing that only three seconds were remaining.

Chip came up behind her.

"Careful," Summer said, "we have a plastic explosive that did not detonate. Evidently, when I jumped on you, the power source malfunctioned and stopped the timer at just three seconds. Let's move away real easy."

The two made it back to the rental car, and Summer picked up her cell phone to call the police. Chip was seated in the passenger side, still trembling. Summer looked back toward the museum, and abruptly a fireball erupted from the device, making a deafening noise. Seconds later, their car was riddled with flying debris.

"Chip, you alright?" Summer screamed as she ducked down behind the steering wheel.

Receiving no answer, she became worried and scooted over to where he was huddled. Summer grabbed him by the arm and pulled him up into the seat. The look of fear in his eyes was unmistakable.

"Summer, you saved my life. If you had not pushed me away, I would be dead right now," Chip said in a trembling voice.

"Damn, I knew I was right all along. Trish is behind Jimmy's killing and out to get me. She could not have orchestrated everything alone. We must find the connection, or next time we will end up dead," Summer yelled.

"Maybe it is just a coincidence that we found the notes from Trish and that they led us to the bomb. It could be someone else who planted the bomb, and we were not even the target," Chip rationalized.

Summer grasped his arm and pulled him to her eyes. "Being naive will only get us killed," she said passionately. "The writing is on the wall. Trish Alcort will go to any lengths to see me dead. Get a grip."

It was obvious Trish had played the first card in her hand as an attempt to kill them both. Even though they had survived, it reminded Summer that Trish was a force to be reckoned with. Summer calmed Chip down and convinced him that the best policy was to not let on to Trish that they had fallen for her ploy. This was a wake up call exposing the intensity of hate and danger they would certainly continue to encounter.

Trish went back to her room and created an e-mail on her PDA for her handler. "American reporters witnessed at Kabul Museum opening box suspected to be dropped by al-Qaeda sympathizer. It is possible they could be working against American interests. Please track accordingly. I require a software program to record keystrokes on any computer within fifty feet. I need to get passwords to break into target system. Subject computer operates on wireless network, Please advise."

The handler happened to be on-line and responded immediately. "The American reporters will be shadowed, and I will update their activities to you as requested. The attached file contains a program to be downloaded to your PDA. This gives your PDA the capability to identify, by IP, and record all keystrokes on any wireless computer within one hundred feet. All passwords will be captured for your use against the target computer to break its security protection."

Suddenly there was a knock on Trish's door. Her first thought was that Summer or Chip were probably naive enough to be returning the dropped notes as a favor. Trish looked out the door, and it was a bellhop. He announced that he had a message for her and shoved it under her door.

Trish recognized the personalized stationary from Curtis Harrison. She intently read the note with the invitation to stay at the estate. She knew she would accept, but she wanted to see how the thing with Chip would play out.

Trish wrote a brief note to accept Curtis Harrison's offer and sent it by messenger. "Curtis, I received your kind invitation to take up a rather permanent residency at the estate. I very much would like to accept your gracious offer; however I have a few loose ends I need to put to rest before I will be free. Please have your conveyance here for my move at about noon on Friday. Fondly, Trish."

Chip excused himself and went back to his room, still distraught after seeing his life flash before his eyes. Summer stayed behind and entered the coffee shop to gather her thoughts. Summer had anticipated that Trish would attempt to kill her, but obviously Chip was not prepared for the dangerous overtones of their mission. She had to convince Chip to meet with Trish and return the notes as if nothing had happened. If Trish knew they had been shaken, she would have the upper hand, and gaining back control would be impossible. Summer knew she had to push Chip to see her plan evolve as anticipated.

Summer stopped by the front desk and scribbled a note to Trish Alcort, falsely identifying Chip as the sender. "Trish, it was so nice to meet you earlier this evening. I do want to take you up on your offer to show me Kabul. I have business in the morning, but if you are free in the afternoon we could have lunch and talk. If your schedule permits, meet me in the hotel restaurant at 1 PM. Chip Murphy. PS: I found some notes that you dropped by accident when we met earlier. I will return them to you tomorrow."

Now all Summer had to do was settle Chip's nerves and convince him to continue following her lead. Her strength and resolve were growing each day. She was even more determined to see justice applied to this evil woman.

CHAPTER 16

▼

Justin Davis was on the phone when he heard a commotion at the reception desk. He ended his call abruptly and proceeded to the lobby area of the AP offices. He saw a well-dressed gentleman arguing with the receptionist while being restrained by two security guards.

"What is going on here? I can hear you way back in my office," Justin screamed.

"Mr. Davis, this man is insisting he speak with you. I told him you were on the phone, and he called me a liar and began to walk into the office area. That's when I called security," the receptionist said nervously.

"Sir, what is this all about? You can't come in here and treat people in this manner," Justin said sternly.

"I am sorry for my insolence," the man pleaded. "I am only trying to find out about my daughter's situation. You have not accepted any of my phone calls."

Justin Davis knew at once who the man was, Trish Alcort's father. Justin had in fact ducked all the calls from him and had returned none. Justin knew that at some point he would have to deal with this state of affairs. The only problem was that since Trish was involved in some sort of secret operation, he could not provide any information. He had already blown it when the receptionist had divulged Trish's location to Summer and Chip. Justin had been forced to beg for forgiveness from Trish for that one. He certainly did not want to provide this man with any details that would get him in further hot water.

"Mr. Alcort, I am sorry. I have been meaning to get back with you about Trish," Justin said, gesturing to the guards to move back. "Perhaps we could discuss this over coffee. I will get my coat and keys. We will be more comfortable away from the craziness here in the office."

Justin walked back to his office. He had no idea what to tell Trish's father. If he gave him her location, he would be in trouble with his boss and who knows who. He was hoping he could skirt the issue and give him just enough so he would leave him alone. One thing was for sure; Justin knew his office must be bugged. He had also noticed that someone had been following him since Trish found out about his little slipup. Letting the cat out of the bag about her location was a major mistake. Maybe he was just paranoid, but men in black suits had been showing up wherever he was, making him increasingly nervous. He could talk more freely out of the office.

"Okay, Mr. Alcort, come with me, and we will have that chat," Justin stated as they entered the elevator.

"Mr. Davis, I need to know where Trish is staying in Afghanistan," James Alcort said. "I have been told that she may be in great danger."

Justin was surprised Trish's father even knew she was in Afghanistan. "I'm sure Trish was told to not tell a soul her location," Justin thought. "She also must have broken the rules."

"I will explain everything to you," Justin said. "You have nothing to worry about. I am sure Trish is in good hands and not in any danger."

Justin unlocked the doors to his ninety-five Ford conversion van with the remote he kept on his key chain. Both men jumped in, and Justin turned the ignition key. The groan of a starter turning down to nothing was heard. The van would not start, so Justin popped the hood.

"Don't worry, Mr. Alcort. This happens all the time. It just needs a little TLC," Justin said, exiting the vehicle.

James Alcort hit the dash with his clenched fist. He was becoming even more frustrated with this sloppy human being. All he was interested in was information. He could care less about going to have coffee in this piece of junk. Alcort decided to get out and give this man a piece of his mind. As he opened the door, he could see a man in a dark suit coming up behind Justin. Perhaps it was his intent to assist in getting the motor running. As the man got immediately behind Justin, he pulled a shinny object from his coat and placed it behind Justin's left ear. All James heard was *pop pop*.

James Alcort was confused, and he marveled at how the man had walked away so quickly. He saw Justin falling from the waist up into the engine compartment, leaving his legs dangling. James ran over to Justin and saw blood gushing from a wound in the back of his head. He felt something dripping from the hood onto his cheek. He rubbed it with his finger and realized it was brain matter. He began to yell.

"Justin, you alright? What just happened here?"

Before James Alcort could ask any more questions, he felt a sharp blow to the back of his head. As he was sinking to the garage pavement, he thought, "It's true; all you see is stars." After that everything went black.

Yasmina was getting more depressed regarding her assignment. She had been sitting for days in the shadows surrounding Curtis Harrison's compound. She had been receiving transmissions without problems since the new electronics had been installed. She could now hide anywhere she wanted, and the transmissions were very clear. She thought to herself how the design and installation had gone so well, and now good information to monitor was just not coming.

The problem was temporary because Trish had gone back to the Mustafa Hotel. Without Trish on the property, Yasmina could no longer keep track of conversations between her and Curtis Harrison. She was hoping to get some tidbit of information that Mr. Harrison might let slip to Trish. The chatter she had recorded to date was nothing more than the normal posturing that new romances go through. Something had to happen, or she would have to change her tactics.

Trish had her phone set to vibrate so the ring would not give away that she was in her room. She could feel that a call was being placed to her, and the caller ID showed it to be from her CIA handler. She picked it up, and it was a text message coming through.

"007 on J Davis completed. Complication. A witness was on site. Observer neutralized. Will update on regular report."

Trish felt a very small twinge of guilt over having Justin killed. She liked him, but he had made the mistake of talking too much. After all, she was now relegated to finding ways to deter her rival because Summer knew her location. Hopefully the notes leading Summer to the bomb had done the trick. Having Justin killed was a small price to pay for the benefits her operation would bring, at least to her.

Trish decided she would have to take the chance of tailing Summer if she had survived the blast, in order to know her exact movements. An easier way would be to separate the two and create enough problems that Summer and Chip would just go back to Boston. All of this would be her contingency plan if they were in one piece after following her notes to the Kabul Museum. Trish decided that, if necessary, the better alternative would be to work on getting Chip under her control. Not only would it thwart their efforts at digging up information about Jimmy, but it would really piss Summer off. That was worth the effort in and of itself. Trish was ultimately hoping to see neither of them again, except in the obituaries.

Summer met Chip at the entrance to the hotel. Soon they were off to army headquarters to meet with Colonel Mathew Hadley. The drive through the streets of Kabul tended to keep Summer sullen. The misery painted on the people's faces was always evident. Life in that part of the world was a constant struggle; nothing like living in the United States. Summer could see the orphans begging on the street. "Everything is relative," Summer thought to herself. "Yes, I was an orphan, but I at least had a warm place to sleep." She was frantically taking notes about what she was viewing. Her plan was to write an article exposing the cruelty toward the unfortunate people caught in the political turmoil of man's greed and war. She had learned about constant pain after losing Jimmy. Her sympathy toward all suffering people had been magnified by the event.

When her mother had died many years ago, she had put a shell around herself as protection against any further hurt. Since Jimmy's death, she had opened up much more to other people's suffering. She had acquired a profound understating that if it were not for the grace of God, she could easily have been born in this war-stricken area of the world. Summer thanked God every day for her blessings and hoped she could make a contribution to help others in some small way.

Chip pulled up to the guard gate at the base, and Summer snapped her mind to the present. After having the car inspected for bombs and weapons, both showed their credentials and were escorted to the colonel's office. The corporal Chip had talked to the day before was seated at the reception desk. He looked up as they both entered. The corporal thought to himself that Chip should have told him he was bringing a beautiful young woman with him. That would really have greased the skids, so to speak. He looked at the long flowing blond hair and bright blue eyes. The lightweight dress she was wearing showed her perfect body. The corporal thought he would get a big thank-you from the colonel for having such a lovely visit. They seldom saw any women's faces, due to the local customs, and never did they see blond hair and blue eyes. The colonel would graciously welcome these two.

They entered the colonel's office. Behind the desk, on the phone, was a middle-aged man puffing a cigar. He raised his untrimmed eyebrows toward his guests. Upon seeing Summer, he immediately hung up the phone and stood with his hand extended toward her. Summer lightly shook his hand, and Chip extended his in a like fashion. The colonel ignored Chip and kept his eyes glued to Summer while not letting go of her hand. Summer broke the trance by speaking first.

"Colonel, thank you for seeing us today. My name is Summer Tolly, and this is Chip Murphy, with the Associated Press."

Summer began to pull her hand away from the colonel. The colonel cleared his throat and realized he was making this pretty young woman uncomfortable. He sat back down in his chair.

"Our visit here today is to discuss a prisoner you have detained at Pul-e-Charki prison, named Abdul-Hakim," Summer said. "He is from Saudi Arabia, and during the war he worked as an interpreter for me and another reporter, Jimmy Murphy, Chip's brother, who unfortunately was killed."

The colonel leaned toward his phone and pressed a button asking the corporal to bring him the file on Abdul-Hakim. They could hear the scream of the dot-matrix printer running in the outer office. The corporal came in carrying the continuous form.

"Here, Colonel, the file on Abdul-Hakim," The corporal announced as he entered the office.

The colonel sat back in his leather desk chair and stopped puffing on his cigar. "Well, your Mr. Hakim is a very interesting fellow," the colonel explained. "He has been arrested as an al-Qaeda member. Not a very pleasant fellow, I must say. We feel he is responsible for numerous bombings and may even be part of the 9/11 attack. What would you want to do with this miserable man?"

"Well, we feel he can give us information to find out more about Jimmy's death," Summer explained. "He was there at the time, and I thought his actions were suspicious."

"There should be no problem getting him to talk," the colonel said. "These types are easy to manipulate, and we have had many successes getting information from them."

"Colonel, we have met with him, and he demands to be released before he talks. We believe that..."

The colonel stopped Summer in mid sentence. "Release is out of the question," he said. "This is a dangerous man needing to be held for life. If that is what you are getting at, then you are wasting your time and mine."

Summer saw that this military man was not going to bend. She looked at Chip and gave him the prearranged signal. Chip pulled out the distasteful eight-by-ten color photographs they had taken at the prison and threw them faceup on the colonel's desk. The colonel gave her a look of contempt for this act and then slowly picked up the photos and began to thumb through them. He hesitated, tapping the last picture on his other hand.

"So you have some photos of my men disciplining these animals. What card do you want to play now, Miss Tolly?" the colonel asked in disgust.

"No cards, Colonel, I just want Abdul-Hakim released to me, and I will agree not to provide these pictures of atrocities to the press," Summer stated flatly.

The colonel rose and carried the photos with him to the window. He stared out, looking away from the two. Suddenly he frantically began to rip the pictures to shreds, hurling them across the room in their direction.

"Now then, young lady," the colonel said. "I did not get these stripes by being bullied by some naive little twit like you. I have no intention of falling for your blackmail scheme, and I could have you arrested for even trying it. I suggest you take advantage of my generosity. I can have you both thrown in the prison with the other traitors. I will forget this little episode, and I strongly suggest you do too."

Chip was shaken by the sudden outburst, but was not surprised. They both rose to their feet as the corporal, hearing the commotion, came and opened the door.

"I am placing my card on your desk," Summer said. "On the back I have put the name of the hotel in which I am staying. By the way, you don't think I am stupid enough not to have copies of the pictures in a safe place do you? I give you twenty-four hours to contact me, or I have the plans in motion to make sure every U.S. broadcasting network will feature them on their nightly news programs. The ball is now in your court, Colonel."

They began to walk out of the office, leaving the steaming colonel. On the way out, Summer turned back and calmly said, "Your operation here smells almost as bad as those cheap cigars you smoke."

They could hear the colonel yelling at the corporal and the breaking of furniture as they quickly exited the building. By the time they got to their car, both were laughing uncontrollably, perhaps from nerves, or more likely because Summer had just put the colonel in a tight box for which all his military training supplied no exit, except of course to follow her demand that Abdul-Hakim be released to them.

Once the pair got past the last security checkpoint, Chip pulled over and slammed on the brakes, creating a small dust storm behind them. He abruptly turned and hugged Summer and whispered in her ear, "You did it, Summer. You are blackmailing the U.S. Army. I am certain he will see things your way once he cools down."

"Chip, being a man, you cannot even begin to comprehend the satisfaction that gave me. Men like him look upon women as inferiors. To be able to beat him in his own arena is the most rewarding thing I could have imagined," Summer said in an excited voice.

Chip slid back into the driver's seat, and Summer continued to stare at him. Chip winked at her and tilted his head, pondering her thoughts.

"We'll get Abdul in our hands and nail Trish's ass," Summer promised.

Chip turned to Summer as he floored the car, heading back to the hotel. "Remind me to never get on your bad side. They say silent waters run deep, and you are a perfect example of a soft exterior and the toughest interior I have ever seen."

CHAPTER 17

▼

Chip was patiently waiting in the hotel restaurant as he checked his watch. Summer had broken the news to him that he would have to meet with Trish. He was so nervous he ate a handful of Tums every five minutes. Summer was much better suited to this type of thing, but he knew he had to pull this off. How do you make small talk with someone who had just tried to kill you? He was not sure, but Summer depended on him, and he would have to deliver.

It was already one fifteen, and Trish had not made her appearance. He wondered if she had received the invitation Summer had written. He was uncomfortable about meeting this beautiful young woman. Chip knew he wore his feelings on his sleeve, and hiding them was not his strong suit. Summer had cringed when he had protested about her scheme, and she had sternly reminded him about the importance of the meeting after they had returned from seeing the colonel. He did understand why Summer had such strong feelings about keeping the museum incident secret, but he also realized that the disdain she had toward Trish went much deeper.

He could definably see they were as different as night and day. Summer had a natural all-American beauty and a simple calmness about her. She wore very little makeup and dressed fairly conservatively. Trish, on the other hand, was striking in an exotic sense. She worked hard at being dressed perfectly and wore the latest fashions. Trish stove to enhance her ample body and had no problem showing off her attributes with skimpy attire.

Chip certainly was attracted to Summer in every sense, but he knew it would never lead anywhere. Trish, on the other hand, was the type of woman he disliked immensely. Her obvious arrogance about her stunning appearance was used to ease men into her web. Chip needed to keep his mind off of Trish's obvious physical beauty and concentrate on getting information. Chip was deep in his thoughts and was startled by the beauty standing in front of him. He stood to greet his guest.

"Trish, I am sorry I did not see you come in," he stated apologetically.

"You must be devising some grand plan," Trish said. "You were deep in thought." She sat down.

Chip took the full measure of her as she was speaking. The long dark hair and tanned skin perfectly illuminated her pure green eyes. "How could such a beauty be so evil?" he thought.

"Yes, I was just thinking about meeting you again," Chip blurted out without thinking.

"Oh, I like a man who gets to the point," Trish purred.

"I'm sorry. That came out wrong. What I meant to say is I find you to be an interesting woman and very intelligent," he attempted to recover.

"Well, Chip, you hardly know me, so I doubt you have been able to quantify my intelligence," she teased.

"I seem to be saying everything wrong. Let's just start over," he said, again apologizing.

"You need to understand me, Chip. I appreciate your attempts at flattering me, but I am smart, and I know that what you are admiring at this point is only my looks. I also notice that you have spent ample time evaluating my cleavage, so I conclude you are a red-blooded American boy. By the way, I love American boys," Trish detailed smartly.

Chip could feel the warmth flowing into his face as a sure sign he was blushing.

"Oh no, did I embarrass you?" Trish asked teasingly.

"Maybe a little. I didn't know I was so transparent," Chip admitted.

"You are a man, and I have a lot of experience with how men react to me," Trish explained.

"A lot of experience, you say?" Chip countered smartly.

"Now I am the one to blush. You may not know this, but I was Miss Rhode Island and have had a lot of practice showing my exterior beauty. The real challenge for any man is to get past my appearance and get to know me as a person. You actually failed your first test, but I will forgive you this time," she said playfully.

Chip became more cautious about what he said after the initial exchange. He was not dealing with the same caliber of young woman he used to entice at the clubs in Boston. He must be careful with her; she was capable of playing him much better than he could play her. Chip kept telling himself to watch his step.

"Before I forget, here are some notes you must have dropped the other day," Chip said, handing her the notes.

"Yes, you mentioned the notes. Could you read my handwriting?" Trish questioned.

"I can assure you, Miss Alcort, I would never examine a lady's intimate items without invitation," Chip said, attempting a double meaning.

"We will see if you get that invitation, Chip. I am still riding the fence on whether I can trust such a good-looking young man."

The waiter brought a bottle of Chardonnay and poured two glasses. Chip looked at the waiter in surprise and began to speak. Trish reached across the table and took hold of Chip's hand.

"I hope you don't mind," Trish said. "I asked the waiter to serve us this wine before I sat down. It is not the best, but for Kabul it will have to do."

Chip took his glass and extended it toward her to make a toast.

"To a very pretty lady who knows what she wants and makes sure she gets it," Chip said bluntly.

"Now you are getting the idea," she said curtly. "Very fast learner, this Boston boy."

"Thank you, Trish. I will be your student any day of the week," Chip said jokingly.

Both began to laugh, and the initial jockeying for position had been established. Chip gazed into her pretty eyes and thought to himself that this could be fun, except that this viper had attempted to kill him less than twenty-four hours ago. Trish stared back and calculated what she could get from him. Both had needs to be satisfied, but strikingly differing ideas.

Yasmina kept her head low as she hid behind her copy of *Omaid Weekly*, the most widely read Afghan publication. She could clearly see Trish with the attractive young man who must have been Chip Murphy. Yasmina was able to get digital pictures using her small Casio Exilim. The camera, being the size of a credit card, could zoom in, displaying their images in detail. Yasmina could tell from their body language that they were playfully teasing each other in the game of amour. She took as many pictures as possible while in their presence. When the waiter took the payment from the duo, Yasmina quietly snuck out the back of the restaurant.

Yasmina hurried to the estate to review the pictures. She was pleased she had thought of a new plan. Her thinking was that she could gain other source information from these Trish Alcort contacts. Also, if required in the future, she could share the pictures with Curtis Harrison to let him know what his new filly was up to when she was out of the barn. She determined she would return to the hotel this evening and track Trish again.

Although she was disappointed that the conversation between Chip and Trish was nothing more than drivel, Yasmina was uncomfortable that Trish seemed to be forming an alliance with this new man. She was already worried that Trish's influence and control on Curtis Harrison might be coming into play. Now she found that Trish was also working on Chip Murphy. The outward appearance was that they were just playing the old game of chicken and the fox.

Yasmina was stressed because she had been hoping for a breakthrough, something really good to report. She was concerned her handler might pull the plug on the operation if she didn't come up with something. The assignment had started off so well by confirming the Curtis Harrison drug connection leading back to the United States. It did not hurt to tie in James Alcort's involvement either. Now she needed something to impress the hierarchy, something really big.

She decided Summer and Chip should not be overlooked in her efforts. Perhaps she could meet with them and discuss their research. Who knows, maybe they had come up with some leads involving the al-Qaeda and Iraq connection that she could use. Yasmina recalled hearing in college that Summer Tolly was Miss Massachusetts. Yasmina decided she would contact Summer and attempt to set up a meeting under the guise of helping her.

Summer heard footsteps coming up the wooden floors of the hallway to her room. She jumped up and peered out her peephole. She could see it was Chip returning from his meeting with Trish. She waited a moment to assure the precocious woman was not accompanying him. To her dismay, Trish was following him closely and entered his room with him.

Summer spent an hour with her eye to the peephole and finally fell asleep inside her room doorway.

Summer was snapped from her sleep when she heard the phone ring in her room. She pulled herself up from the floor and tripped toward the phone next to her bed. She took a quick look at her watch and was amazed it was now morning.

"Hello," Trish said.

"Yes, Miss Tolly, You don't know me, but I am a local woman who has some information that you might be interested in obtaining," Yasmina said.

"Who is this, and what type of information are you talking about?"

"My name is Yasmina. I think it best we meet, and I can tell you more completely. Could I possibly see you in two hours?"

"Yes, where do you want to meet?"

"The coffee shop at the hotel. See you then."

Summer did not know what this woman could possibly be able to tell her, but as a reporter, she knew any lead could be important. Although she was so infuriated at Chip she could scream, she hoped the suspected dalliance was successful in getting information. If on the other hand he was stupidly thinking with his little brain, then he better have life insurance, because she would surely kill him on the spot. Summer knew she would have to control her emotions and tell him about the meeting. She took a deep breath and called Chip's room.

"Well, how was your date with the beauty queen?" she asked sarcastically.

"Summer, I did not call you last night after the meeting because I thought you probably were asleep. The meeting was fine, nothing special, and she is exactly as you described, very shallow. I could not get anything out of her," Chip responded, trying to not create waves.

"I'll bet you got something out of her," Summer said. "How about we meet at the coffee shop in an hour and a half, and you can fill me in on all the details. Also, I got a strange call that I need to talk to you about,"

Chip was a bit perplexed by Summer's attitude. Why was she so persistent about what Trish had to say? She had already told him not to expect Trish to say anything. What possible value did the exasperating evening with Trish have?

"Fine, I will be there, but I hope you will not be disappointed. There is really nothing to report," Chip answered in a condescending tone.

Summer hung up the phone and again told herself to control her hate for Trish. "Chip was not doing anything wrong," she thought. "He was only trying to get information. Trish is such a conniving bitch that I don't want to see Chip get sucked in. He may still have doubts that Trish is the one who planted the museum bomb, pegging us as targets." Summer must make sure that Trish did not turn his head and convince him she was innocent. Summer lay across her bed and whispered, "I hope Chip is different from most men. If not, I may have to play her little game and do the thing I hate most, use my femininity to hold his interest." She buried her head in her pillow and moaned.

Yasmina reflected to herself, "now is the time for me to spring the whole plan into action. If I don't make my move now, Curtis Harrison will either become suspicious or hurry to take James Alcort out of the picture." This could screw up the detailed plans she had made. Yasmina decided to call Curtis Harrison's office phone to speak to him.

"Yes, Yasmina, what do you need?" Curtis answered.

"I would like to talk to you about something very important. Do you have the time now?" Yasmina pleaded.

"Yes, come on in if it is important."

During the short walk to his office, Yasmina tried to get all her thoughts together. She had to be careful to provide him with just enough information to get him nervous, but not so much that it caused him to doubt her as his security chief. It was a balancing act she had to play, and one slip could cause a treacherous fall. Yasmina lightly knocked on his door.

"Yasmina, is that you?" Curtis answered.

Yasmina slowly opened the door and proceeded to sit down across from her boss. "Mr. Harrison, I am sorry to disturb you, but I am very concerned for your safety," she explained in a worried voice.

"Go on, Yasmina, you can tell me anything." He could tell she was uneasy.

"I enhanced and reran the security video of the other day when you and Ms. Alcort were down by the river. What I enhanced is the flash from across the river, and it is evident that it occurred much before you were alerted. In fact, I observed the bodyguards seeing it a good fifteen minutes before they reacted. At first, I thought they were just slow to take action, but then I saw what appeared to be a signal from our previous head of security. Nothing happened until he threw down his cigarette, and only then did the guards spring into action. I brought a DVD with me, and would like to show it to you."

"If what you are telling me is true, I did the right thing by killing the bastard. Indeed, please show me the video at once," Curtis exclaimed in a concerned voice.

Yasmina went to the entertainment center and carefully loaded the DVD she had produced. First she played it fully through for Curtis while pointing out the abnormalities. Then she slowly played the portion back and forth where she claimed the head of security was giving the signal. Curtis rose from his seat and stood within a foot of the fifty-two-inch plasma TV.

"My God, Yasmina, you are right. There is a conspiracy going on here. Who was it across the river? It could have been a sniper, or an assassin trying to get a clear shot at me. I can actually see that jackal signal them. I knew it, you rotten bastard. I am happy I killed you, you traitor," he shouted at the screen.

"Mr. Harrison, I know this is very upsetting, but with our electronic security, it may be wiser to plant some devices around the areas the guards frequent and get more information on their plans. I am not certain the treacherous deeds were confined to the dead chief. If we don't move against these traitors now, we may never find the vile person behind this hideous plan."

Curtis Harrison walked slowly toward his beautiful young protégé. He took both of her hands in his, probably the first time they had touched in years, and spoke from his heart.

"Yasmina, you are more to me than you can ever imagine. Words cannot express how I feel at this moment. You are the only human in the world I can trust, and you are the brightest as well. I claim to mentor you, but today you are the teacher. I will follow your advice. Place as many devices on the property as you desire. I must find the ones behind this plot to bring me down," Curtis expressed soulfully.

Yasmina said nothing. She took her DVD and walked out of the office. She gave Mr. Harrison a slight bow and held her exuberance till she reached her office. She could not contain her glee. She had him right where she wanted him, and now she was going to call the shots. The way she was able to seamlessly edit the DVD to make it appear as a conspiracy was brilliant. She was proud of her accomplishments and would be rewarded soon.

Trish called the front desk and summoned a bellhop to assist her with the mountain of bags for her move to the Harrison Estate. She had called the local florist to have two dozen red roses delivered to herself at the hotel. Trish gave the concierge a nice tip and instructions to make sure, although the flowers were addressed to her, that they were delivered to Summer's room.

Trish entered the limo and began conniving how she could now reel in the fish named Curtis Harrison she had so expertly hooked.

CHAPTER 18

▼

Summer was waiting in the hotel bar as prearranged. She had had a long talk with herself about the fact that she needed to control her emotions. Summer could not put her finger on why she had such a strong reaction to Chip's meeting with Trish, but she had convinced herself it was nothing more than her distrust of this manipulative woman. Summer did decide to wear her red dress that plunged at the neckline and was revealingly slit up the side. She determined it a necessity in order to keep Chip's attention and thwart the attempts made apparent by Trish to garner his attention. Chip walked into the bar, and Summer put her best smile on her face.

"Have you been waiting long?" Chip asked, looking at his watch.

"No, I just arrived and ordered us a couple of cocktails," She calmly stated.

Chip was taking all of Summer in and appreciating her very appealing outfit. He suddenly realized he was staring at her. "You look wonderful tonight. You remind me of that song, "Lady in Red" I think it is called."

Summer thought to herself that the extra effort certainly did pay off. Chip was finally seeing her as an attractive woman. She thought, "of course this is just to assure he won't get sidetracked by Trish."

"Thank you. That is a nice compliment. This old thing travels well, and I am running low on casual clothes," Summer said, covering her intentions.

"Well let's get down to business. Did you hear anything from our colonel?" Chip asked.

"No, not yet, but I don't expect to hear anything until the last minute," Summer said confidently. "I'm sure the colonel will have to stew over his situation and maybe break some more furniture before he calls me. I really expect him to call with affirmative news.

"I received a call this morning from a local woman named Yasmina," she continued. "She claims she has information for us, and we are to meet her in the coffee shop in about thirty minutes."

"Interesting. I wonder what she could possibly have for us." Chip wondered, hoping the conversation would stay away from his meeting with Trish.

"I am praying she can provide us with information about Jimmy's killing," she said. "At least this would give us another source."

"I think you're correct. But for now do you think we should concentrate on getting Abdul-Hakim in our hands?"

"No doubt about it. He is our main lead. But you have to look at this as I would when writing a story. You take all your leads and information, throw it against the wall, and see what sticks."

On the other side of the bar was seated an Afghan woman dressed in traditional garments, reading a paper. Summer and Chip barely noticed her presence because she blended into the local scenery. Yasmina folded her newspaper and turned toward the wall as she left the bar to conceal her face. Yasmina wanted to get a feeling for whom she was about to meet by seeing them beforehand. The cautious nature of her ways always seemed to serve her well. The two appeared to be very American and a bit naive. Her gut feeling was they could be trusted. She proceeded to the coffee shop for their scheduled meeting.

Chip and Summer moved to the coffee shop, and as they were about to sit were summoned by a woman in a burka. The woman approached them and extended her hand.

"Miss Tolly, I am Yasmina."

Summer shook the young woman's hand and turned toward Chip to make her introduction. "Very nice to meet you, Yasmina. This is Chip Murphy. I am working with him here in Afghanistan."

"I am sure you are wondering how I acquired your name and what type of information I may have on your behalf," Yasmina started. "I work for a gentleman by the name of Curtis Harrison. Recently he has become involved with a woman I believe you may know."

"Don't tell me. Trish Alcort," Summer said in disgust.

"Yes, then you do know who I am talking about," Yasmina continued. "She is staying with Mr. Harrison at his estate just outside the city. I am concerned over their liaison because I am chief of security for Mr. Harrison. Could you tell me about Miss Alcort and perhaps, if you know, what her intentions might be regarding my boss?"

Summer looked at Chip and was wondering if this young woman concealed in the burka could be trusted. Obviously Summer wanted to warn her about Trish and the underhanded way she operated. Chip was giving Summer a look she translated as "be cautious." Summer was still very upset with him over the episode she had witnessed of him taking Trish to his room. Summer decided to throw caution to the wind.

"Trish Alcort is a person I have known since my college days. She is not to be trusted and uses people, men in particular, for her own bidding. She is a reporter for Associated Press, as am I, but I am certain she was involved with the death of my boyfriend," Summer detailed in monotone.

"I think what Summer is trying to say is that Trish Alcort is a loose cannon, and we wonder what type of activity she may have been involved with," Chip stated, trying to cover.

Summer turned toward Chip, and from the look in her eyes, he knew he had crossed the line.

"Chip, I speak for myself and don't need for you to interpret. Trish Alcort is a vile woman, and I warn you her intentions toward your boss are unhealthy," Summer stated factually while kicking Chip hard under the table.

"I appreciate your honesty, Summer. I see my instincts are correct. It seems she is attempting to influence my boss by using her physical attributes. My boss is a very wealthy man, and I would not want to see him hurt," Yasmina explained.

"If there is money and a man, Trish will not be far behind," Summer said convincingly.

"Then could I ask you a favor? It may be in our mutual interest to work together to break up this liaison," Yasmina suggested.

"How would you suggest we accomplish separating the two?" Chip questioned.

"I look at things from the perspective that anything is possible. Therefore, I will chronicle the possibilities, but please do not think I would support the more severe," Yasmina explained.

"Okay, we understand," Summer answered.

"The first consideration," Yasmina said, "would be to eliminate Trish Alcort. In this way, we would be assured she would have zero effect on my boss. Also, it would give you a sense of retribution for her alleged involvement in your loved one's death."

"Oh, no, I could never be involved in killing her…although I must admit it has crossed my mind in fantasy," Summer answered.

"Again, please keep in mind that these are just possibilities. Do not judge me by the information I am relaying," Yasmina stated in a staunch way.

"The second would be to create a rift between the two by inserting a third party. This could be done by artificial means and would work if one of the parties thought it to be factual. In other words, we could make one of them think the other is being disloyal, and perhaps it would separate the two," Yasmina reasoned.

"I like the idea, but if Trish is playing Mr. Harrison for money, would she care if he had other women as long as she gets what she wants?" Chip interjected.

"I recommend we look at this from Mr. Harrison's perspective. If we were to convince him that Trish was seeing another man intimately, well, then he might make the break," Summer offered.

"Yes, Summer, I think you are very wise to consider it from his view. I know him very well, and although he would be upset, I think he might try even harder to win her heart. She has already had that effect on him. He has many beautiful young women at his disposal, but she has worked it so that he wants only her. We need to find a much stronger way that he would find utterly despicable," Yasmina stated in a thoughtful way.

"You said Mr. Harrison has many women?" Summer asked.

"Yes, many, and he has curtailed his activities because of Trish," Yasmina answered.

"We know Trish would not care if he were unfaithful to her as long as she got what she wanted. We know he would not break up with her and send her away because of a supposed affair. He would probably just watch her more closely and keep her confined to the estate. What else is there that we are missing?" Chip wondered.

"Wait a minute. Yasmina, you said Mr. Harrison could be described as a philanderer. What would any sexually active man be more fearful toward than losing a lover?" Summer asked with a twinkle in her eye.

Yasmina and Chip looked at each other, wondering what could Summer mean. After a few minutes without response, Summer began again.

"Disease. HIV or AIDS. That would be what he would fear most, if he thought Trish was HIV positive. I bet he would move her out in an instant," Summer stated, pleased with herself.

"Brilliant, Summer. He would dump her in a New York minute," Chip congratulated.

"I can easily set this up because I have full access to her suite. First I can plant HIV prescription drugs in her room with her name on the pill bottles. Then I can have falsified medical lab results printed. All of this I can do through a friend of mine who is a doctor. Finally, I can break the news to Mr. Harrison and show him the damaging evidence. He trusts me, and he will evict her promptly," Yasmina said.

"Great. We have some business to take care of, and by the time we get back maybe Trish will be pushed out into the public where we can get at her," Summer concluded.

"I will take care of everything," Yasmina said, "and if you give me your cell phone number I will advise you when I have completed the scheme. You both seem very nice, and our joint effort will have mutual benefits."

Summer separated from Chip. Chip was going to take a walk to get his mind around how all of the plans would fall into place. Summer admitted she was tired and decided to retire to her room to do some reading and get an early night's sleep. She was still upset with Chip about what appeared to be a late-night encounter with Trish in his room, but she decided to confront him on the issue later when she had rested. A good sleep was all she needed.

Summer saw something sitting outside her room as she approached. As she got close, her pretty smile filled her face, savoring her victory. She could see a bouquet of the most beautiful roses she had ever seen sitting just outside her door. She knew it was Chip's way of apologizing to her, and she was certain he now realized she was in charge. She opened her door carefully and centered the roses in the middle of her round table. She looked and found a small card attached to one of the long stems. She held it up and beamed with excitement to read Chip's feelings.

"Dearest Trish, Thank you so much for the most exciting night of my life. Your beauty is surpassed by your passionate lovemaking. If I die today, I have lived the ultimate moments of my life. I hope to see you again soon. Yours truly, Chip."

Summer grabbed the vase and flung the entire canister out her open door, smashing it across the hallway. Once again, Trish was playing with her mind, and she was in no mood.

Chip was walking just out front of the hotel and heard the crash. The direction indicated that the noise had come from Summer's room. Thoughts of possible danger to his partner frightened him. He ran up the stairs to her room, finding the door wide open and flowers scattered throughout the hall. He looked into the room and could see Summer's face filled with anger.

"Summer, what happened? Are you okay?"

Summer rolled her eyes, holding the card in front of her. She tried to regain her composure, suddenly becoming embarrassed thinking he might take her reaction as jealousy. Summer knew her reaction was hate for this woman, but she wanted to be cautious that Chip did not misinterpret her anger.

Chip took the card from her hand and read what he had supposedly written. He threw his arms around Summer and comforted her. Summer pulled away and walked to the other side of the room.

"Summer, you have to believe me. Nothing happened between Trish and me. She made an attempt by asking to use my laptop computer in my room, but I did not have anything to do with her. Anyway, you know we were just plotting against her with the Afghan girl. I only want her for information about Jimmy," Chip explained in a soothing way.

"Besides," he continued, "who else would deliver flowers to your room other than Trish herself? Think about it. Only Trish loves Trish that much. She is just trying to put a wedge between us and hopes we will go home and forget about Jimmy."

Summer began to realize that Chip had taken her outburst in the wrong way. "You have to understand. My reaction does not have anything to do with you. It is because Trish is an Olympic-class conniver. The outburst is my frustration about how I want so desperately to nail her," Summer said while hitting the wall.

"You mean you knew this was a sham all along?" Chip asked, disappointed.

"Well, Mr. Murphy, you write a pretty mean love letter, but I knew it was Trish," Summer said, breaking into a laugh.

Summer peeked over her shoulder with her long blond hair flowing and winked at Chip. Her tight-fitting red dress accentuated her figure while Chip looked on in total confusion. It seemed to him it was impossible to understand her, but for some reason he was even more anxious to try.

Trish Alcort again settled in at the Harrison Estate. She could not wipe the smile off her face, imagining Summer's reaction to the flowers she had sent herself and had delivered to Summer's room. She was sure it was a Kodak moment indeed when she read the gushy note supposedly from Chip. Summer might fool Chip about her interest in him, but as a woman, Trish was sure Summer was head-over-heels in love with him. Trish got the greatest joy in life by stirring the pot and letting it boil over by upsetting unsuspecting victims.

Trish received the software and installed it on her PDA, allowing her the ability to steal passwords off Yasmina's computer. She had it set up and was patiently waiting for Yasmina to begin using her machine. Trish also had a pair of night-vision binoculars at the ready. She was confident she could get the passwords off the wireless network for Yasmina's computer. Her big concern was that the communications center's door had a push-button combination lock. The only way to get that combination was to physically see Yasmina enter it, using night vision.

Trish's PDA unexpectedly came to life, and the program to record the passwords by keystroke was clicking away. She looked out to the back veranda and could see a woman in a burka heading toward the communications center. Trish was not able to identify the woman and thought it could not be Yasmina because she never wore a burka. The night vision worked great. She could now see that it was Yasmina's face. The woman began to punch in the combination on the door to the secure building. Trish wrote down the numbers for future reference: #-3-3-8-2-3.

CHAPTER 19

▼

The sound of Summer's cell phone aroused her from a sound sleep. She fumbled around the nightstand to find the ringing device. Summer flipped open the phone while looking at her watch, wondering who would be calling her at six in the morning.

"Hello, this is Summer," she answered in a sleepy tone.

"This is Colonel Hadley's assistant, the corporal you met yesterday," the voice explained.

Hearing it was the message from the colonel she had been waiting for so anxiously, Summer jumped to her feet. "Yes, Corporal. What information do you have for me?" Summer asked, dreading the possible bad news.

"The colonel has given your proposal much thought, and although he is not pleased with the situation, he has decided that in the best interests of the United States, he will meet your demand."

She could not believe what she was hearing. The canned response by the corporal was exactly what she had hoped. "This is good news. Where can I pick up Abdul-Hakim?"

"Wait a minute, Miss Tolly. The colonel has a small condition."

"What is that?"

"He wants all copies of video and photographs you took at the prison."

She thought for a moment, and considering that the colonel had no idea about the complete set secured in the States, she agreed.

"One other thing that the Colonel requires. He demands that after you are through with Abdul-Hakim, you contact me, and I will arrange to have him picked up," the corporal stated emphatically.

Summer mulled the new condition over in her mind and determined the old saying applied: "possession is nine tenths of the law." She decided it best to meet the colonel's demands and worry about giving Abdul back later.

"You have a deal. When can we meet, and where?" Summer demanded.

"Place the items we discussed into a valise and leave it with the front desk at your hotel. We will pick up the case and inspect the items. If acceptable, we will release Abdul-Hakim at that time. The exchange can take place at 9 PM tonight. A car will arrive at the hotel's main entrance at that precise time," the corporal explained.

"I will be there. Relay to the colonel that his statement about this being good for the United States is baloney. The only one benefiting by hiding the prison abuse is him."

"Yes, and of course you benefit from getting Abdul-Hakim, the interpreter, whom you feel is implicated in your boyfriend's murder," the corporal spewed as he hung up the phone.

Summer flipped her phone closed and reflected on what the corporal had just said. It was true; by blackmailing the colonel, she would get access to the interpreter and the information she needed to convict Trish of Jimmy's death. Sometimes the ends do justify the means, whether it was finding the killers of her boyfriend or getting information from al-Qaeda prisoners. Things in this dangerous world never seemed to fit into tidy boxes, and they always must be considered from differing perspectives.

Trish Alcort spent the evening recording Yasmina's keystrokes on her PDA. Now she had a complete set of the passwords necessary to break into Yasmina's computer. Also, she had the code to the communications center and would be able to have physical access to the file servers as well.

After Trish had completed her investigative work, she had a late dinner with Curtis in the lavish surroundings of the dining room within the main house. She spent most of her time throwing out sexual innuendos, reeling him ever tighter into her web. When he began to kiss her, she turned her head and only allowed a peck on the cheek. She could tell he was frustrated, but this was her little game of give and take she played so well. She expected Curtis to give, and she would take. Sex was just the lubricant to keep the ebb and flow going.

Trish decided tonight she was going to withhold sex from Curtis. In this way she could control him better by using the push-and-pull technique she knew so well. Trish proceeded down the hallway to her suite. She looked back while opening her door, and she playfully called to him, "night-night bad boy." Trish pulled down the straps of her evening gown, allowing it to drop briefly exposing her bare breasts. She held her finger to her mouth and cooed, "Not tonight, my love."

Curtis exhaled completely and strode toward his suite. He wanted nothing more than to have this woman again tonight, but he was not going to beg. He was fearful about losing all his dignity.

Trish was surprised the lights were still on in the communications center building as she looked out her veranda. Yasmina must have been working late. Trish checked her PDA, and it was still recording the keystrokes made by Yasmina typing away on the file server. Trish decided she had better use her memory stick to create a copy of the important information flowing to her PDA. She had not thought about it, but observing the information being captured by Yasmina using the file server had an additional benefit. Trish could tell, just by looking at her PDA, when Yasmina was working in the communications building. In that way, Trish could keep tabs on Yasmina. Trish was ecstatic over this windfall. She decided to take the opportunity to search Yasmina's room.

Trish carried her PDA in one hand, constantly checking to make sure that Yasmina was still typing on the file server. She approached the door and tried the handle. It was locked. Trish was prepared, having her credit card at the ready. She slid it carefully into the crack by the latch. The door popped open, and she entered the room. Suddenly the typing stopped on her PDA. Her heart sank, and she scurried to make her exit. Just as she was about to close the door, the typing resumed.

Trish used her available hand to begin rummaging through the drawers. In the back of Yasmina's underwear drawer, she found a wooden box. She opened it and revealed a chrome handgun with a pearl handle. She removed it from the box and began to inspect it. Trish could see an inscription engraved onto the barrel of the weapon. She read it to herself.

"Continued success in our endeavors. James Alcort."

Trish knew her father was aligned with Curtis Harrison, but why would this Afghan girl have a gun from her father? Trish looked out the window toward the communications center in wonder and noticed the lights dim in the building. Trish put the gun down the front of her waistband. She carefully replaced the box that had contained the gun and rearranged the bras and panties neatly as they were. Trish quietly exited the room and snuck back to her suite.

Trish held the chromed gun, thinking about how to interrogate her father. Trish needed to find out what the connection was between him and Yasmina. Perhaps it was nothing, and the gun was originally given to Curtis Harrison. Maybe he gave it to Yasmina, or she stole it. Regardless of the events surrounding the gun, Trish knew her father would be worried not having heard from her in several days, and she did not want him to "call out the army," so to speak.

She was confident that she was adept at lying to her father, but she did not want him to ask too many questions. Her father was smart, and when he began asking questions in rapid fire, Trish at times got flustered. Trish decided she would have to control the conversation.

The satellite-phone system at the estate worked very well, and conversations sounded as though they were made from a local connection. Trish dialed the number for her father in Rhode Island.

"Hello, Alcort residence," a female voice answered.

"Jasmine, it's Trish. Is daddy there?"

There was a silence on the other end of the phone, and Trish began to wonder if she had become disconnected. Finally a tearful voice responded.

"Miss Trish, we have been trying to get hold of you," Jasmine said. "Your father is missing,"

"Wait, what do you mean, missing?"

"He went into Boston and met with your boss, Mr. Davis. Something bad happened. A robbery, they suspect. Anyway, the police found Mr. Davis, but your father is missing."

"What did Justin Davis tell the police about my father?" Trish demanded.

"Oh, no, Ms. Trish, he could not tell the police anything. He had been shot in the back of the head and was dead. Oh, I am so worried about Mr. Alcort," Jasmine cried.

Trish abruptly hung up the phone.

She stormed out of her room and proceeded down the hallway toward Curtis Harrison's suite. Along the way, she brushed past Yasmina returning from the communications center. Yasmina could tell Trish was in a tizzy about something. Neither spoke to the other, but Yasmina decided she would follow in a minute and hide outside Curtis's door to eavesdrop.

Trish knocked loudly once and threw the double doors open to gain access to Curtis Harrison's room. Curtis was just nodding off and had the TV still turned on. He sat up startled and reached into his nightstand drawer to pull out a revolver.

"My father is missing. This is not your doing, is it?" she demanded in anger.

"No, it is not part of my plan," Curtis responded, surprised.

"Well, I know I agreed we need to get my father out of the way, but you must include me in your plans," Trish shouted.

Curtis returned the gun to its storage place and walked over to close the doors behind her. He led her to the patio and sat with her at the small table.

"We do need to talk, Trish. I desperately want you to be part of my operation and plans. I can't have you losing your temper and shouting information that could be heard by others. There are many little ears around here, and we cannot be certain who can be trusted," Curtis calmly explained.

Curtis reached across the small table and took her hand. Trish's hand was still trembling from her anger. He rubbed it softly and began to speak again.

"Look into my eyes, Miss Rhode Island," he began.

Trish grudgingly looked into Curtis's eyes.

"We can be a team of the greatest power ever seen in the world. We can acquire tremendous wealth and ultimate power. The key to our success is absolute trust between us. If we can achieve that, then I have put into place a plan that will exceed your every dream," Curtis said in a convincing voice.

Trish thought about it for a minute, and she realized she was perhaps being a bit impetuous. She felt, without any doubt, that Curtis had the ability to bring her to a new level in her life. Super wealth and power was her ultimate goal, and this man was her ticket. Trish stood up and leaned across the table toward him. She kissed him fully on the mouth and began to speak.

"Curtis, I am sorry I lost my temper. Now, let us get down to business."

"I would rather take you in my arms and carry you into my bed," Curtis said hopefully.

"Business first," Trish said bluntly as she sat down again.

"The first issue we must contend with is your father. I know who is holding him in Boston, and I have made arrangements to have him released to us. Then I am leaving it up to you to figure out how to get him out of the way," Curtis explained.

"We must go to Boston, and I will take care of my father. I just came across something that I think daddy will get a real bang out of," Trish stated in a determined tone.

Curtis stood up and walked around to Trish. He picked her up in his arms and carried her to his bed. He gently laid her down and with his strong tanned hands ripped open her shirt. Curtis proceeded to make love to her with a new sense of passion.

CHAPTER 20

▼

The dark-colored Humvee pulled to a stop at the front entrance to the Mustafa Hotel. Although nighttime, the star on the doors and hood identified it as U.S. military. Summer and Chip had been waiting in the coffee shop just adjacent to the lobby. This location allowed them a perfect view of the front entrance.

The corporal, known to them as Colonel Hadley's assistant, strode up to the front-desk clerk. The valise containing the pictures and video was handed to him, and he returned to the Humvee. Suddenly, as the Humvee drove away, the back door opened, and a man was pushed out tumbling to the ground. Summer rapidly darted from her seat and ran to the man. She grabbed the man's arm and helped Abdul-Hakim to his feet. Chip stood about ten feet back and opened the lobby door as Summer forcefully escorted Abdul into the hotel.

Summer had already devised a plan for handling Abdul. She determined it best to take him to Chip's room, have Abdul shower, and then she would order room service for him. Both restrained their anger, knowing that the old axiom "you get more flies with honey than vinegar" applied here. Summer decided that if she did not get the information about Jimmy she needed, she would turn to plan B and use stronger tactics. For the time being, she would try to do this in a civilized way. Once Abdul finished showering, the three sat down at the small table in the room and began to talk.

"Mr. Hakim," Summer said, "I have kept up my part of the deal and have had you released. I am sure you can appreciate how difficult it was for me, considering the charges against you. If it were not for me, you would have rotted in that jail. Now I expect you to reciprocate by telling us who was behind Jimmy's death."

Abdul-Hakim continued to eat as if it were his last meal. He would look up at Summer as she spoke, but he never put his fork down or stop shoving food into his mouth. Finally she became exasperated, stood up, and knocked the plate out of Abdul's hand.

A surprised Abdul exclaimed, "Wait, I will tell you what you want to know. I was hired by a woman from your AP office to guide you and Jimmy and be your interpreter."

"I know that. Otherwise I would not have found you. Now tell us who was behind placing the bomb that killed Jimmy," Summer shouted in anger.

"I am telling you, but you are not listening. It was the young beauty queen who set up the whole thing, and she ordered us to get rid of you, Summer. Jimmy was just collateral damage."

"Why would Trish Alcort want to kill me at that time? I know she hates me, but I can't imagine she was that upset about my assignment."

"The problem was not with you, personally," the interpreter explained. "It had more to do with your insistence that we venture to the north. When she found out about it, she was adamant that you be eliminated."

"I am still very confused. What is it about the north that concerned Trish?"

"Trish was not certain that you and Jimmy didn't know you were very close to our leader. She could not take the chance that it was by accident you were within a thousand meters of him. Regardless of how it happened, she called the order for us to do the hit."

"What leader? We did not know anything, only that the fighting had moved to the north. That was the only reason we directed you to head to the area," Summer stated incredulously.

"Osama Bin Laden was only a short distance away in the foothills. We all were sure you and Jimmy knew of this and were going to divulge his location. Trish Alcort was acting as a double agent or something and ordered to have you both killed," Abdul informed.

"We did not know of Bin Laden's location," Summer jumped up and yelled angrily. "You killed Jimmy for no reason, you bastard."

"You must understand that I did not set up the bomb. In fact, I was duped because they told me to get you two out of the area because of imminent danger. I knew nothing about the mine until you hit it. Please forgive me, I beg you," Abdul cried as he knelt at Summer's feet.

Chip moved to comfort Summer as she broke down into tears. He held her and continued to repeat softly in her ear, "Jimmy was at the wrong place at the wrong time."

Abdul realized the hospitality shown by these two might be wearing thin and decided to change the subject. "I can tell you where all al-Qaeda are located, even Osama himself, if the money is right."

Summer turned her attention back to the informant. "First I want to know where Trish is located. We have been told she is staying with a Curtis Harrison. Then you tell me how I can get to the evil man himself who caused my boyfriend to be killed. There is no money. If you ask again I will begin chopping off your fingers," Summer warned in a believable voice.

Abdul-Hakim had seen tough people before, and he surmised she was not in the same league with them. The concern he had, though, was that there are times when even calm people get into stressful situations and explode. The backlash from her blowing up might be worse than he could imagine. Abdul thanked Allah for making him a free man and decided it was best to give Summer the information she was seeking.

"I have heard of the man, Curtis Harrison, although the heroin, not al-Qaeda, has funded much of his operation. The story is that he has an estate just outside of Kabul." Abdul spoke slowly.

"What about Bin Laden?" Summer questioned.

"Osama Bin Laden is not anywhere near where the Americans have been looking," Abdul said. "He is not hiding in the mountain caves, nor has he moved to Pakistan, nor is he staying here at the Mustafa Hotel. If you understand that the drug business supplies al-Qaeda with money for weapons and that in return al-Qaeda offers security for the drug dealers, then it follows that Osama Bin Laden is hidden by the dealers. I know he has visited a very large compound outside of Kabul, on the river, owned by the Englishman. This is firsthand information because al-Qaeda has their own people inside to protect him."

"Show us where this is located," Summer insisted.

"I am happy to show you, but my most recent information is that they are preparing to move Bin Laden out of the country. There is an ally in the western hemisphere working with al-Qaeda. The plan is to mobilize al-Qaeda troops in an attack on the United States."

"Do you know where they are moving Bin Laden?" Chip asked.

"Not exactly. In prison we have the latest information, but this plan is very confidential. I have been trying to determine for myself what country in the western hemisphere would be supportive of al-Qaeda and have enough of an al-Qaeda presence to allow for troops to attack the U.S.," Abdul stated uneasily.

Summer and Chip decided to speak alone so they could compare notes and determine if Abdul was truthful or just lying to escape their grasp. Both are concerned that he had been very open and wondered why he would tell them the information, particularly about Osama Bin Laden. Chip checked the window lock, and Summer made sure the door to the room was closed tightly behind them as they entered the hallway. Chip stood with his hands against the wall behind Summer.

Summer began to speak first. "I knew Trish was behind the whole thing. She set us up and killed Jimmy. Her relationship with Harrison must be connected with the money supplying al-Qaeda. But I don't know how she has the power to pull all of this off."

"It smells like CIA to me," Chip said. "They are the only ones capable of pulling strings like this."

Chip continued, "I don't get it. I hoped he would talk, but it is as if he wants to divulge everything. He may be a really a good liar, or perhaps he just wants to tell us what we need in hopes he will not have to return to Pul-e-Charki Prison."

"Chip, you are not getting it. This man will say or do anything to get out of a mess. He would probably tell Trish or al-Qaeda where we are if he could get money or avoid this sticky situation. He cannot be trusted," Summer said with confidence.

"I don't disagree with you, but it fits with the information the young Afghan woman, Yasmina, told us the other day about Trish staying with Harrison. Now we just need to know where his estate is located. Let's go back in and pressure him to give us something we can use, the exact location of the estate."

They walked back into the room, and Abdul was sitting in the same position but was sweating profusely. The napkin from his meal was now soaked from his use on his brow. Summer noticed the man's discomfort and felt that now was the time to get the facts out of this man.

"Okay, Abdul, you have told us a nice story. Now I need facts. If you know a country in the western hemisphere is prepared to support Osama Bin Laden and al-Qaeda in the attack, who are they?" Summer asked while placing her hands on Abdul's shoulders from the back.

"I tell you, I don't know. When they would talk on the phone, it would be in a foreign language. I did not understand it, but it sounded to be Italian or maybe Spanish. I am not sure. The only other detail is that al-Qaeda evidently has a large concentration of forces in that country. Otherwise they could not plan an attack. Al-Qaeda has over eighteen thousand troops throughout the world, but they are very scattered. It is unheard of to find a hundred in one place, let alone more. I just cannot figure it out," Abdul confided.

"Okay, let's make a list of what we know," Summer interrupted.

"First, the country is in the western hemisphere," Chip said. What country in the western hemisphere would be against the United States? It just does not make sense."

"Well, just a minute," Summer interrupted. "Cuba and Castro have long been an enemy of America, and it is just ninety miles south of Florida. Second, you said they were speaking a foreign language, like Italian or Spanish. Spanish is the official language of Cuba. And third, there is a large concentration of al-Qaeda in Cuba. Up to two thousand at one time."

"Wait, al-Qaeda in Cuba?" Chip questioned.

"Guantanamo Bay, Cuba," Summer said. "It is where the U.S. has taken all the al-Qaeda prisoners from here in Afghanistan. They had over two thousand at one time, and I know of no releases."

"Yes, but that is a U.S. Navy base. I agree it is in Cuba, but how could an attack be carried out on a U.S. Navy base?" Chip asked, wondering.

"You have the largest concentration of al-Qaeda anywhere in the world, a dictator that has hated America for decades, and Osama Bin Laden having drug money to support the effort. If Bin Laden were to combine the prisoners in Guantanamo Bay with the Cuban Army directed by Castro, the navy base could easily be overrun. Don't you see they could launch an attack on the U.S. quite easily through South Florida or the remote Florida Keys? It is the perfect marriage of two narcissistic dictators, both having an equal hatred of America.

"I will tell you one more thing," Abdul interrupted. "Al-Qaeda has obtained large quantities of nuclear waste from the old Soviet Union. They have developed these into what you Americans have referred to as dirty bombs. Their intent is to infiltrate and place these bombs in large cities in the U.S. One can devour and contaminate several large city blocks, I am told."

"I am confused," Summer said. "Why would you want to share this information with us, or are these just lies to save your own skin?"

"I found while I was held prisoner in Pul-e-Charki prison that my al-Qaeda brothers did nothing to effect my release. You have saved me, and all I want to do now is go back to the beautiful mountains of my home and be with my family. I am too old now and will leave the holy war to the young," Abdul claimed with tears streaming down his face.

"One last thing, Abdul, and then I will let you relax," Summer said. "Show me on this map the exact location of where Osama Bin Laden has been hiding at the Harrison Estate."

Abdul looked hard at the map and finally took the pen from Summer's hand. He circled the exact location showing Curtis Harrison's estate.

Summer demanded that Abdul come with her and Chip to the circled location. The three proceeded to find Osama Bin Laden.

CHAPTER 21

▼

Curtis Harrison entered Yasmina's office and interrupted her phone conversation to one of the heroin plant managers. She looked up as he entered, knowing it must be important because otherwise he would never distract her from the drug business. Yasmina quickly dismissed the party on the other end of the phone. Curtis looked toward Yasmina as she hung up the phone.

"What is it Mr. Harrison? I am working," Yasmina said, a bit disturbed.

"I am sorry to interrupt, but we have an emergency with my guest Trish Alcort," he explained.

"How can I help?"

"Trish just found out that her father is missing and insists she go to Boston to see what has happened. Also, I found out her boss was murdered while in the company of her father. It is feared her father was also killed, but his body has not been found.

"I plan to take my plane. The flight restrictions have now been lifted. Call and have the jet readied while I finish up some details here. Also, please help Trish get ready for travel."

"Yes sir, I will take care of the arrangements at once."

Curtis walked out of her office, and she immediately began dialing numbers into her phone.

Once he had returned to his office and was out of sight, he picked up the phone and placed a call to his long-time business associate.

"Trish Alcort has discovered that her father is missing," Curtis said. "I was able to convince her it was not of my doing. She has agreed that if her father is released to her, she will take care of getting him out of the way."

"How did she put everything together?" the associate questioned.

"That is not important now. Only thing is, she knows. I am going with Yasmina and Trish to Boston in my private jet. I have an idea that would literally kill two birds with one stone," Curtis proudly announced.

"I am not familiar with the expression 'killing two birds, one stone,'" the associate stated.

"Just follow my thinking," Curtis said. "Have James Alcort moved to the presidential suite at the Colonnade Hotel in Boston. Tell him we have found his daughter and that we will bring her to him. Once at the hotel, have him execute the money transfer to our Swiss account. He has already agreed to ten million, but he expected to borrow it from me against future drug profits. I checked his accounts, and he has about seven million liquid. Have him transfer everything he has, or he won't see his daughter. Once the transfer is accomplished, dress him in traditional Arab garb. Have him facing with his back to the door looking out over the balcony. Drug him so he is asleep."

"I don't understand. Why are we doing this?" the associate asked.

"I plan to use him as a decoy to help us continue with our business. His daughter is under the impression she will take over his business once he is out of the way. Also, please send me all of the case files related to killing Justin Davis and abducting James Alcort. I will review these during the flight to Boston."

"I will make all of the arrangements. Just don't get yourself tangled up with the Boston police. I have connections, but if you are caught by them, it can be messy," the associate warned as he hung up the phone.

Yasmina knocked softly on the guest-suite door where Trish was located.

"Miss Alcort, this is Yasmina. Can I come in?"

"Yes, Yasmina. Please enter," Trish responded.

"I have spoken to Mr. Harrison, and he has arranged to take us on his jet to Boston. He told me about your father. I am sure he is as concerned as you are in finding out about your father. Can you be ready in a half hour?"

"Yes, I will be ready," Trish promised. "Does he know what happened to my father?" Trish asked in a false sweet voice.

"I suspect he is making phone calls as we speak to establish what might have happened," Yasmina concluded.

Yasmina walked out of the room, and Trish was proud of her acting abilities. Curtis had told Trish that Yasmina did not know about their impending business and certainly nothing about their plan to take James Alcort out of business. Yasmina was a smart girl, but not close to the intelligence quotient she and Curtis possessed. Trish would follow the plan exactly as they had intended.

During the direct flight to Boston on Curtis Harrison's Citation Mustang, he reviewed the material he had received from his associate. He decided to organize the information for his best advantage and present only the distorted facts he gleaned from the material.

Curtis leaned toward the front of the cabin where Trish was seated across from him. He took her by the hand and pulled her closer to the empty seat next to him in the back. He pressed the intercom button and asked Yasmina to close the door separating her and the pilot from the aft cabin. Curtis wanted his privacy both for business and personal reasons.

"I made some calls to the U.S. and have come up with some interesting information. First, I think your father will be delivered to us at the Colonnade Hotel. Because of his connections in Afghanistan, I had a bit of a problem obtaining his release. I have made arrangements through a contact in Boston who assured me your father will be drugged and unconscious. Normally these types only want money, and I can handle most anything they demand," Curtis said.

"Why did you have him drugged?" Trish inquired.

"I am not certain of how you intend to take care of your father, but an unconscious person is always easier to deal with," Curtis explained.

"Very good thinking. It will make my job less stressful," Trish said, smiling.

"The last thing I want for my lady is stress," Curtis teased.

The two began to romantically kiss, and Trish was invited to join an elite new club, which she eagerly accepted. At thirty thousand feet, even with the impending doom relating to her father, she gladly joined the "Mile High Club."

The two were just regaining their composure after their tryst when they heard a voice on the intercom. It was Yasmina.

"We are within fifteen minutes of Logan International, Mr. Harrison. We will be landing shortly. You may want to buckle up now."

Trish laughed at the double meaning of Yasmina's message. Obviously Yasmina was referring to the seat belt when she said buckle up, but it could also have referred to Curtis's pants still around his ankles. Curtis turned to Trish, wondering what was so funny.

"Did I miss something?" he asked, perturbed.

"Just a very small joke," Trish quipped.

Curtis looked at the beauty sitting next to him and got dressed. He decided not to pursue the question in his mind. Quite honestly, he was a bit afraid of the answer.

"We will be staying at the Four Seasons Hotel, and I will get further instructions at that point in time from my contact," Curtis said.

The arrival into Logan Airport occurred at 6 PM Eastern Time. Customs officials boarded the private jet, and all occupants were quickly released to the waiting limousine.

The entire fourteenth floor of the Four Seasons was reserved for the entourage
of six people. Yasmina and Trish were escorted to adjoining rooms in the suite
Curtis Harrison occupied. Yasmina changed into her casual attire and entered the
living area of the suite. Trish stayed in her locked room, sitting on the edge of the
bed, handling the chrome-colored handgun she had taken from Yasmina.

Curtis Harrison made all of the final arrangements for the setup. His associate
called and informed him that James Alcort would be in the presidential suite at
the Colonnade Hotel as planned. Curtis was proud he could make these arrangements without much difficulty. He saw Yasmina in the central living area of the
suite and summoned Trish. Since Yasmina was not part of the plan, he had con-
cocted a story to tell her in order to cover his and Trish's real intent.

"I have some incredible news. I have located, through my sources, the location
of the man responsible for the abduction of your father, Trish. He is staying at
the Colonnade Hotel, and we can surprise him there and get the answers about
your father," Curtis explained with glee.

Yasmina listened closely to this information but was very skeptical because
Curtis Harrison never did any of his own dirty work. She was doubtful about
Trish being able to handle any type of dangerous situation and was wondering if
she would become unglued.

"Are you sure my father is still alive?" Trish asked.

Curtis thought carefully before answering and decided to make the entire
event more dramatic for the benefit of Yasmina. "I am concerned the ruthless
man we are going to meet may have done harm to your father. These people are
animals and in no way adhere to our standards of civility," Curtis stated while
pausing on key phrases for effect.

Yasmina, detecting that something was just not right about this situation,
decided to try and back out of her involvement. "I don't see any need for me to
attend. I will stay here if it pleases you."

"It does not please me, Yasmina," Curtis stated in a huff. "You know that I
may need assistance with the language. We all will go. Call for the car now,
please."

Yasmina knew something bad was about to happen, but not going along with
her boss at this point would be too damaging to her overall assignment.

"Yes sir, I will summon the car at once," Yasmina conceded.

Once Yasmina had exited the suite to get the limo, Curtis was able to finalize the details with Trish.

"Academy Award material?" Curtis asked.

"Pretty good, but I still think your diction could be more polished," Trish teased.

"You are a tough critic, but the important thing is that Yasmina bought it. I want her with us in case something goes wrong. Not only is she the most resourceful person I know, but if needed she would gladly take a bullet to protect me," Curtis explained.

"Can she be trusted to keep her mouth shut?" Trish asked.

"I assure you she is completely loyal. If I were to ever find anything conflicting my belief, she would be eliminated," Curtis assured.

Yasmina went down to the lobby of the hotel, and before requesting the limo, she called her handler.

"Yes, Yasmina, how can I assist you?" the handler answered.

"I am in Boston," Yasmina said. "Something big is about to happen. Curtis Harrison is here with the AP reporter, Trish Alcort. He indicates we are going to pick up her father who was abducted. I can't talk long, but I need strategic support to be ready at the Colonnade Hotel."

"I cannot supply you with any support. All operatives are absorbed in other assignments. You must handle solo," the handler answered.

"You don't understand. This is an emergency," she yelled.

"No, you don't understand. Lack of planning on your part does not constitute an emergency on mine," The handler concluded.

The phone went dead, and Yasmina determined once again that the CIA was not taking her seriously. Every time she got close to a major breakthrough, the company not only did not provide support, but also puts up roadblocks. Frustrated, she decided to make another call.

"Hello," the voice on the other end answered.

"Summer, this is Yasmina. I intended to plant the evidence against Trish Alcort showing her to be HIV positive, but I have been forced to travel. In fact, Mr. Harrison and Trish Alcort are here with me in the United States," Yasmina explained.

"The U.S.?" Summer asked, stunned.

"Yes, please listen. I have only a short time. I have been informed that the medical records and prescription bottles are ready to be picked up from my doctor friend in Kabul. Would it be possible for you to pick up these items and deliver them to Mr. Harrison's estate so they will be waiting for me upon my return?" Yasmina requested.

"Yes, I am sure we could accommodate," Summer replied.

"The health clinic is named Qala-e-Qazi and is in the village. I will call and have the package ready to be picked up under your name. Also, I will tell security at the estate to expect your arrival," Yasmina detailed.

"I will find it and make the delivery," Summer confirmed.

"Do you need directions to the estate?" Yasmina questioned.

"I can ask the concierge at our hotel."

"Thanks, and I will contact you upon my return."

Summer hung up the phone, turned to Chip, and said, "Well, we have just received an invitation by the chief of security at the Harrison Estate to visit. What could be easier?"

CHAPTER 22

▼

Summer gathered the package at the Qala-e-Qazi Clinic and took Abdul with her and Chip on the forty-five minute drive to the Curtis Harrison Estate. They wanted to make sure Abdul was not providing them with false information to save his own skin. Along the way, Abdul insisted that the owner of the property, Curtis Harrison, had long been involved in the heroin drug trade. Also, Abdul detailed for the duo how Harrison used his funds to secure a peaceful coexistence with al-Qaeda. Abdul was careful to only suggest that Osama Bin Laden had stayed at the compound, but would not hazard a guess as to whether he could be in residence at that time. Finally, he offered information about the most recent resident at the Harrison Estate, creating some concern for his al-Qaeda associates.

"I have been told the American beauty queen has taken residence at the Harrison Estate," Abdul said. "This confirms the information you indicated you had received. She may be a reporter, but one thing is for sure; she is making al-Qaeda very nervous. Curtis Harrison is known for his penchant for beautiful women, and an American is way too dangerous for al-Qaeda."

Summer and Chip began to develop a plan to garner further access to the estate. The delivery of the package to Yasmina would get them in the door, but they wanted to explore the many notions floating around in their minds. Since they were certain Trish was in residence, they hoped to investigate the compound and Trish's complicity to illegal acts.

It was agreed that Summer would take the car to the entrance gate alone and ask to deliver a package for Yasmina. Chip and Abdul would attempt to gain access by hanging under the car's belly until it was through the gate. Then they would roll into the shrubs by the main building.

One hundred and fifty feet before the grand entrance to the estate, Chip and Abdul took their positions under the car. Abdul complained about being part of the plan but quickly changed his attitude when he saw the decisive look in Summer's eyes. Summer moved the car slowly to the closed gates and extended her left arm to push the buzzer on the voice box. Simultaneously, the two security cameras on pillars holding the gate moved to focus on her face.

"Mr. Harrison's residence, how may I assist you this evening?" the voice from the box questioned.

"Yes, I am a personal friend of Yasmina's," Summer stated. "She asked that I deliver a package for her."

"Your name, please," came the response.

"Summer Tolly."

"Yes, Miss Tolly, I have a message to expect your arrival. Please hold your passport picture to the lens of the camera at the gate for confirmation."

Summer dug out her passport and met with their wishes. After a few minutes, the security cameras zoomed back and forth to focus on her more completely. The voice responded, "That will be fine. Please proceed up the drive until you see the main house. I will meet you at the door."

As Summer proceeded up the winding drive to the fountain area just at the main house, she noticed a number of dimly lit profiles of men carrying what appeared to be automatic weapons. Suddenly her palms grew cold and damp as she realized they had never made a plan as to how Chip and Abdul were to exit the property. Summer tried yelling and stomping through the floorboard of the car to Chip, but to no avail. The noise of the engine running and the tires on the cobblestone driveway covered her attempts at communication. She determined it best to stall as long as possible, giving the two men enough time to make an inspection of the other buildings and additional time to allow retreat back under the car for their exit from the property. She would have to tap some reserve of inner strength to pull this one off.

Summer could see the main entrance and pulled the car as close to the driveway edge as possible to allow Chip and Abdul the cover needed to make their exit from under the car. Several lights popped on automatically as she walked toward the huge front doors.

A female in a burka answered the door and requested, "Please give me the package."

Summer had purposely forgotten and left the package inside the car, giving Chip and Abdul more time. She was thinking on her feet and decided to put her acting capability to the test. She suddenly fell over on her side, pretending to completely pass out.

Chip and Abdul waited for their chance and dropped from the bottom of the car just as the woman in the burka bent over to assist Summer. They rolled easily into the low foliage.

"That's my girl," Chip whispered as he watched Summer on the ground. He thought it ingenious how she had created the diversion.

Chip led Abdul around to the back of the main house. He could see a large unoccupied pool and entertainment area. Night had fallen an hour earlier, but most of the other buildings were dark and seemed to be empty. Chip took his small penlight out and headed toward the first door he could see. The entrance was surprisingly unlocked, and the two men entered quickly.

The building was an enormous filming set of some type. It was very similar to what Chip had seen previously when his family had vacationed at Universal Studios. His flashlight showed it to be constructed as a landscape. Huge artificial boulders were piled to form what appeared to be caves. Chip could see the many rows of lighting hanging from the ceiling some twenty feet in the air.

He walked toward the center of the stage area and came across a teleprompter. He had seen this kind of device before and knew it was used to display words that a newscaster or actor were to speak. He decided to turn on the device.

"Abdul, watch the door. I want to see what's on this thing," Chip demanded.

The pale blue light given off from the teleprompter illuminated the stage area. The words appeared in what Chip thought to be Arabic. After the first sentence, Chip noticed there was also a small English translation written below. He began to read the lines.

"The angles of death have visited the great American city and have ravaged the twin brothers. The giant will be slain by the righteous in this holy war. Al-Qaeda will send more death and destruction to the headless giant. I command all Islamics to enter this holy war and fight to the death for almighty Allah and myself, Osama Bin Laden."

"Holy Jesus," Chip said. "That's it. Osama Bin Laden has been making his propaganda tapes released to the media from here. It's a perfect setup. The CIA has spent hours attempting to analyze the geological features in the videos to determine where Bin Laden might be hiding. The features they have studied for hours are only fake foam rocks."

"See, I told you Osama Bin Laden was staying here. Now you believe me, and I can go home to my family in the mountains?" Abdul pleaded.

"Not yet. We have to get back to the car before Summer's fainting act gets discovered," Chip warned.

Summer artificially came to in a fog. Her eyes slowly focused on the woman in veils bending over her offering a cup of water. She could see inside the residence upon opening her eyes.

"Miss, please drink a little water," the woman implored.

Summer moved her arms behind herself and sat up to meet the waiting cup. She then took the cup into her own hand. "I am so sorry. I don't know what happened," she explained.

"Just sit still and sip a little. You will be fine in a minute," the woman replied.

Summer acted as though she had regained her faculties and realized she must be creating some suspicion. The looks she was receiving from the armed men showed she was viewed as an intruder. She had to think quickly.

"I forgot the package in the car. I will get it at once," Summer explained.

A strongly built man holding an Uzi machine gun stepped up to her and followed her out to retrieve the package.

"Yasmina is away with Mr. Harrison," the man said. "They had some business in the States. She will not be returning for a few days."

Summer could sense she was making the group anxious. She felt the best thing now was for her to exit quickly. "I will call her in a couple of days. Thanks for your help," she concluded, handing him the package.

Summer, upon entering her car, saw two additional men holding their weapons in the ready. She hoped that Chip and Abdul were already concealed under the car. She proceeded to drive back down the long driveway toward the gates. Once she had exited the property, she looked behind to make sure she was not being followed. Once assured she was alone, she jumped from the car and bent over to see both Chip and Abdul in their hiding place.

"It's okay. We are safe now," she advised the two.

The two men pulled themselves from under the car and began to brush themselves off.

"You should get an award for that performance. It was perfect and gave us enough time to inspect the other building," Chip complimented.

"That was quite a performance, I must say," Summer replied. "I counted on the false belief that women faint unexpectedly. I think it had them fooled, and they were just happy to see me leave. Did you find anything?"

"We have found undeniable evidence that Bin Laden was there," Chip said enthusiastically. "In fact, we found a teleprompter with the exact message he made on Al Jazeera TV two weeks ago. I believe this is the place where he has been hiding, and Curtis Harrison is directly involved, along with Trish. This is huge."

"We need to track Trish down," Summer said. "She may be able to lead us directly to the man himself. We must make her talk. She can provide us with many answers."

"Although complicated, I will call the AP office. They will know what's up with Trish, or at least what she has told them. I think we need to make a quick trip to the U.S.," Summer said with a slow inquisitive drawl.

CHAPTER 23

▼

Trish and Yasmina stood next to the elevators as Curtis Harrison spoke to the front-desk clerk at the Colonnade Hotel. Trish could tell by the body language of the clerk that Curtis must have made him a tempting offer. Curtis had explained to the two during the ride from the Four Seasons that he would bribe the clerk and get the key for the presidential suite where James Alcort could be found.

The young man nervously looked around the lobby and slid the stack of money Curtis had laid on the marble counter into his pocket. The magnetic room-key card was then handed across to Curtis where the money had just been. Curtis walked swiftly to the young women. The three of them entered the elevator, and Curtis placed the key card into the slot indicating the presidential suite. This would take them immediately to the top of the hotel and open directly into the vast suite.

The elevator doors opened, and the three entered the dimly lit suite. They could see the lights of the city flickering through the floor-to-ceiling windows. Trish reached into her Gucci purse and placed her hand on the chrome pistol. Curtis grabbed each of the women by their upper arms and placed his finger to his lips.

"Quiet. See the man sitting in the chair looking out over the balcony?" Curtis asked.

The two women look and noticed a man dressed in traditional Arab garb sitting looking out the window.

"I will go behind him. Yasmina, you and Trish take either side. I think he might be asleep," Curtis instructed.

The three crept silently, and Trish paused, realizing her high-heeled custom Franco Sarto shoes were clicking on the marble, making too much noise. She grabbed onto Curtis for support and removed them, putting the shoes to the side of the room. Trish nodded to Curtis, indicating she was ready to proceed toward the Arab man. Trish once again found her way into her handbag and held on to the gun tightly. When the trio was within a foot of the man, Curtis bent down, taking the man's face into his hand while turning it toward the dim light. Trish was startled to see her father's face and positioned herself directly to his right side.

"Wake up, Mr. Alcort," Curtis yelled at the man.

Trish was getting more nervous by the second and pulled the gun from her purse. She intended to have it pointed at her father to be ready for when he would awaken. She then could force him to accept her demand to give up the business. She still was unsure how the gun worked, so she tried to cock it by pulling back the slide.

"BANG!" The gun fired.

"My God, Trish, what the hell are you doing?" Curtis yelled as he jumped back away from the shot.

Yasmina ran over to Trish as she was looking at the gun in a perplexed and surprised manner. Yasmina said nothing to her but slowly took the gun from her hand. Yasmina then leaned over the seated man and could see in the low light that blood was gushing from a hole in the right side of his head. Trish slowly melted to the floor, seeing what she had done, and put her hands over her mouth in disbelief.

Curtis walked back to the man seated, and he could see the blood gushing from his head. Trish continued to peek through her fingers at her father in disbelief. Curtis pulled James Alcort's head up and removed his headdress. Trish's fear turned to panic as she could now fully see the death on her father's face.

"No no no no no, please God, no," Trish began to mumble as she crawled toward the slumping body. "Daddy, no. Please, daddy, it was an accident,"

Yasmina looked directly at Curtis in wonder. He had a very strange expression, as if he was not entirely surprised. She could tell he was worried, but it was certainly not a reaction one would expect from someone who had just seen a daughter kill her own father in cold blood.

Curtis turned toward Yasmina when he felt her eyes upon him. "Get her away from him," he said. "We have to get out of here. Someone may have heard the shot."

Yasmina pulled Trish away as she melted into a pile.

"Yasmina, give me the gun," Curtis instructed.

She handed him the gun, and he placed it into his pocket.

"How is it that her father is here dressed in that way?" Yasmina asked Curtis.

"That is not important now. I can't explain everything to you, but help me get him over the balcony before the police arrive."

Yasmina and Curtis struggled with the lifeless body, and with a timed heave threw James Alcort's body off the balcony. The two watched as it cartwheeled fourteen floors down. Even being over 150 feet above, they could hear the grotesque splat as the body hit the pavement below. The impact caused the body to flatten and dismember.

The trio exited the suite using the back stairwell. Yasmina had to struggle to keep Trish moving on her bare feet as they descended the stairs. Finally they were in the night air and could hear sirens advancing from a distance. Curtis pulled his cell phone from his pocket and summoned the limo. Yasmina shoved Trish into the backseat, and they proceeded toward the Four Seasons Hotel.

Curtis Harrison made a call after they returned to the hotel suite. Yasmina had taken Trish into her room, and he was now alone.

"We have had an unforeseen event," Curtis said. "Trish Alcort was in possession of a gun and unexpectedly shot and killed James Alcort. I told her it was her responsibility to get her father out of the way, but I did not expect she would pull a gun and shoot him on the spot. I attempted to make it look like a suicide by throwing the body off the balcony.

"There are some loose ends you need to clean up," he continued. "The front-desk clerk can ID me, so take care of him. Make sure to pull some strings so this thing does not get investigated. If they examine the body, they will find the bullet hole."

"I will take care of it," the voice at the other end replied, "but I told you the Boston police are a problem. Keep the girl under control."

The *Boston Globe* was delivered promptly at 7 AM outside the door of Curtis Harrison's suite at the Four Seasons. He was awake all night trying to determine how his plan had backfired so terribly. The result of having James Alcort out of the way was positive. Curtis just did not like messy things, and this could get that way if not handled properly. When he heard noise in the hallway, he peeked out and retrieved the paper. He unfolded it with a swift shake and read the headlines.

"Prominent Rhode Island Man Falls to Death Fourteen Stories at the Colonnade Hotel

"James Alcort, a prominent Rhode Island businessman, was reported falling to his death from the presidential suite of the Colonnade Hotel late last night.

The coroner ruled the death a suicide pending a further medical autopsy of the dismembered body. It was rumored that Mr. Alcort was under federal investigation linking him to the illegal importation of heroin from Afghanistan. An unnamed source indicated he apparently took his own life, leaping over 150 feet to the pavement below. In an unusual twist, our source indicated that Alcort was dressed in traditional Arab clothing.

"In a related incident, police report that Michael Sheehan of South Lynnfield was found dead inside the office area of the Colonnade Hotel as well. He was reported to be the night front-desk clerk. Initial indications were that he died of an overdose of illicit drugs. Police theorize he may have attempted to conceal drugs when he heard the sirens approaching. Unfortunately, he attempted to swallow six crack cocaine rocks leading to his death. Toxicology reports are expected to show the overdose, and the cause of death is to be announced within the next day."

Curtis Harrison smiled seeing that his associate had taken care of covering up the problem of James Alcort's murder and had also disposed of the front-desk clerk he had bribed to get access to the suite. Now his only problem was to control Trish and give Yasmina some answers to get this thing behind them. It would not be an easy task, but, as always, Curtis knew that in some twisted way it would work to his benefit.

Curtis entered the adjoining bedroom occupied by Trish. Yasmina was sitting in a seat by the window. Trish had her head buried in her pillow, and Curtis could hear her sobbing softly.

"It was a terrible accident," he said. "I have taken care of everything, and the police have reported it as a suicide. I have already made arrangements to fly your father's body back to Rhode Island for the funeral to take place within the next day. Is there anything I can do for you, Trish?"

Trish turned over and brushed away her tears. "Yes, there is something very important you can do for me," she choked out between her tears. "Explain to me how my father ended up being there dressed as an Arab."

Yasmina looked directly at Curtis, wondering how this horrible thing could have happened.

"These people are ruthless. I can't tell you how sorry I am, but I do promise you this: I will find who is responsible and get you the answers you desire," Curtis answered in no uncertain terms.

Trish rolled back over, sobbing again, and did not reply.

Curtis walked to the door and turned back to Yasmina. "Please leave her alone," he said. "I have to talk to you."

Yasmina told Trish that she would return and followed Curtis into the living area of the suite.

"Yasmina, I know you are upset. I assure you I had no idea Trish had a gun or what she was going to do. Trish seems to be saying it was an accident, but I am not sure what happened myself. I thought I was doing a good thing by helping her find her father. It could not have turned out worse," Curtis said with a false-sincere voice.

Yasmina knew that the story he was unfolding before her was not true. The coincidences were just too much for anyone to ignore. She knew that the fact he had planned to use Trish to regain control of distribution in the United States must have be the real reason behind the whole thing. The aspect that perplexed Yasmina the most was regarding the gun Trish had in her possession. It was dark, but it seemed to be the same type of gun Curtis had given her. Why did he give Trish a gun as well? If he had indeed planned to have James Alcort killed, he would not have done it in this way. Curtis Harrison would have been far away from a killing and would have had his lackeys do his bidding. The more likely scenario was that he was trying to get Trish indebted to him, and his plan had backfired when she shot her father. Yasmina felt the best approach now was to not ask questions and go along with the story Curtis had offered.

"I know you had her best interests at heart," Yasmina said in a consoling voice.

"I need to be alone with Trish and get some things answered for myself," Curtis said as he walked into Trish's room.

Trish sat up, and Curtis closed the door behind him, locking it carefully. Smiling, he ran to her and jumped on the bed. "Well, Miss Rhode Island, you really did put on a show. I was not sure how you were going to get your father out of the way, but you proved your loyalty today," Curtis praised her.

Trish put her arms around him and whispered in his ear, "Well, Curtis, when I say I will take care of something, I mean it. I believe we have cause for celebration. We have just acquired, by majority vote, ownership of the U.S. East Coast distribution. A shame we had one dissenting vote, but I hear he flew off and will not bother us anymore," Trish said in a wise tone.

"You are simply amazing. Not only are you the most beautiful girl in the world, but you also have ice water in your veins. Remind me to not cross you," Curtis stated, praising his partner.

"I think I just made it clear to never double-cross me, Mr. Harrison," Trish stated flatly. "You can see I show no mercy."

"I have a surprise for you. I set up a Swiss account in your name and have transferred seven million dollars into the account so you have some pocket money. Call it my thanks for helping me with my problem and as something to seal our future," Curtis stated proudly.

"Well, Curtis, I see you are a man I can appreciate. You know what a girl likes, this girl anyway," Trish said in appreciation.

Curtis was particularly proud of the fact that the seven million dollars was actually the money James Alcort had given to his associate for the ransom assuring his daughter's safety. Curtis thought to himself that Alcort was dead, so why not take the credit for this generous gift of his money? Curtis thought he really had outdone himself this time.

"We must keep up the front that this was a terrible accident," Curtis said, "and you must mourn as any good daughter would. We will have the funeral, and then it will be behind us."

"Oh, I think you can see I have adapted to my role well," Trish said proudly. "I can cry at a moment's notice. It should be very sad."

"There is just one thing I need for you to answer for me. How did you get the gun I gave to Yasmina?" Curtis questioned.

Trish moved closer to Curtis and pushed her breasts into his chest while speaking directly to him an inch away. "Well, I am a very resourceful woman, and, being your business partner and more importantly your lover, I must be concerned about any dangers that might befall us. Yasmina must understand her position as a servant. I will keep a close eye on her for the both of us, my love," Trish purred to him.

Curtis Harrison did not get a direct answer, but Trish had begun to unbutton her blouse. Curtis's mind had just shifted from business to pleasure, and he upheld his motto to never mix the two.

An hour later, Yasmina saw Curtis leave Trish's room. She returned to Trish and helped pack up her things. A doctor arrived and gave Trish a sedative that helped her to settle down for the short trip home to Providence, and enough extra to get her through the anxiety of the next couple of days. Yasmina actually felt sympathy for Trish. She knew it was some type of a setup or accident, but she could not imagine killing a father under any circumstances.

No matter how awful the recent events had been, in reality it worked into Yasmina's assignment well. Now with James Alcort out of the picture, the U.S. distribution of heroin would be tied more closely to Curtis Harrison. Now maybe the CIA would take a more aggressive posture toward this evil man. Yasmina hoped she would be the beneficiary of this event by finally gaining deserved stature with her CIA superiors.

CHAPTER 24

▼

Summer looked at her watch as she was driving back toward Kabul from the Harrison Estate. She was anxious to call Justin Davis to find out about Trish's trip back to America. She knew it would be a tenuous situation at best, since he probably realized by now that Chip had tricked him into getting Trish's location. She was comfortable that Justin would understand her dilemma in needing the information. Justin, being Trish's boss, should have close tabs and know where she was headed.

"It is 9 PM here, so that would make it early afternoon in Boston," Summer said. "If I wait until we get back to the city, I might miss Justin. He normally darts out of the office right at five."

"Pull over, and I will drive," Chip offered. You can make the call on your cell phone."

Summer pulled her cell phone out and turned it on. She could see that although the outskirts of the city had mediocre signal strength it should work okay. She eased the car to the side and skidded to a stop. Abdul woke up in the backseat in a daze. Summer and Chip traded positions, and she placed the call.

"Good afternoon. Associated Press," a female answered.

"Sally, you won't believe who this is," Summer bubbled.

"Oh my God, it's you, Summer. I have thought about you so often," Sally replied.

"Listen, Sally, I would love to catch up, but I am calling from Afghanistan, and it is expensive. I need to talk with Justin. Is he in?"

"Oh Summer, I thought you knew. Justin was killed in a mugging."

Summer dropped the phone to her side in disbelief. She slowly picked it back up to her ear and heard Sally asking if she was still there.

"Yes, I'm still here. I am sorry. I didn't know. How did it happen?" Summer inquired.

"It happened here at work. He was leaving one night with Mr. Alcort, Trish's father. They were getting into Justin's van when evidently someone tried to rob them. Justin was shot and killed, and Trish's father ended up missing."

"Did they find Trish's father?"

"It is the strangest thing. In the *Boston Globe* today is a front-page story saying they found Mr. Alcort at the Colonnade Hotel. He had committed suicide by jumping fourteen floors."

"Listen, Sally, I will call back when I have more time," Summer concluded.

Summer sat in a daze, trying to take in everything she had just heard. She tapped her cell phone on her knee as Chip kept glancing over, waiting to hear the news.

"Well, are you going to tell me, or should I start guessing?" Chip asked sarcastically.

Summer turned in her seat, tucked her ankle under her, and leaned over toward Chip. Tears were now streaming down her face.

"Justin is dead…killed by muggers. I can't believe it, and I never got to thank him for coming to see me. Then she told me that Trish's father committed suicide last night at the Colonnade Hotel. He disappeared when Justin was killed," Summer choked out.

"None of this is making any sense," Chip said. "It seems peculiar that we were told by the staff at the Harrison Estate that Trish was in the U.S. There is no way Trish could have known her father was dead before she went back to the States. Trish was already there before her father committed suicide, if it was suicide. Something is really strange."

"I hate to interrupt, but it seems to me this smells like a CIA operation," Abdul offered from the backseat.

"You may be right, Abdul. It appears this is way more than an unfortunate run-in with a mugger. Then Trish's father conveniently shows up dead, and they rule it a suicide?" Summer questioned sarcastically.

Summer pulled herself up straight in the seat and brushed her long blond hair away from her face as she said, "I bet Trish is involved with this somehow. I am convinced her association with Curtis Harrison is for her own personal gain. If she is associated with the CIA, as you contend, Abdul, then she is just using her position to grease the way to making money. She is obliged to show up at her father's funeral. We need to get back to the States at once and see what is going on here. Curtis Harrison must also be connected with Jimmy's death, and I want to know who made the ultimate call to have him killed."

Summer curled up next to the passenger door as they drove. She reached down with her hand, twirling her long blond hair. She exhaled and stroked her hair as she looked down at the phone still in her hand. It seemed that Summer was trying to connect everything she had been bombarded with the moment before. Chip was feeling emotions he could not explain. He felt sad for Summer, and he coveted the idea of being close to her. Tears filled his eyes, and the road became blurry. He rubbed his eyes hard and pulled his slumping body up. He would have to draw upon her strength to get through what had become a complex, exasperating, and dangerous mission.

As soon as Chip and Summer returned to the Mustafa Hotel, they called the airlines to find the first flight back to the States and Rhode Island. He agreed with Summer that they would be certain to find Trish at the funeral and should confront her. If she was working for al-Qaeda through Curtis Harrison, she could give them the current hiding place of Bin Laden. On the other hand, it was more likely she would not be coerced into giving up any information. Summer's idea was to challenge Trish by making her think she had evidence against her. Lighting this fuse would either force Trish to blurt out information in anger or blow up. Either was acceptable to Summer, and she felt there was nothing to lose.

Summer accepted the concept that Trish had found a way to acquire wealth and would do anything, including killing her own father, to gain an advantage. Summer determined she would have to trust Abdul and leave him in Afghanistan. She realized that if they took him with them, Trish would immediately recognize him and know he was feeding Summer information. Abdul promised to return to his home village and continue to gather information to pass along to them. It was a gamble trusting this corruptible man, but she had no choice.

Summer and Chip were able to leave Kabul and get to London. Flying west to New York, they continued to gain time. They would be in Providence, Rhode Island, by ten in the morning.

A meeting was called by the CIA director to review the Afghan operation. The reports recently filed by the two field operatives had caused him continuing concern. The handlers for Trish Alcort and Yasmina sat motionless, awaiting the director's arrival. The assistant director and other supervisors entered the conference room and did not speak to the handlers. Both knew this was a very bad sign. The director arrived, and as a courtesy each in the room stood until he took his place at the head of the table.

As he approached the table, he took a piece of paper, crumpled it to his head, and did a complete turn, slamming it down on the table.

"Well this is quite messy, isn't it?" the director shouted, throwing the waded paper toward the middle of the table.

The assistant director took the paper and smoothed it with his hand on top of the flat surface. He read the notice.

"Disperse only to security-cleared personnel as required.

"Local FBI office, Boston, reports back on CIA request to intercede in investigation of victim James Alcort found at Colonnade Hotel. FBI took over investigation, convinced local Boston PD it was a suicide case. FBI investigation suspects professional hit by foreign assets. Alcort involved in Afghan heroin distribution. Subject found on street fourteen stories down from suite, with bullet to the right skull, shot from distance of approximately two feet. Subject handgun not recovered. FBI investigated suspicious circumstances relating to concept of suicide by jumping. Autopsy of dismembered body found bullet imbedded in skull fragments. Investigators found through confirmed sources and military records that James Alcort was left-handed and could not have shot self with right hand creating injury to right skull. Theory of suicide by shooting and falling from balcony not corroborated by evidence. Please advise as to how to proceed. This seems to fall under your jurisdiction. FBI, Boston bureau."

Gasps were heard from the others as they began to put the pieces together in their minds.

"I am going to ask a very simple question," the director said, "and I expect a direct answer. Who called in the FBI on this? Remember, I will be checking."

Yasmina's handler had not expected that his friend at the FBI would inform his superiors. The cleanup operation should have been on the "Q-T" and should not have gone any further than his agent friend. He had to think on his feet. Otherwise he could be facing a mandatory retirement. When one retired from the CIA under these circumstances, one didn't receive a gold watch. In fact, the parting gift was more of the lead variety, a bullet to the back of the head.

"I have advised you about the young Afghan woman I have had working with me undercover at Curtis Harrison's estate," the handler said. "I feel we are very close to uncovering facts that could lead us directly to Bin Laden. She called me last night and indicated there had been a shooting and that James Alcort had been killed. She was there when it happened. She only had a few minutes before the Boston PD would arrive. In order to not compromise our operation, I had to react quickly, and I had a friend of mine from the FBI intercede."

The director and the others in the room did not respond. The supervisors looked at each other, and with knowing nods each of them gave their unspoken approval.

"Okay," the director said, "we have been rough on you today. We all agree you did the right thing by protecting our important asset who is providing intelligence about Curtis Harrison. I will contact my counterpart at the FBI and bury this thing."

"Thank you, sir. I appreciate your support on this issue," the handler said in a relieved voice.

"Don't be too thankful yet," the director said. "We need to continue to gather information on this possible conspirator. Keep on this girl like glue and find out everything you can from her. If required, use the information about her complicity with James Alcort's murder as a wedge to apply in order to get her to divulge new information. Do you know her current location?"

"Yes, I am certain of her location, and I will be going to her directly from here. I promise you I can be relied upon to get the information I know the agency needs."

The handler exited the hidden back room where they had been meeting and returned to his rental car parked nearby. He entered the address of James Alcort's residence into the GPS unit in the car, and he paused while waiting for the detailed map. Once displayed, it showed him the route from Boston to Providence, Rhode Island. He suddenly began to shake uncontrollably when the magnitude of what had just occurred hit him.

The handler thought to himself, "That was a close one. I was waiting to feel a bullet enter my head from behind at any moment. I knew if I told them just enough of the truth they would back off. I am smart enough to know that if I denied any connection I would be eliminated and my body never found. I need to be careful now because they will be more vigilant than ever. I must now revise our plans."

The director did not have to give the order. Two of the men attending automatically followed the handler to the garage and pulled out behind him. They would assure that the agency was not being snowed by this clumsy agent.

The meeting room now only contained the director, assistant director, and three supervisors.

"I am disgusted with the performance of our assets in Afghanistan," the director said. "I told all of you that if they were unable to make the required connection between al-Qaeda and Iraq I would pull the plug. The suggestion that we use two agents within the same operation seemed like a good idea at the time. I would have thought that if they were worth their own salt they would have discovered each other by now. Tell me, what do we know at this point?"

"Trish Alcort has requested and has been provided technical support to gather intelligence on Yasmina, our other agent. At the same time, Yasmina has requested support to gather information on Trish Alcort," a supervisor offered.

"Son of a bitch. So we are using our limited resources by having our own agents investigate each other?" the director bellowed.

"Mr. Director, I think you summarized it best in our last meeting on this issue. We have created a kludge by having two agents working the same assignment with neither of them knowing about the other. If we can't trust our own resources and must have them keep tabs on each other, then we should find different agents," a supervisor summarized.

"I said it before; the drug connection is a DEA problem," the director said. "I cannot impress upon you enough that our only mission now is to connect al-Qaeda to Iraq. This is what our commander in chief promised the American people before getting into the Iraq War. If we don't make the connection, he is going to look like either a liar or a fool. I don't think I need to remind each of you that this is an election year." By this point, the director was shouting.

In unison the group replied, "Yes sir."

"Now, pull the plug on both of these operations, and have it done like yesterday," the director concluded.

The men exited the room and made the appropriate calls to the agents following the handlers. The missions had been scrapped, and the handlers would soon be swimming with the fish in Boston Harbor.

CHAPTER 25

▼

The group of people gathered near the freshly dug grave was sparse at best. Trish sat in a folding chair positioned on artificial turf next to the casket suspended above the muddy hole. The rain from the previous night had turned to a slight drizzle. Seated next to her was Yasmina, dressed in a conservative black dress. Behind the two stood Curtis Harrison. Summer and Chip stood off to one side, and the remainder of the group were those friends not intimidated by the presence of men dressed in black suits surrounding several black SUVs parked across the way. The mention in the *Boston Globe* about James Alcort's involvement in the drug trade forced the more timid to remain at home.

Summer took in the whole atmosphere carefully and began to whisper her thoughts to Chip as the minister began the service.

"I suspect the man behind Trish is Curtis Harrison," Summer spoke into Chip's ear. "The pretty Afghan woman next to Trish I'm not certain about, but is probably Yasmina. Since we only saw her in a burka, it is hard to say for certain it is her."

"That's her," Chip said in a hushed tone. "Look at her eyes. No question about it.

"I can't believe all the Feds here," he continued. "I suppose they are trying to establish who might have been in partnership with Alcort. Watch the guys next to the SUVs. They have earpieces, and I am sure the one to the left is taking pictures with a small digital camera concealed in his palm."

Summer looked toward the men Chip was describing, and in her peripheral vision she saw a man duck behind a large granite monument nearby. She refocused her line of sight and could see the man positioning himself, holding what appeared to be a cell phone.

"Look at the guy over there. What could he possibly be doing?" Summer said in a hush in Chip's ear.

Chip bent back a bit, and with both of them looking toward the man in wonder, the Fed suddenly raised himself to his knees and made a gesture to the others gathered by the vehicles. Abruptly the men all jumped into the parked conveyances and quickly proceeded to leave.

"That seemed like the guy we were watching received a phone call and motioned for everyone to leave," Chip observed.

"Yeah, they shot out of here like a bat out of hell," Summer agreed too loudly. The group listening to the minister's kind words all turned around to look at her, and she began to turn red with embarrassment. Summer bowed her head as if in prayer, and when the group returned their gaze to the minister, she again looked to where she had seen the spooks driving away.

As the service ended, Trish placed a handful of dirt on the top of her father's coffin as a final gesture, and Yasmina assisted her back toward the waiting limo. Curtis Harrison followed close behind. The trio walked directly toward Summer and Chip. Summer, realizing this might be her only opportunity, knew she would have to confront Trish. It did not seem appropriate at the burial, but giving the suspected killer condolences was not an Emily Post recommendation either. Chip took one of his old Gillette business cards from his wallet and scribbled a note on the back, saying, "Call me. Summer," with her cell-phone number. He handed the card to Summer as they had prearranged. As the trio got closer, Trish gazed up and had a look of amazement as she saw Summer. She paused for a moment before her.

"Trish, I am so sorry about your father. I know how difficult a loss like this must be for you, even though you probably have already cleaned out his bank accounts," Summer said with feigned sympathy.

"How dare you say something like that to me, you white trash? You are not welcome here," Trish blurted out.

"I am onto you, Trish. I have the evidence to put you away, and as God is my witness, I will," Summer promised in a stern voice.

Trish did not respond and turned her green eyes to Chip.

Chip did not hesitate, and his natural instincts kicked in as he reached to her and hugged her while he whispered into her ear, "Trish, Summer and I are onto you. You need to come clean or we'll contact the authorities."

Trish slowly stepped back from Chip and then pulled him close again. Her eyes were filled with anger as she spoke into his ear. "I am the authorities in this world, you bastard. How brazen of you to threaten me. You should be the one in fear. Show me you comprehend by kissing me on the cheek when I pull away, and perhaps I will spare your little girlfriend," Trish stated violently.

Trish pulled back, holding on to Chip's arms. Chip leaned over to her and kissed her lightly on the cheek. Trish batted her eyes in a knowing way at Summer as Yasmina began guiding her to the waiting limo. Summer placed the business card having her phone number into Yasmina's hand without anyone else noticing.

Summer could not resist one last shot as Trish walked away.

"Let's do lunch," Summer needled.

"Oh, you will get your lunch alright, Summer Tolly," Trish answered sarcastically.

Summer could not hear what Chip and Trish had discussed and suddenly felt a pang of concern as she saw him kiss her. She did not speak until the others were out of range.

"What was that all about?" she inquired.

"Listen, I told her we are onto her and that we will tell the authorities if she does not come clean. She then threatened us and said she would do you harm. She asked me to show her that I understood the threat by kissing her on the cheek. We know Harrison is connected to al-Qaeda, and obviously she has made a partnership with him."

"You are crazy. First you threaten Trish without my input, and then you kiss her? You have to be careful, and I expect to be consulted on every turn," Summer stated confidently.

"Well, what do we have to lose at this point?" Chip stated, upset.

"Our lives are what we have to lose," Summer answered without hesitation.

Summer took it all in and knew the importance of having Chip as a partner. She was not comfortable with him making any decisions without her knowledge. The trip was successful if only for the opportunity of seeing Curtis Harrison in person. Also, challenging Trish might make her come back out into the open where she could be watched more effectively. She still was a bit miffed at the kiss, but understood why it was necessary. Summer began to speak and tried to cover her dissatisfaction by joking.

"I'll give you that one, Mr. Murphy, but if you are going to be with me, you better keep your lips to yourself," Summer blurted out.

As soon as the words left her mouth, she wished she could either take them back or crawl in the hole with James Alcort. Chip took a step back, wondering if he had really heard what he thought he had heard. Summer immediately noticed how uncomfortable he was acting.

"I'm just kidding you. You know how I am," Summer said in a teasing mood.

Chip tilted his head to the side and looked at Summer as she swung her long blond hair and turned to walk away.

"I only wish I could be with you," Chip said in a muffled tone.

Summer had walked ten paces away and flipped her hair, turning to look back at him over her shoulder. "What was that?" she yelled.

"I said I wish we could put this all together," Chip replied, covering his tracks.

Trish, Yasmina, and Curtis each rode in separate limos. Yasmina reached forward to the center of the limo where the power-window buttons are located. She depressed one of them, and the darkened glass separated her from the driver. Yasmina took out her cell phone and called her secure number to speak with her handler. Never had there been an instance when her handler had not answered on the first ring. Finally there was a voice message.

"The number you have reached has been disconnected. Please check your number and try your call again later."

Yasmina's heart sank. She knew what the message meant. Her handler was gone, eliminated. She would never know if it was by accident or design. Regardless, she had no lifeline. Standard operating procedure was for agents to have no CIA contact other than their handler. Since this important link was broken, she would just have to wait and see if she was ever contacted again.

This was a sure indication that she must now be more vigilant than ever about her security. Yasmina suspected that Trish had broken into her room and stolen the gun she had used to kill her father. Yasmina had planned to inform Curtis about Trish's clandestine activities, but now that seemed impossible. Yasmina knew Curtis Harrison would believe the beauty he was sleeping with over her. She had to be careful and discredit Trish in another way by using the AIDS evidence she had planned with Summer.

Yasmina looked at the crumpled card Summer had given her. Her first thought was that the two unlikely Americans might be her only hope for survival.

Trish threw her cell phone across the back of her limo. She had just received the same seemingly innocent message about her handler's phone being disconnected. Like a spoiled brat, she was pouting about the fact that she alone would be responsible for figuring out a way to have Chip and, more importantly, Summer killed. Using the CIA to do her bidding would have been much safer and more convenient.

Curtis Harrison watched the multicolored hills roll by as his limo proceeded to T. F. Green Airport, where he would be departing for Kabul on his private jet. His cell phone rang, interrupting his calm.

"Hello," Curtis answered.

"It is your partner. We must meet as soon as possible. I have explosive information you need to hear at once. When can we meet?" the man asked exuberantly.

"My friend, what is all the excitement about?" Curtis inquired.

"I was receiving an update over the phone from Yasmina's handler, and suddenly I heard a commotion and two gun shots. The phone went dead, and when I tried to call back, I got an automated message saying the phone had been disconnected. I strongly suspect that our CIA connection was assassinated," the man described with worry.

"Okay, the main thing is that he was able to get the James Alcort killing under wraps. He has been a valuable asset, but we can manage without him. In fact, it makes my need to deal with Yasmina even more imminent. It is unfortunate that she has decided to work with the CIA behind my back. The good thing is that through your connections we have been able to thwart her every move and use her by feeding her false information," Curtis said as he attempted to make lemonade out of a lemon.

"I will meet you in Kabul at our regular place as soon as I arrive from Miami, in about eight hours," the voice stated seriously.

"I will be there, and be ready for the surprise of your life. I have been successful in acquiring our ultimate product. This makes selling heroin look like child's play," Curtis stated and flipped his phone closed.

CHAPTER 26

▼

Yasmina fumbled through the package she had received from Summer in her absence. The seven prescription bottles containing Agenerase, Combivir, Crixivan, Epivir, Emtrivam, Fuzeon, and Hivid each had Trish Alcort's name prominently printed on the labels. These were the most common medicines used to treat AIDS. The medical report, in Trish's name as well, gave the definitive diagnosis of full-blown AIDS.

Much had changed since her meeting with Summer, when they had devised their plan to divulge this artificial information to Curtis Harrison. The loss of her CIA handler put a real crimp in her plans. If she were to proceed with the idea to break Trish and Curtis apart, she would be without CIA support. Also, without having the resources to keep track of Trish outside the estate, she was concerned that Trish could do even greater damage.

Yasmina decided she would have to put the ruse on hold until she was assigned a new handler. She felt the only avenue to stop Trish Alcort was to stay close to the situation and create no waves. The gun was an issue she was most concerned about. She wavered over the idea of stealing it back from Trish. She pondered her options and decided she could enlist the assistance of Summer and Chip if required. Now was the part of the job she hated most. The waiting.

The meeting place had been designed several years ago during the war. Only Curtis Harrison and his associate knew the place and how to access the cave. Both men knew they must never be seen together. That would bring the wrath of multiple nations down upon them. Curtis heard the steel access door slide open and looked up to see his friend. Both men shook hands and then embraced each other.

"I am sorry to be running late. Some of us have to fly commercial, and considering the added security, the flights always seem to run late," The Latino man explained.

"I am forever at your disposal, Mayor Lopez. I am certain you would not have delayed our meeting if it were within your control," Curtis Harrison stated emphatically.

"You know our business has worked well and has been mutually beneficial," the mayor said. "Through our business efforts we have been able to supply al-Qaeda and Cuba with the funds required to exact their revenge on the United States. In the meantime, we have been able to amass a fortune. The bombing and killing of our major heroin-business rival at the Mustafa Hotel has nearly doubled our fortune."

"I have been dedicated with assisting Bin Laden in order to avoid any conflicts with our business," Curtis said. "I have also used Yasmina's CIA handler when needed to have special operations performed to alleviate our adversaries. Just recently we were able to extinguish our American distributor and cover it up by using the handler."

"The introduction of Osama Bin Laden to Fidel Castro was a stroke of genius," Mayor Lopez said. "My home country now has provided safe haven for Osama to run his operations, and Fidel has now offered strategic support and military might where needed. In return, you have run the heroin business professionally and have made us both rich. I trust you as my brother and know we will continue to prosper."

"Yes, my friend, it is all true. We have made a true alliance that goes far beyond our material success. I also trust you without question and feel you have something heavy on your heart. If I can help, please do not hesitate," Curtis said in an assured tone.

"I am concerned about losing Yasmina's handler. He was our only contact with the CIA. The deep cover I now enjoy as Mayor of Miami could be jeopardized without clandestine support. Our plans for my future political career are now in question," the Cuban mayor complained.

"My friend, we must look to nature to see the wisdom of our plan. In the wild, a juvenile male lion will look to acquire a pride of his own. The only way to accomplish it is to steal it from an older male. In nature you will see that the young lion will attack the alpha male in order to take over a coveted pride. The remainder of the pride, comprised of many females and young males, never does anything to assist their challenged leader. If the young male wins the contest by killing the alpha male, then he becomes the new leader," Curtis described.

"I understand the wisdom, but the tremendous strength and many numbers of the American military far exceeds the combined forces of al-Qaeda and Cuba," the mayor pointed out.

"That is exactly my point. Cuba and al-Qaeda must think like the young lion. Attack the leader, bring down the head, and the American people will follow," Curtis explained.

"But how do we proceed to assure that our plans for advancing my political career are not compromised?"

"That I have assured with the next phase of our mission. I told you on the phone I had some exciting news. I have finally been able to acquire enough nuclear-grade materials to manufacture five dirty bombs," Curtis boasted.

"That is excellent news. How do we proceed?"

"I have cleared the plan with Osama and Fidel. I am taking delivery of the materials here in Afghanistan. I will then transport them to the Bahamas, and Osama and Fidel will take delivery in Cuba."

"When does this happen?"

"We will have the bombs delivered into Cuba by the end of the week," Curtis promised.

"Then is there a plan to strategically place and detonate these bombs?"

"That is the best part of the plan. Three of the five will be held in Cuba for future use. The other two will be transported to you in Miami. The use of the bombs is a strategic move to assist in your career," Curtis divulged.

"I like the way you think, my friend," the mayor stated, sitting up taller in his seat.

"Used properly, your political stock will increase in value a thousandfold," Curtis promised.

"I am not certain how this event alone will be enough to assure my aspirations for the presidency," the mayor relented.

"I agree, but we have other plans to insure that you can easily win the election. Just look at the popularity of the former mayor of New York. One step at a time leads to a thousand-mile journey," Curtis philosophized.

"How will the operation be executed?"

"Remember I told you about the new, resourceful young woman I have working with me now?"

"Yes, the beauty queen," the mayor said.

"Trish Alcort is her name, and she has made the ultimate commitment to our cause. She is known as an aspiring Associated Press reporter. Her cover fits perfectly with the coordination of the operation. She will be briefed and will assist you with every detail. She inherited a waterfront home in Miami from her father after he took a nasty fall and did not recover. This will work well within our strategy. She also has immediate access to the press and can release information beneficial to our cause," Curtis assured his friend.

"I now understand your analogy to the young lion. The president of the United States is the older alpha-male lion. I am the young juvenile attempting to take over the pride, or the United States, per se. I will attack the leader directly, and when I win, the Americans will follow. The analogy is perfection," the mayor congratulated his friend.

"The only difference is that you will have the strongest lioness as your partner. Trish Alcort has the capability to bring any man to his demise," Curtis assured.

"How does the plan unfold?"

"Trish will coordinate the Miami procedure. I have negotiated the financial issues with Osama and Fidel."

"I was so excited about the future plans that I forgot about the money we are acquiring through this transaction."

"That is why you have me, my friend. I never forget about the money. I too will support the mission of our friends, but I also have to eat," Curtis explained.

"I understand what you are saying. You are the business person in our relationship," the mayor said.

"The five valises will be paid for by wire transfer to our Swiss account at the time of delivery in Cuba. They will wire one hundred million for the five. I also have a commitment for five additional until the time we can get no more. We are paying a small fraction to the Russians for the product. Believe me, my friend, we will become wealthy enough to retire from the drug business in a year," Curtis promised.

"The Cuban Americans watch my every step in Miami. I have to be cautious so that they never discover I work for Fidel. They make many demands on me and expect special concessions, being that they think I am one of them. Of course they are the ones who got me elected, and I must bow to their demands," the mayor complained.

"There is an old American saying: 'Keep your friends close and your enemies even closer.' I suggest you go along with their demands. Make them love you as a good friend. Their support will be required in the next election," Curtis advised.

"And their votes in the future presidential run as well," the mayor concluded.

"I am going to personally deliver the materials to Andros Island in the Bahamas, using my jet. Then I have arranged boats to do the transport to Cuba. I am taking Trish Alcort with me, and she will travel on the boats with the delivery. I am also taking Yasmina with me. Since her handler has been relieved of his duties, she is of no further value to us. I will assure there is no possibility of her divulging information she may have discovered about our operation," Curtis explained.

"Yasmina was close to you, like a daughter, and I am very sorry she ended up being a traitor. My thoughts are with you, my friend," the mayor said.

Curtis jumped up from his seat and hugged the mayor. Their agenda was working perfectly. Curtis's only concern was that the mayor's political aspirations made him an impatient person at times. The way to win this war was through a patient stalking of the prey. Just like the young lion.

CHAPTER 27

▼

The sound of the Bell Jet helicopter was unmistakable. Yasmina jolted from her sound sleep and ran to her window to see the slow dissent of the copter at its landing site just beyond the pool. She checked the digital clock next to her bed and wondered who would be traveling at two thirty in the morning. Yasmina decided to pull on her black jeans and sweatshirt and sneak out to where all the activity was taking place. She grabbed her digital camera just in case.

Yasmina skirted the pool area, using the lavish greenery to conceal her while tiptoeing toward the helicopter pad. When she was within twenty feet, the engine whined to a stop. She could see Curtis Harrison exiting the copter with Trish following directly behind.

Three security guards began unloading five aluminum suitcases. Each one was clearly marked with the international caution notice and logo for nuclear materials. Yasmina began to wonder why Curtis Harrison would be making a clandestine trip without her knowledge. Also, what would be the purpose for carrying nuclear materials? None of this made any sense, and when she heard Trish tell Curtis that she would she him in the morning, Yasmina knew for certain Trish had gained full control over Curtis Harrison.

Yasmina began to take pictures as quickly as possible. Her camera had a low-light lens and could easily see the nuclear cases in the dark morning hours. She was happy she had remembered to bring the camera, since she noticed the two mounted security cameras trained on the helipad had been covered with dark cloths, rendering them useless.

Yasmina made it back to her room without detection. She reviewed the many pictures and placed the camera in its docking station attached to her computer.

She moved the mouse on her computer and uploaded the pictures for future use, not currently having a handler to send this damaging evidence to.

Yasmina began to search for the card Summer had given her the day of the funeral. She had about given up when she finally found it still in the pocket of the outfit she had been wearing that day. She unrolled it from the used Kleenex she had wadded in her pocket with it. The front had the Gillette Company logo, while on the back she found a cell-phone number with a note, "Call me. Summer." She looked at the clock next to her bed, as if the time would have mattered, and opened her cell phone. She entered the handwritten number.

"Hello, who is this?" Summer answered in a sleepy tone.

"I am so sorry to call at this hour, but I need to talk to you. This is Yasmina."

"Yasmina, where are you?" Summer asked while jerking up to sit on the edge of her bed.

"I am in Kabul, back at Mr. Harrison's estate."

"What is the matter? You sound scared."

"I am afraid. I know they are plotting against me, and I have just witnessed them unloading some sort of nuclear materials they flew in."

"Listen," Summer said, "I can meet you in the morning. We need to cover everything you know."

"I can't," Yasmina said nervously. "Curtis Harrison is taking me and Trish Alcort on a get-away trip to Andros Island in the Bahamas in the morning."

"Andros Island. What could he want to do in the Bahamas?"

"He told me it would be good to get away and lie on the beach. He also said that the scuba diving is wonderful. I took it all to mean we are just getting away to relax. Now I am suspecting he has other plans. Seeing him and Trish with nuclear materials is way too strange. That is why I am calling you for help. Could you go to Andros in case I need your help?" Yasmina begged.

"I will be there. If you need me, just call the number I gave you. Be safe, and don't confront them directly. It may cost you your life," Summer concluded.

Summer did not hesitate a moment. She called and woke Chip, telling him of the strange phone call from Yasmina. Summer convinced Chip they needed to go to Andros Island and see what Trish was conjuring up with nuclear materials. If she could connect Harrison and Trish directly, she could go to whomever necessary in the government to stop what appeared to be an al-Qaeda operation.

Summer knew they would have to leave at once flying commercial because Curtis Harrison's private jet could fly direct. She wanted to be sure they arrived ahead of Trish in order to establish a plan to keep a watch over her activities.

Summer agreed with Chip that it could just be a vacation trip, but she knew Yasmina would not have contacted her unless she was really afraid for her life.

The flight to Andros Island took most of the night and the following day. When they landed at the airport, both of them looked about the area to see if Curtis Harrison's unmistakable private Citation was on the tarmac. They agreed he must not have arrived and were pleased they could make the necessary arrangements. The airport lobby contained racks of tourist flyers, and Summer noticed several offering helicopter tours of the island. She thought this would be the perfect way to follow Yasmina, Trish, and Curtis from a distance.

The taxi took the pair down the bumpy road to a flat spot next to the ocean. The ocean twinkled in aquamarine, and differing hues could be seen for miles till they turned deep royal blue further offshore. A helicopter came in for a landing, and the sunburned tourists exited the noisy machine, carrying cameras, towels, and sunscreen. The pilot was the last to exit, and Summer walked directly to where he knelt to check the fluids on the engine.

"Excuse me, sir," Summer yelled.

The man turned. He had a perturbed look on his face until he saw the beauty summoning him. He then made a big bright smile showing his white teeth against his dark skin.

"Ya mon, wat ya tinkin?" the native man replied.

Summer walked closer to the man as Chip stayed back. They knew ahead of time that Summer would have a much better way with the locals than Chip would. Unless of course they were women, he had teased Summer.

"We would like to rent you and your helicopter for the next couple of days," Summer replied, figuring out the man's lingo.

"Whew, ya mus bin rich or somtin, pretty lady," he replied in a surprised tone.

"Not rich, but I can pay you five hundred dollars a day," she replied as she walked closer and put her hand up over his head on the side of the copter.

The local man, known as Cory, struggled to his feet. He was ready to tell her to take a swim. He made two hundred dollars a flight for twenty minutes and could do ten a day. Why would he want to take only five hundred for a day? Cory took a big breath to begin his case for a higher fee.

Just as he was ready to rant and rave, Summer pulled her hair back with her other hand, bent toward him, and said in a sweet, low way, "Pleeeeeease. I really would like to spend several days with you."

It was too much for Cory to deal with, seeing her tight halter top straining to hold her taut breasts, and he blurted out, "Okay, no problem," before he could get his bearings. It was just the thought of being near her for two days that stirred his primitive needs. Then he saw Chip walking toward them, and he knew he had been had. Anyway, in the Bahamas, a man was of his word, so the trio got into the helicopter and began to explore. Along the way, each conversed via headphones and microphones. Cory now understood they were going to find and follow some people. This made him happier, since it was a fun departure from his normal canned tour. They flew toward the airport.

The engines of Curtis Harrison's jet were thrown hard into reverse. The powerful aircraft came to a stop just short of the crystal-clear water at the end of the runway. Yasmina, Trish, Curtis, and three security guards exited the plane. It was a short ride in the open-air jitney to the hotel and marina on the other side of the island.

Yasmina threw her bags on the bed draped under mosquito netting. She walked out onto the wooden porch overlooking the marina where sportfishing boats bobbed at the rickety docks. She picked up her cell phone and dialed Summer's number.

The suite at the desolate resort was not up to the standards Curtis Harrison had become accustomed to. Trish complained to him about the "shabby" accommodations, but, being in a remote location, there was little to do but make the best of the situation.

"Curtis, there is something we need to discuss. Being concerned for your safety and mine, I have been keeping a close eye on Yasmina," Trish began tenuously, knowing his close relationship with the Afghan girl.

"You have nothing to worry about with Yasmina. She is loyal to me to the end," Curtis retorted.

"Well, I have something to show you. After we picked up the nuclear materials last night, I thought I saw Yasmina near the helipad. Being of a suspicious nature, I decided to check her computer to see if she had sent any e-mails regarding what she may have seen. This is what I found in her out-box, ready to be sent."

Trish threw a folder containing photographs onto the king-size bed where Curtis was seated. Several came out and slid across the bed. Curtis picked them up and could clearly see that they were pictures of him and Trish taken next to his helicopter. Close by were the aluminum cases with the nuclear warning signs clearly displayed.

"How did you get these?" Curtis demanded. "Yasmina is the best tech person around. How were you able to break into her computer?"

"Well, I can tell you about the technology I used, but it is the result we need to concentrate on," Trish replied.

"This is a disaster. I have three Intrepid go-fast boats waiting in the harbor to deliver the bombs to Cuba. If she sends this to CIA or FBI, our plan is sunk," Curtis screamed.

"We need to get rid of her before she has a chance to send them. I am now even more certain that my suspicions about her were true. She is working against you and is quite possibly an agent of the United States," Trish exclaimed in a matter-of-fact way.

"Well, it seems the time has come for me to part ways with Yasmina. I know exactly how to terminate her employment," Curtis said in a sinister voice.

Chip and Summer were flying about the island in the helicopter they had rented. Summer had her cell phone set to vibrate and could feel she had a call. The sound of the helicopter made it difficult to talk.

"This is Yasmina. We have landed, and I am now at the resort. I saw them unload the nuclear cases I told you about last night. They may have transported them to the harbor, and I can see them guarding three boats. The boats have multiple outboard engines and look fast. I am sure they are going to be transporting the nuclear materials on them."

"Yasmina, I am having a tough time hearing you, but I understand your message," Summer shouted over the noise. "We are in a helicopter over the harbor and can see the three boats you are talking about. It appears they are heavily guarded."

"Yes, they have three security men with automatic weapons. I am sure you cannot get near them. Just keep an eye on the boats and track them if they leave the harbor," Yasmina suggested.

"Where are you going to be later?"

"Mr. Harrison has arranged a scuba-diving trip with me and Trish in the morning. I will call you after we return, and you can update me."

"Should we call the Coast Guard or something?"

"Not yet," Yasmina said. "They need to be out to sea before the U.S. Coast Guard can intercede. Hang tight. We will get them."

"Be careful. These people are ruthless," Summer warned.

Yasmina knew what Summer had said was true. She had always known Curtis Harrison was tough and broke the law on many occasions. It seemed, though, that he had always subscribed to the belief there was honor among thieves. The addition of Trish Alcort to the caldron seemed to provide a catalyst that was creating the possibility of a massive explosion.

CHAPTER 28

▼

Yasmina headed down to the marina. Curtis had told her to be there at 8 AM for their scuba-diving trip. She had no interest in scuba diving and had never been before in her life. She knew that trying to explain her absence would be impossible and that just disappearing would cause Curtis Harrison's security people to tear the island apart looking for her. She would have to go along with his plan even though she was very nervous. She was hoping the only reason Curtis was taking her out to sea, away from the island, was to allow the nuclear material to begin its trip without her notice. She still did not know for sure what the planned final destination for the materials was, but she counted on Summer to keep track for her.

Yasmina hoped and prayed that Summer, with Chip's help, could get the whole operation on film. Then she could turn Curtis Harrison in to the U.S. government and get him incarcerated permanently. She saw the sportfishing boat named *Bubba's Baby* in front of her.

"Ya mus be pretty lady friend o Mr. Harrison," the local man hollered from the transom of the boat while lifting scuba tanks onto the back deck.

"Yes sir, I am. Is this our boat?" Yasmina asked.

"Ya mammm. Yor for da day anyway," the friendly captain replied. "Let me help ya aboard. My name be Bubba."

Yasmina observed all of the equipment and convinced herself that Curtis was indeed serious about doing this diving trip. Her fears that he might do her harm began to subside. Yasmina's concentration was interrupted when she felt the boat move as someone came aboard behind her.

"Good morning, Yasmina. Beautiful day for a dive, wouldn't you say?" Curtis Harrison stated in a happy mood.

"Yes, if you like that sort of thing," Yasmina replied.

"Now, Yasmina, you will enjoy this. Trust me," Curtis assured.

Curtis looked around the back deck and then stuck his head inside the boat's cabin. "Where is our special guest? Trish not here yet?" Curtis questioned.

"Trish is fashionably late. She is probably getting her hair done and nails polished," Yasmina described insolently.

"Yasmina, you need to remember your place and be more respectful," Curtis scolded.

"I am sorry, sir. You misunderstand. I have an appreciation of the things important to this American woman. She takes so much of her time worrying about her appearance," Yasmina attempted to explain.

"I know she will be here shortly. She is looking forward to getting some sun and seeing the beautiful waters," Curtis offered.

Curtis was silent for a moment and then called for one of his security guards. He whispered something in his ear, and the security guard began the walk up the pier to the hotel. A few minutes later, Yasmina could see Trish being escorted down the dock. She was blowing on her fingernails, as a funny confirmation that Yasmina was correct about the reason for her delay. The guard loaded the beach bags onto the back deck as Curtis provided a hand to Trish, who struggling to hold on to her floppy hat while stepping aboard.

Curtis turned to Bubba and said cheerfully, "Crank it up. Let's go diving."

The diesel engines started with a cloud of white smoke as the lines were thrown into the cockpit of the fifty-foot sport fish. Bubba goosed the engines, and they were off toward open water.

On the way out of the harbor, Yasmina noticed several of Curtis Harrison's security men still standing guard next to three Intrepid go-fast boats. Each boat had triple three-hundred-horsepower outboard engines. Yasmina thought how smart she was to know what Curtis's intentions were. He planned to take her and Trish out off the island so the nuclear material could begin its journey. She hoped Summer was able to coordinate the filming of the event to seal Curtis Harrison's fate.

Summer arrived to find Chip already strapped into the open-cockpit helicopter. The pilot helped Summer into the copilot's seat. He buckled her in and walked around the aircraft. Summer turned to talk to Chip, and when she got no response, she could see him motion to the headphones. She put hers on and began to speak.

"Chip, were you able to get a video camera with a telephoto lens?"

Chip tapped her on the shoulder and held up the compact device. "I also got an infrared lens so we can film during darkness," he said.

"Good thinking. I am pretty sure they will make the transfer of the cases from the Citation at any time. Yasmina thought the transfer had been made. She was not sure, but it was hard to hear her over the sound of the helicopter yesterday."

The helicopter vectored from its position near the water's edge and flew toward the airport. Once there, they could barely see men moving around the cargo compartment of Curtis's jet. Chip took the video camera and switched it to record mode. He could now clearly see the shiny aluminum suitcases with the international nuclear-caution logo on their sides. He was able to get extreme close-ups of them even though they were at fifteen hundred feet altitude from where the airplane was parked.

They followed at distance as two golf carts they had seen at the plane carried the deadly weapons to the marina. Once there, Chip filmed the entire process of loading them onto the go-fast boats. The camera was so precise and clear that the registration numbers of the boats could be identified without a problem. Summer began to speak over the intercom attached to everyone's headset.

"This is great," she said, "perfect evidence for catching Harrison in the act."

"I agree," Chip said. "We have the nuclear materials being loaded from Curtis Harrison's plane onto the boats, but we still have not been able to put him on tape with the criminal cargo."

"Curtis is going scuba diving this morning with Yasmina. At least that is what he is claiming. He might be planning to meet up with the boats as they leave," Summer explained.

"Well maybe, but the top speed on these three boats is much faster than any sport fish I've ever witnessed. Maybe the best thing is for us to find the boat Harrison is on and see what develops. I have all the incriminating film I need on these guys. What was the name of the boat Harrison is supposed to be on with Yasmina?"

"*Bubba's Baby* is the name Yasmina mentioned," Summer answered.

The helicopter pilot, hearing the conversation, headed out southeast over the open ocean. He knew the captain, Bubba, personally and where he normally took people to dive. After about twenty minutes, the pilot could see the wake of the big sport-fish boat. He turned to the others and pointed down.

"Der's *Bubba's Baby*," he said. "I stay back some so they no see us. I git real close wen dey anchor. I guessen they be bout fifteen minutes away from place Bubba dive."

Curtis Harrison was sitting on the flybridge next to Trish while the captain let her steer. Occasionally he would look down into the cockpit to see if Yasmina was still sitting in the large Marlin-fighting chair. Curtis felt his cell phone vibrate, and he pulled it from his shirt pocket.

"Yeah, what you got?" Curtis asked bluntly.

"Sir, the reporters are not in their rooms," the voice explained in a concerned tone. "The tip you got from the concierge was correct. They flew in commercial yesterday from Kabul. This could be a problem."

Curtis Harrison pulled the phone from his ear and tapped it on his leg. It was a nervous habit he had developed, used when he was trying to think. Suddenly he realized his security guard was still on the phone, shouting his name.

"Sorry, I am thinking," Curtis said. "Go to the airport and see if they are there. They can't be too far. You can only fly out or take a boat. Find them. It is important."

"One more thing, Mr. Harrison. When we were loading the materials onto the boats, I noticed a helicopter hovering about a half mile away. I'm sure they were too far away to see anything, but I thought I should mention it to you," the security guard said.

Hearing the bad news, Curtis Harrison hurled his cell phone off the flybridge into the deep blue water being cut by the shape of the sport fisher. Curtis now realized there was a distinct possibility that Yasmina may have tipped off the CIA, and they could be in pursuit. It was now imperative he get some answers. He instructed the captain to anchor at once. The captain protested, since it was not his normal stop, but pulled the engines into neutral when he saw the wild expression in Curtis's face. Curtis scrambled down the ladder to the cockpit where Yasmina was seated.

Summer pointed out to the others that *Bubba's Baby* was slowing down. The pilot took a wide turn so as not to come up on the stopped vessel. Chip began to zoom in on the target, and he could see Yasmina and Curtis talking on the back deck. Chip asked the pilot to get a better angle so he could reveal all of Curtis Harrison's face.

The captain dropped the anchor using his electric windlass. He followed Curtis down the stairs and began to attach diving gear to the tanks lined up by the side. Trish glided down the stairs and went into the boat's cabin. Curtis went up to Yasmina's side and began to speak.

"Having a nice time? It is a great day for a dive," Curtis said coolly.

Curtis went over to the five-gallon buckets positioned along the back of the boat. He popped off the top of the first one, and the wretched smell of rotting fish hit him full force. He took the large ladle and began scooping the bloody mixture into the water next to the boat. He then lifted the whole bucket and poured it all into the water. The captain heard the splash and turned to look at what had caused it.

"No, no, mester. Ya attrack sharks wit dat. Dat for fishin later. No man wanna dive in blood chum. It be suicide," the captain protested.

Curtis turned to the captain, and he could see the captain's confusion and concern. "Come here and take a look," he said. "If we get some sharks in, maybe we should go ahead and fish,"

The portly man came to the side of the boat. "See here," he said, "they be circling right now. I seez three big mako." The captain pointed at the dark shapes in the water.

Suddenly the back door of the cabin crashed open. Trish, running full force, pushed the captain over the transom, and he hit the water with a splash. Yasmina attempted to stand, and Curtis held her tightly by the wrist. Trish, after she had pushed the old captain overboard, turned her attention toward Yasmina.

Chip saw the commotion on the boat and, having the advantage of the telephoto lens, was the first to see that someone had been pushed overboard.

"My God," he said, "someone just pushed the captain over, and I can see at least a dozen sharks circling him."

"You're right. Get closer," Summer demanded, grabbing the camera with the long lens away from Chip.

The helicopter began a long loop back toward the boat's position.

Yasmina began to struggle against the tight hold Curtis had on her, and she turned to Trish. "Trish, I don't understand. Why did you push the captain overboard?" she squealed in total confusion.

Trish stepped toward her and grabbed her other arm as she tried to struggle free from Curtis's grip.

At the back of the boat, the captain surfaced and began a mournful scream. "Save me. Des killers got hold a me. Plez mista," he begged.

The captain's head was jerked rapidly down and disappeared into a swirl of bloody pieces. After a moment, his head suddenly popped up, having been decapitated from his body. Yasmina turned her head and vomited violently onto the deck. A large twelve-foot Mako surfaced and swallowed the captain's head in one gulp.

"My God, the sharks ate the man alive," Summer yelled into her mouthpiece.

Fortunately Chip could not detect the gory details as well as Summer could with the zoom lens. He and the pilot were still in shock at what they were certain was a man's torturous death. The pilot made another wide swoop and turned back toward land. Summer could tell they were moving too far away to get the details she needed on film.

"Come on, man, get closer. I can't see anything this far off," she yelled at the pilot.

"I jus seen me buddy ate by sharks," the pilot said. "I gotta go back. I no want to see no more."

Summer and Chip simultaneously shouted at the pilot until he finally turned back toward the boat.

Curtis and Trish yanked Yasmina from the fighting chair. She began yelling and kicking, trying to get away. Both of them took hold of her upper arms and lifted her slim body till her feet could no longer reach the deck. They positioned the struggling woman next to the transom of the boat. Curtis took her by the chin and forced her to look into his eyes.

"Trish showed me the photos you took the other night of us at the helicopter. Well, little lady, you just made the biggest mistake of your short life," Curtis growled, looking into her fearful eyes.

"Wait, I am only protecting you. I will tell you everything. Please don't hurt me. I am begging you," Yasmina pleaded.

"You have three seconds to tell me who you are working with and why you took those pictures. One, two…" Curtis began.

"I am working with you, only you," Yasmina moaned.

"Feed her to the fish," Trish prodded.

The two lifted the wrangling girl over the edge of the boat and dangled her legs over the side while she violently splashed the water. The swarm of sharks beneath her began to stir as she kicked the water.

"I would guess you have about a second to tell me something that would convince me to save your life. Now tell me what you have been up to, and we will pull you back in," Curtis demanded in a harsh voice.

Yasmina glanced down and was able to pull her legs up just as a ten-foot hammerhead slammed at her, hitting the back of the boat and leaving a large tooth imbedded there. She let out a long mournful scream and began to talk.

"It was not my idea. It was Trish. She wants to take your money," Yasmina yelled in a fearful tone.

Not convinced, the two then lowered her deeper into the water, up to her waist.

"Wrong answer. After all I have done for you. You are an ungrateful, conniving girl. Tell me the real reason you planned this thing. Are you working with the reporters?" Curtis shouted.

The sharks made a swirl in the water, and Yasmina felt a strong tugging on her legs. The clear water turned to a scarlet red below her. The two could barely hold on to her as the sharks grinded through her flesh and bones. Yasmina threw her head back and howled like a wounded animal.

"Now tell me while I can still save you," Curtis demanded in a shout.

Yasmina only had a blank stare on her face as he got closer to hear her reply. Once Curtis was within six inches of her face, her head snapped toward him. She spit blood directly in his eyes and said in a level tone, "I will see you in hell, you bastard."

Swiftly one of the largest sharks jumped up and pulled her torso from their grip. She disappeared into the water, and Curtis could still see her eyes wide open as she was pulled to the depths in the crystal clear waters. Intense bleeding finally obscured the view of her demise as if the curtain had fallen at the end of a play. The two backed away from the transom, and Curtis wiped his hands clean on his shirt.

The helicopter had been directly overhead while they tortured and killed Yasmina. The pilot and Chip had buried their heads deep in their laps when they first saw them holding Yasmina over the edge of the boat in the shark-infested water. Summer kept filming, with tears running down her face at seeing the lowest form of man and woman. She gagged several times and at the end only barely held the camera in position as Yasmina fought to keep the sharks from grabbing her legs.

"My God, is she okay?" Chip asked, knowing it was unlikely.

"You scum," Summer yelled, slamming her hand against the window of the helicopter.

Summer looked again into the lens and could see that Curtis and Trish must have heard the rotors from the helicopter. They both looked up, and she got a perfect identification shot of them while they were wiping the blood from their hands.

"Go back to land. We got what we came for," Summer stated into her microphone in a low voice.

The helicopter banked and swiftly flew back toward Andros, leaving sight of *Bubba's Baby.*

One of the three Intrepid fast boats pulled alongside of *Bubba's Baby,* and Trish Alcort climbed aboard. She was exhilarated after the grotesque killings.

Now she could make the trip with the nuclear bombs and assure their safe delivery to the desperate leaders. Trish did not care about the intent of the bombs, only hoping she would acquire considerable wealth and power through their delivery.

CHAPTER 29

▼

The helicopter roared low over the crystal water toward the airport. The trio knew Curtis Harrison and Trish had been aware of their presence in the helicopter when they killed the captain and Yasmina. These evil beings probably also suspected that photos were taken of their crimes.

Summer noticed the unmistakable white wakes of three powerboats leaving the harbor. The pilot turned to get a better view, and Summer was able to zoom in and film the boats as they made their way. Finally the helicopter landed at the airport, and the three looked toward Curtis Harrison's Jet Citation in disgust.

"We have to get a charter flight and follow those boats. If I can get film of them actually making delivery, we will have everything we need to nail Curtis's and Trish's coffins shut," Summer said excitedly.

Bahamas Executive Air operated a fleet of three Cessna 210s out of Andros. Summer and Chip arrived at the small office and asked the local lady about availability. Chip and Summer were able to acquire one of the planes and a pilot to leave within the hour.

The small plane shot off the runway, and they were over open water within minutes. Summer gave the pilot a rough idea of the direction the go-fast boats were last seen running. The plane followed the line from Andros, skirting down along the Cay Sal bank. Finally the pilot announced over the intercom that he could see the three go-fast boats. They were headed southwest and on their current track would make landfall at Varadero on the northern coast of Cuba. This location was a relatively short driving distance from Havana.

The plane flew low, and Summer was able to get close photos of the three boats using the telephoto lens. Flying from the Bahamas to Varadero was not unusual, since several commercial flights made the journey daily. Therefore the Cuban government was not alarmed by the small plane coming into its airspace.

Summer saw two larger vessels cruising down the Cuban coast toward the go-fast boats. She alerted Chip. The pilot circled the plane closer to the larger vessels. They were Cuban Coast Guard boats heading directly toward the trio of fast boats. Finally the two larger vessels came to a stop, and the three boats from Andros slowed down and tied alongside the gunships. After a matter of thirty minutes, the three smaller boats had been hoisted aboard the larger ships, which then steamed toward the Cuban island. There was no doubt that this was a planned operation. When the two ships entered the breakwater at Varadero, Summer instructed the pilot to land at the airport.

The pilot paid the Cuban customs agent enough money to make any clearance problems disappear. Summer and Chip grabbed the nearest taxi for the short trip to the harbor. They arrived just as the two ships carrying the three go-fast boats were tying to the docks. The sun was setting, and Summer attached her ultraviolet lens for night vision. A caravan of black limos stopped on the dock next to the ships. Men dressed in military fatigues and carrying automatic rifles exited the vehicles first and inspected the area. Summer carefully taped the activities. The men seemed to group tightly around one of the limos, and a man in army fatigues exited, followed by a man in Arab garb. Summer refocused her camera to reveal the identity of the men.

"My God," Summer blurted out. "You are not going to believe who this is meeting the boats. Fidel Castro is the one in the army clothing, and I am certain the man in the Arab clothing is Bin Laden."

Chip craned his neck to see the dark shadows on the dock. He pulled the camera from Summer and yelled at her, "Let me see."

Both of the men disappeared behind a group of soldiers keeping close quarters to protect them. Summer then trained the camera on the officer walking down the gangway, followed by three men carrying the aluminum suitcases with the nuclear logo. Summer was able to get a close shot of the cases being loaded into the trunk of the vehicle carrying Castro and the man thought to be Bin Laden. The doors were closed, and the stream of black vehicles disappeared into the twilight.

Summer and Chip summoned the taxi waiting for them and returned to the airport. The pilot was poised at the wing of their small plane while a worker finished fueling. They got into the plane, and Chip huddled around Summer. On the small screen attached to the video camera, Summer started the replay at the point where she had thought she saw Bin Laden with Castro.

"What do you think?" Summer asked Chip. "Here, I will pause it."

"I can see the man dressed in Arab garb, but his face is partially concealed," Chip offered.

"I am certain it was him. I have seen plenty of photos to know for sure," Summer said. "And we have enough on Harrison and Trish to put them away for life. The nuclear suitcases could be used against the U.S. if built into dirty bombs. I say we need to take what we have and notify whoever is in command of the U.S. Navy Base at Guantanamo."

"But can we trust them?" Chip asked.

"I agree that is a problem," Summer said, "but we have no choice. I don't know who is behind this operation, and we could be walking into a trap if we provide this evidence to the wrong person.

"I think the base commander has the most to lose," Summer continued. "If Castro and Bin Laden use their forces to overrun the base, then he and his troops would be slaughtered. The base commander is sitting on the bubble, and he is closest to where this is all going down. We have to take the chance, or the entire world could end up at war ninety miles from the United States."

The two nodded their heads in slow agreement, still worrying about the possible outcome. The pilot entered the cockpit, and Summer asked him to set course for Guantanamo. The plane lifted off the ground, and they followed the north coast around to the town of Baracoa. This was the closest they could land to get to the U.S. Naval Base. They took a taxi to the gate of the base, and the taxi driver threw gravel at their backs while making a hasty departure from the area. The ten-foot wire fencing with razor-sharp barbed wire seemed to extend forever. The entrance had two small structures barely large enough for one man. The shore-patrol guards on duty ran out, pointing their rifles at them after hearing the taxi speed away.

"Stop, or you will be shot on the spot," both soldiers ordered.

Summer and Chip raised their arms and were escorted onto the base.

"We need to see the base commander," Summer announced. "It is an urgent national-security issue."

They were placed in the back of a jeep with armed guards and taken to the base buildings. The guards frisked the intruders and escorted them into the reception area. Soon an officer appeared before them.

"Are you Americans?" the officer asked.

"Yes, we are Americans, and we have some vital information for the base commander," Chip answered for the two.

"I am sorry, my name is Commander Brown. I am in charge here. What could be so important at this hour?"

"I want to show you some video. We work with Associated Press and have some incredible information we feel you need at once," Summer explained.

The commander would have thrown them off base a long time ago except that seeing the beauty of Summer made him want her around longer. He did not see women of this caliber in Cuba very often. The commander escorted them into his office, and he comfortably put his hand on Summer's back to guide her along. Chip took a seat, and Summer walked around the commander's desk to show him the video on the camera screen. Several times, even the tough Commander had to look away. Finally he sat straight up in his chair and asked Summer to stop the tape.

"Is that Castro and Bin Laden?" the commander barked.

"We know it is Castro, and we agree that the Arab man is Osama Bin Laden," Summer responded truthfully.

"My Lord, when did you take these pictures?" the commander demanded.

"About two hours ago. They took delivery of nuclear materials we can see are contained in the suitcases," Summer explained.

The commander sat patiently as Summer detailed the connections, people, and devices that had brought them to his door. On occasion the commander would shake his head in disbelief, but he knew the video could speak for itself. Finally, when all the tape had been reviewed, the commander made a decision.

"We have to kick this upstairs and fast. If any of this is accurate, al-Qaeda and Cuba could have nuclear bombs built and delivered within a week. I am going to call the commander at NORTHCOM. I am sure he will assign assets at once, and I expect we will have some brass coming our way soon. Until then, I am going to have accommodations set up for you at the bachelors officer quarters. I will have multiple copies made of the tape. You two rest up. You will have a busy schedule in the next thirty-six hours," the commander promised.

Chip heard a knock on his door. He opened the door and saw Summer standing there dressed in one of the army-green T-shirts they had been issued. Even in the olive-colored shirt, she was a vision of beauty. The bottom edge of her white bikini panties showed slightly as she walked past him. Summer sat on the edge of the bed. Chip left the door open and positioned himself across from her.

"Chip, I have never been so relieved. I know Trish could have easily killed me, or you, if she were not so distracted with her own greed," Summer exclaimed.

Chip reached over and smoothed her long hair away from her eyes. "Summer, it is over now," he assured her. "We are safe."

"I pray they find them and the bombs before something like 9/11 happens."

"We have the right people working on it, and now it is out of our hands. You need to just relax and take a deep breath."

Summer pulled her hair back and took several deep breaths. She turned toward Chip and began to speak in a hesitant way. "Chip, I am not certain we can trust everyone in our own government. Not because anyone would want another 9/11, but because the bureaucracy cannot react quickly enough to imminent dangers. They probably will study the tape for weeks in nauseating detail. The attack could happen and be over before they can react."

"We have no other options," Chip said. "Trust me on this. We need to hand it off to the authorities."

"Chip, there are always other options. We have to do everything possible to make sure we get to the right people. I have a fear in the pit of my stomach. It's something I cannot explain, but I had the same feeling the day Jimmy was killed."

Chip felt she needed comforting and could not be restrained any longer. He placed his left hand on her cheek and turned her mouth toward his. They embraced as his tongue excitedly explored hers. His other hand began to pull at the T-shirt covering her perfect body. She stopped him and paused while looking into his eyes. Then she crossed her arms in front of her and pulled the shirt off over her head, revealing the most perfect breasts Chip had ever seen. His other hand began to violently pull at her bikinis while she undid his belt and unzipped his pants. She straddled him underneath her thighs, and they kissed each other randomly about as they melded together.

"Summer, I love you, my precious baby," Chip extolled in passion.

Summer heard the words she feared. She was enjoying his comfort and lovemaking but was not ready to commit to another. She had found herself and was not ready to give up her newfound independence.

The passion subsided as both met their ultimate pleasure. Summer got up and began to talk. "Chip, I am so sorry," she said. "It is just because of the things we have been through. I was overtaken by the moment."

"Shut up, Summer," Chip said while kissing her hard on the lips.

Summer got up naked and threw her arms around his neck and jumped up, wrapping her legs around his chiseled body.

Chip continued to hold Summer in that position, and while still kissing he carried her to the door and slammed it shut with his foot. A moment later a hand reached out of the crack in the door and a "Do Not Disturb" sign was placed on the handle.

CHAPTER 30

▼

The sound of reveille woke the pair. Chip leaned over to Summer and kissed her deeply with passion. Neither got much sleep, as they had awakened and made love again and again, seeming to be insatiable. They had also discussed the many issues surrounding their tape and the worrisome deeds it depicted. Suddenly they heard a pounding on their door.

"Sorry to disturb you, Mr. Murphy, but the CO is ready for you in the situation room," a male voice stated.

Summer scurried off the bed and began to gather her T-shirt and bra scattered about the room. Chip pulled on his pants and walked toward his lover.

"Did you happen to see a white pair of bikini underpants around here?" Summer playfully asked.

Chip pulled the front of his pants open and looked down. "Just old boxer shorts here."

Chip grabbed Summer again and they rolled onto the bed kissing. The pair was interrupted by another knock on the door.

"Yes, I am coming. It will be just a minute," Chip yelled.

"I need to speak to you. I have important information for you," the voice replied.

Chip straightened his pants and opened the door. Standing in front of him was a middle-eastern man holding an eight-by-ten manila envelope.

"Please let me come in," the man pleaded.

Chip looked back to make sure Summer was presentable, and he opened the door wider, letting this mysterious man into the room.

"My name is Tamer from Turkey. I work for the FBI, and I am an interpreter here interrogating the al-Qaeda prisoners. I have these documents obtained from the Taliban incarcerated here," the man explained.

"I don't understand. Why would you give us these documents?" Summer asked surprised.

"The documents are directly from al-Qaeda," the Turkish man said. "They indicate that a highly placed U.S. politician is involved with the dirty bombs. I have sent numerous translations to FBI headquarters, and nothing ever happens. I am hoping that since you are reporters this information coming from you will have greater weight within the government."

"Why do you think your translations of the al-Qaeda prisoners' confessions are not being utilized?" Summer questioned.

"The official excuse is lack of staff. In fact, I know my superior has deliberately destroyed some of my translations. The translation-department head is using this tragedy in an effort to get more funding and increase the size of the department. In the meantime, important intelligence is being purposely ignored," the man stated factually.

"This cannot be true. If what you are saying is accurate, then in an attempt to build a bureaucratic empire, some in the FBI are inadvertently aiding al-Qaeda," Summer stated harshly.

"I am happy you understand. This must be stopped." The strange visitor hastily made his departure when the sailor knocked on the door again.

The commander was at the head of the table in the situation room. In front of the conference center was a fifty-six-inch plasma TV. Seated around the table were his staff, an FBI operative, and two empty chairs. The commander turned to the sailor guarding the door.

"I thought you told me you woke Murphy and Summer. Where the hell are they, sailor?" the commander barked.

"Sir, I am sorry, but I did wake Mr. Murphy. Miss Tolly was not in her accommodations, so I thought she was on her way," the sailor responded.

There were sounds in the hallway of a female and a male talking. Summer and Chip entered the room, carrying the envelope they had just received.

"They are here, sir," the sailor proudly announced.

"I can see that, you numbskull," the commander snapped.

The commander turned toward the two as Chip pulled the chair out for Summer to sit.

"Happy you could make it. Sleep well?" the commander asked sarcastically.

"A restless night worrying about catching these criminals," Summer replied, irritating the seasoned navy officer.

Chip nodded in agreement as he grabbed for Summer's hand under the table. She pulled it away, giving him a look indicating he was being too presumptuous.

"Okay, let's get down to work," the commander stated without emotion. "I have had the tape duplicated, and we flew a copy to Washington during the night. We have a videoconference with the secretary of defense and the Joint Chiefs of Staff at O seven hundred. I expect the FBI director may also sit in, depending on their take of the video. Any questions before I place the call?"

"We have some additional information for the FBI," Summer said. "We have documents that seem to imply a top U.S. politician may be involved. We will interject this information during the call."

"Okay then, hold on to your seats. I think this could be a wild ride," he warned.

The plasma TV showed a conference room filled with people. The main conference table held the important personalities of the U.S. government as predicted by the commander. The secretary of defense tapped his coffee cup with a teaspoon and began the meeting.

"We have reviewed the tape provided to us at O one thirty hours by Commander Brown of Guantanamo Bay Base. Thank you, Commander Brown, for your prompt attention to getting us this vital information. Also, special thanks to Miss Tolly and her team that gathered the intelligence. You have acted beyond the call of duty and represent what is good in every American," the secretary congratulated.

"Excuse me, Mr. Secretary, please acknowledge the vital role played by my counterpart, Chip Murphy, who also risked his life for this information," Summer interrupted.

Both rooms were hushed, as all knew it to be a real "faus-paus" to interrupt the secretary.

"Yes, of course, Miss Tolly, I did not mean to leave anyone out."

A nervous laughter turned into a round of coughs, getting things back on track.

"As I was saying, this is an interesting piece of information. I concur with our experts that the suitcases could be used as dirty bombs. Terrorists could wreak havoc with our major cities with these types of devices. Second, I concur with our experts that Cuba and Bin Laden might be in cahoots. Finally, we see that a Mr. Curtis Harrison and an unidentified female were responsible for two deaths in the Bahamas. We consider this to be a Bahamas issue, and we will not intercede because it is out of our jurisdiction," the secretary concluded.

"Excuse me, Mr. Secretary. The woman in the photos is Trish Alcort. I have proof she killed others," Summer stated loudly.

"Yes, again my thanks to you, Miss Tolly. You need to understand that we at the Department of Defense do not investigate murders. We are looking at this thing from a national-defense perspective. I assure you that the murder investigations have been turned over to the appropriate authorities," the secretary answered, getting impatient.

"Now, I want to read a statement from our commander in chief to detail what we are doing with this new information."

The secretary began to read the prepared statement.

"Good morning, everyone, and a special thanks to the reporters who captured the interesting intelligence on tape. I have instructed the FBI to place an urgent worldwide Interpol notice for the capture of Curtis Harrison. It distressed me beyond words to think of the possibility of future terrorist acts upon the American people. Mr. Harrison will be captured shortly and brought to justice. The Marines have landed reinforcements at Guantanamo and will attempt to secure the suspected nuclear material before it can be developed into a destructive device. We have fortified our presence in the waters surrounding Cuba and have sent a force to secure the Straits of Florida. I hope to receive a positive report within hours describing our success at thwarting this danger. We have already begun to address the part Fidel Castro may have in this plot, and we will take decisive action once his complicity has been determined. Finally, we will make every effort to root out Osama Bin Laden and hopefully capture this murderous man. Again, my thanks to all involved, and when time permits I would like to personally meet you two fine Americans responsible for stopping this horrible plan. May God bless us all."

Summer and Chip looked at each other, realizing that with the president's message the meeting might be ending. Summer began to speak.

"Excuse me, sir. I want to bring to your attention that we have documents needing to be translated. The partial translation seems to indicate that a high-ranking U.S. politician is somehow involved with the delivery of the nuclear materials."

"Please have these documents forwarded to us at once," the FBI director said. "We will give it the highest priority to have the complete translation done immediately. Thank you again for your assistance."

The screen of the TV went blank, and everyone in the room, except Chip and Summer, began shaking hands, slapping backs, and congratulating each other. The commander finally realized that the two were left out.

"Listen, you two, again our thanks. I have been instructed to send you to the Naval Air Station in Key West, Florida. This is a precautionary procedure to make certain you are protected until we round up any threat from Harrison. We will be ready for your transport at O nine hundred."

Summer looked at Chip. "I think we were just sold a bunch of baloney," she said. "They do not believe what they have seen, and it sounds to me they are not going to do much of anything. I think the whole thing was only for show."

"Well, I guess we will have to see what they do. Anyway, there are worse places to hold up in other than Key West."

The meeting in DC did not end when the teleconferencing equipment was turned off. The secretary of defense had left the room with direct orders for the FBI director to figure out the next move.

"The reason for the dog and pony show was for the reporters," the FBI director explained. "The president agreed that you don't want to piss off the Associated Press. By the same token, he wanted to make sure we keep them under wraps till we can see if this story has any validity. Sending them to Key West will keep them busy and away from their word processors."

"When do you think the Translation Department at the FBI can translate the documents they are sending?" one of the joint chiefs asked.

"Speaking for the FBI, I don't see anything here that is of a national-security issue," the FBI director said. "The Translation Department is grossly overworked since 9/11. We need additional staff to handle the load. The best we can hope for on these new documents is several weeks. That is if we really consider them to be important enough to go to the top of the heap. All we have is Fidel Castro meeting with an Arab man, a video of aluminum briefcases, and a known drug dealer disposing of a body in Bahamian waters. The young girl providing the information does not have a clue for certain what she has witnessed. She is unreliable at best. All of this seems to be way outside our jurisdiction. Maybe the CIA would want to sniff around, but they probably will kick it over to DEA."

"Good idea. Let's do that. Kick it over to CIA on the covert-operations angle," the joint-chiefs member suggested.

"Consider it done."

Trish patiently waited for a call from Curtis Harrison for the next step of the plan. Three of the suitcases containing nuclear material had been successfully handed off to Fidel Castro and Osama Bin Laden. She now was waiting in the

Cuba customs office while the last Intrepid boat was being refueled for the trip to Miami. She was not pleased that she had been relegated to the task, but she understood the final phase of the operation required her firsthand oversight. Her cell phone rang.

"Hello, I hope this is who I think it is," Trish stated.

"Well, Miss Rhode Island, enjoying your Cuban holiday?" Curtis asked, expecting her ranting.

"I have seen better garbage dumps than this place," she replied. "I am anxious to get back to civilization."

"Well, then I have good news," Curtis said. "There is a small blimp called *Fat Albert* containing radar equipment located in the Florida Keys near Key West, and it tracks all the boat traffic within the Florida Straits. I have made arrangements for it to be disconnected from its tender, and therefore the radar disabled, within the next hour. You will then have a clear shot to Government Cut at Miami.

"The plan is to go to your father's waterfront home," Curtis continued, "or should I now say your home? Give the three men with you on the boat one thousand each in cash and send them on their way. Then call this number: 470-9547. That will put you directly in touch with my friend the mayor. He will meet you at your home, where the bombs are located on the boat you arrived in."

"Okay, I understand. Are you sure we can trust Mayor Lopez fully by giving him the two suitcases of nuclear material?" Trish asked.

"Without question. Just follow the plan, and everyone will be happy. Within the next twenty-four hours, you and our friend the mayor will have accomplished a huge victory," Curtis assured her.

"Well, I always wanted to be victorious, but I hope you have not forgotten about my payment," Trish answered.

"My goodness, you do cut to the chase. Yes, I have the money waiting to be transferred into your Swiss account once you pull this off. Then I thought we could take six months and travel. How does that sound?" Curtis asked.

"Sounds great. Think of me, and remember how well I fill out a bikini, Mr. Harrison. Give you any hints of where I want to vacation?" Trish asked in a sweet voice as she hung up the phone.

CHAPTER 31

▼

Summer and Chip spent the waiting time swimming, canoeing, and snorkeling
from the Naval Air Station Marina. They were anxious to see Key West, which
was only a stone's throw away, down Highway One. The Navy still endeavored
to keep them under wraps for their own protection, but more importantly in case
the Defense Department or the FBI had further questions. Also, the malicious
release of the spy and radar balloon, *Fat Albert*, concerned the brass. The
half-inch stainless-steel cable had been cut, and the small blimp carrying radar
equipment was adrift. Now the ninety miles of open ocean between the Florida
Keys and Cuba was wide open for drug smugglers. Additional patrols were
ordered, but they could not come close to the coverage a radar unit fifteen hundred feet in the air could offer. They considered the vandalism a prank by local
teens.

Chip had seen a navigation chart at the NAS Marina and had seen what
appeared to be old deepwater submarine pits. He thought it would be an adventure for him and Summer to kayak the short distance from the marina to the pits.
He also thought it would be romantic.

The evening sun began to dip below the thin lines of clouds in the west. The
ocean was painted pink and calm as Chip pulled the double kayak to the water's
edge. The shallow water of the Keys twinkled with the light evening breeze. Chip
looked up and could see Summer alternately walking and skipping toward him.
Her skin had become golden tan from the many idle days playing in the water
and was dramatically contrasted by her blond hair. Her charm exploded from her
smile, and Chip felt a warm glow envelope him as she grew near. Chip had asked

the commissary to pack a picnic, and he had wrestled a bottle of wine from the bartender at the Officers Club. Chip wanted everything perfect.

The two explorers paddled together under the bridge carrying traffic on the Overseas Highway. Occasionally they would coast for a few minutes while watching the brightly colored fish swim under their kayak. The water turned from a gin color to ink blue when they entered the submarine-pit area. The water had been deeply dug out by the Navy many years ago to hide submarines from enemy air photography. Chip steered the vessel quietly onto the secluded beach. The couple laid out a blanket, poured a glass of wine, and embraced, watching the setting sun.

"I have something for you, Summer," Chip said softly while reaching into his pocket.

Chip produced a golden four-leaf clover held securely on a golden chain.

"My God, Chip, that's Jimmy's. He never took it off, and I used to tease him by saying that when we married he would have to pass it along to me for my good luck," Summer explained as tears fill her eyes.

"I know what you told Jimmy. He confided to me that he intended to indeed give it to you as an engagement gift. He said that at that moment, if you were to say yes, he would have used up all his luck. Giving the clover to you would symbolize his good fortune. He told me he would be blessed by you and honored by your sharing your life with him. The day before he went with you to Afghanistan, he had me make two promises to him. First, if anything ever happened to him, I promised I would look after you. Second, no matter what happened, he wanted you to have this clover as a symbol of his love for you."

Summer began to weep silently as she played with the golden clover in her hand. Chip pulled himself to his knees and brushed her hair back from her face.

"I love you, Summer, and I want to be with you always. I have had a hard time dealing with Jimmy's loss and have resisted you because I thought it wrong to be with you. I put Jimmy's clover in my wallet the day we left for Afghanistan and forgot I even had it with me. The morning after we made love for the first time, I found it lying next to my wallet. I did not remove it, and I knew it must have been Jimmy's way of letting me know it was okay. Now I am convinced Jimmy wants us together."

Summer leaned back and realized that her fears were being fulfilled. She did love Chip and was comfortable that Jimmy would approve. The problem was that she was not ready for any commitment while there were so many unresolved issues.

"I admire you, Chip. I thank you for your help with finding Jimmy's murderer, but I just don't..."

"Don't say anything. Let me show you this," Chip interrupted.

He dug through the wicker basket and produced a candle. He lit it and placed it on a plate between him and Summer. In the twilight, Summer could see that placed on the candle was a bright shiny object. Suddenly she realized it was a diamond ring. She gasped and covered her mouth with one hand.

"Summer, the candle represents the light of Jimmy's soul that brought us together. Taking the diamond ring from the candle shows you that from my brother's soul he wants us to be together. Summer, if you marry me, the love we share will only enhance our memories of Jimmy."

Summer stood and walked to the water's edge, wishing that Chip had not put her in this predicament. He came up behind her and put his arms around her waist.

"What is it, Summer? What are you afraid of?" Chip asked in an understanding tone.

"I have relied on other people all my life. Every time I did, they were taken away from me. First my mother died, and then Jimmy. I have found through this process that I did not know myself. In fact, I was not even sure if I could do anything without Jimmy or some other man. I have found strength I never knew existed, and it is inside me. Today I need to explore the person I have never met, which is myself," Summer concluded.

"I understand and will not pressure you. When the time is right, we will know," Chip answered.

"When, or if, the time is ever right is something I will know," Summer replied.

Chip gathered the blanket and the other picnic items and loaded them into the kayak. They paddled back to the harbor slowly, without a word spoken, and went to their own rooms for the night.

Summer and Chip were summoned to the base commander's office. Summer felt they were again going to be asked to answer the same questions they had been fielding for the last four days.

"I have received a memo from the secretary of defense's office that I think you will be pleased to hear," the commander said. "They have received reports through Interpol that place Harrison back in the Middle East. They have not captured him, but intelligence indicates it is imminent. Our main concern has been for your safety. Knowing he is not in the United States, we feel comfortable releasing you from our protection. We do ask that you not travel outside the country until an arrest of this terrorist has been accomplished. With that said, are there any questions?"

"Does this mean I can go home?" Chip questioned in an upbeat mood.

"Yes, you can go home as soon as you can make the necessary arrangements. I have staff available to coordinate any travel plans you may have," the commander concluded.

Chip hugged Summer. "We did it," he said excitedly. "Two regular people have brought down the most intricate terrorist organization ever conceived by man. I am proud of you."

"I don't want to be negative, but what about the bombs and Trish Alcort, and do you really think they will get Curtis Harrison and Bin Laden?" Summer questioned.

"One thing at a time. We have to trust our government. Right now, all I know is that we can be free of all this drama. Let's enjoy it and ask questions later," Chip answered, trying to change the subject.

"Chip, I agree with you, and this whole ordeal has been physically and emotionally draining. The problem is, I must finish what I have started. It is not enough for me to turn everything over to the government and hope it will all get resolved. I am committed to assuring it gets the attention required," Summer said.

The two hugged and held on to each other, realizing the magnitude of what they faced. Summer finally began to pull away, and Chip pulled her back tightly.

"I told you I would help you in any way possible. What is our next move?" Chip asked without hesitation.

"I am suspicious about the radar, *Fat Albert*, being cut loose, disabling all security of the Florida Straits. The navy seemed to dismiss it as a prank, but having the nuclear devices in Cuba, what better way to get them to the U.S. than by boat in the open waters to Florida?" Summer asked with concern.

"I did not even think twice about the coincidence," Chip said. "You have a valid point."

"I say we go to Key West and dig up some information on why the intelligence radar was disabled and who did it," Summer suggested. "I think we will find it is somehow connected to the bombs."

Summer told the navy driver to take them to the southernmost city at once. There she hoped to find the connection to stop a possible deadly attack. She knew she had to try.

The Intrepid arrived at the dock outside the extravagant waterfront home in Miami that now belonged to Trish. She amused herself by thinking how she had accelerated her inheritance by killing her father. The home was over fifteen thousand square feet, with an elaborate waterfall cascading down to the pool. The interior was crafted using the finest Italian marble accenting the soaring ceilings over twenty feet tall. Trish paid her traveling companions, and they were on their way. The boat containing the bombs sat quietly bobbing at the dock behind her palace. She called the number Curtis had given her.

Mayor Lopez was expecting her call and was at her home within fifteen minutes. He was accompanied by four police cruisers, and the SWAT team was following close behind. The mayor and police were led to the sleek boat docked in Trish Alcort's backyard. The mayor called the local network affiliates, and their news trucks rolled in behind the caravan. Once the area was secured by SWAT, the news reporters were allowed to film the mayor going onto the boat, expecting to find a large cache of drugs or illegal aliens. Instead, the mayor emerged from the cabin of the boat carrying two aluminum cases with nuclear materials logos attached to their sides.

The film crews jockeyed for position, and one female reporter was inadvertently bumped into the canal. The cameras with their bright lights began to film the triumphant mayor and Trish Alcort as they held the cases before them. Due to the uncertainty of the cargo's contents, Hazmat professionals took control of the suitcases and secured them. Mayor Lopez and Trish Alcort sat down by the pool and began their interviews with the ravenous media.

CHAPTER 32

▼

Summer and Chip entered the lavish old-world lobby at the Casa Marina Hotel. Chip requested a single room. Summer interrupted, assuring that he realized their tryst and her refusal of his offer of marriage was sincere. Summer, although she loved Chip, did not want to encourage his interest at that time.

"Make that two rooms, and can I ask a question?" Summer interjected. "I am a reporter, and I would like to meet some military people. Where do they socialize?"

"The best place would be at a bar called Finnegan's Wake," the desk clerk replied. "The Navy and Coast Guard people normally meet there just after the sunset celebration at Mallory Square at about eight."

The Irish pub was packed with clean-shaven heads as the two entered at eight fifteen. Summer instructed Chip to sit on the other side of the bar so she could encourage some conversation. It did not take long for her plan to work.

"Hey, pretty lady, I haven't seen you around here before," a young Coast Guard man commented.

"If you are military, I will buy you a drink," Summer offered.

"Oh, you like a man in uniform? Next time we meet, I'll be sure to wear my whites," he replied.

The two had several drafts, and Summer was determined to stop the small talk and get down to the big question.

"Do you know anything about that radar thing they call *Fat Albert?*" she asked, playing dumb.

"Sure, it can see the entire Florida Straits. We use it to keep track of smugglers and drug dealers. Why you ask?"

"I saw it from the airplane when I was flying in one time, and the lady next to me said it was called *Fat Albert*, but she was not sure of the purpose. I understand it got loose?" Summer asked innocently.

"Yeah, they say some kids cut it loose, but I don't buy it. I worked on the thing, and the cable could not be cut without a welding torch. I say smugglers or drug runners cut the cable."

Summer confirmed her thesis. The removal of the "eye in the sky" meant only one thing to her. The bombs were going to be transported into the country by boat through the Florida Straits. She abruptly got up from her bar stool and proceeded to the other side where Chip was seated, staring into his beer. The young man called behind her, "Something I said?"

Summer grabbed Chip by the shoulder and was about to tell him her findings when she noticed something on the TV above the bar that caught her attention.

"Chip, look. Trish is on TV. I wonder if they caught her," Summer said excitedly.

Summer yelled for the bartender to turn up the volume, and he handed the remote to her.

She grabbed the remote and turned up the volume to overcome the sound of the noise in the bar.

"Mayor Lopez. How did you get the lead that a smuggler had arrived here in Miami?" the reporter questioned.

"Well, I take these things seriously, and I am a man of action. So when Miss Alcort called to report that a boat had docked at her house, I personally took charge of the investigation," the mayor answered.

The reporter asked the station to cut to the film clip showing the mayor and Trish recovering the cases.

"Mr. Mayor, do you know what is in the cases? We can see from the film they are marked as radioactive."

"I turned them over to Hazmat for their investigation, but from the looks of it, we think we have thwarted an attempt to smuggle nuclear materials into Miami. If it is true, then I think we have just witnessed the avoidance of a catastrophic event that could have exceeded the devastation of 9/11," the mayor boasted.

"Miss Alcort, how did you discover the smugglers?"

"I was reading a book on my veranda when I heard the sound of a high-powered boat coming. I could hear them speaking in Spanish, and they suddenly pulled to my dock and tied up quickly, and three men ran away into the night. I knew to immediately call the mayor's office because I know him to be a man of action and integrity. You can see the results. He single-handedly may have saved Miami or our nation from whatever these evil men intended," Trish stated in a convincing way.

Summer put her arms around Chip for comfort, seeing his eyes well up with tears.

"My God, Summer, what does all this mean?" Chip asked in a somber way.

"I suspect it means that Trish and Harrison are using the bombs as a ploy. Their plan could be to propel this mayor into national prominence. He could be the politician referred to in the documents we gave to the FBI. We were so convinced they were intending to use the bombs to cause destruction that we never considered the possibility of the ultimate publicity stunt," Summer spoke in a hushed voice.

"We have to notify the authorities. We cannot let her get away with this sham." Chip insisted.

"Who would you trust? They all promised us, from the top down, that they were following up on the leads we gave them. I doubt if they would do anything," Summer stated caustically.

"Then we have to trust ourselves. You are a reporter. If you can't make the government listen to you, then you go to the press. No politician wants bad press," Chip proclaimed.

"I'll call the ABC affiliate covering the story in Miami. I will offer them explosive news surrounding the event," Summer suggested.

"What could we possibly offer other than our word against a sitting mayor of a major city?" Chip questioned.

"How about our film showing the transfer of the cases and Trish Alcort killing Yasmina? I would think it would devastate her credibility, and they will listen to our story," Summer suggested.

"You are about to piss off some very powerful people and make some heads roll. You ready to take on the world, Miss Tolly?"

"I'll make the call," Summer stated without hesitation.

The mood at the FBI was close to panic. The director had just been notified that the aluminum cases did in fact contain active nuclear devices. That the discovery had been coordinated by the mayor of Miami made things even worse. Now, with a politician involved, the mayor's "spin doctors" would blow the hype surrounding the incident way out of proportion.

The president on down was on the chopping block for everyone's callous disregard of Summer's claims. The documents from the reporter were buried on someone's desk in the FBI Translation Department. The other evidence had been sent over to CIA, but little was done due to other priorities, and it was kicked over to the DEA. Now was the time for damage control.

The meeting of the Defense Department, CIA, FBI, and DEA was unprecedented. The president demanded a conference to discover how such an utter failure of intelligence could have happened. Every department director had instructed their staff members to work overtime and create documents to cover their own rear ends. The falsified reports flowed like the vapor from which they were created. Each produced "documented" proof that the intelligence had been passed along to another department. In other words, they all were blaming each other. The president finally spoke out of frustration.

"You guys sit here and blame each other for your own lack of professionalism. Now I have egg on my face. I can't think of a more embarrassing incident a president might have to endure. Hell, I would be happier if I were caught with my pants down on top of a young aide in the Oval Office. The coup de grâce is that the young punk independent mayor from Miami falls into the mess and comes out the hero. I would not doubt he is over filing his paperwork at the Federal Election Commission to run for president. I demand you all get together and make this thing go away. I don't want to hear anything more about that Cuban mayor. Understood?" the president yelled.

Summer hung up the phone after she talked with the news director at the ABC network affiliate in Miami.

"Well, what did they say? Do we have an interview?" Chip asked in excitement.

"No, we don't," Summer stated calmly.

"Why not? What happened?" Chip prodded her.

"The news director at ABC in Miami had another call he took, and he put me on hold. When he returned, he told me that the mayor of Miami and Trish are going to appear on the Oprah Winfrey Show. If we could convince her to show the tape as part of her interview with Trish, it would get national exposure. So I just hung up," Summer explained.

"Absolutely. If we could get to the producer, it would be earth shattering."

Summer and Chip cut their Key West trip short and were on the next plane to Chicago. Summer convinced the producer of the Oprah Winfrey Show that they would not be disappointed in the footage she had of Trish Alcort killing Yasmina. Also, they could show the footage of the whole incident involving the nuclear materials.

Summer and Chip arrived in the windy city that evening and met with the producer promptly. Summer reviewed the film, and the producer agreed that it was devastating to Trish Alcort. The producer stopped short of believing that the entire incident was designed to enhance the Miami mayor's political career. However, in good journalistic fashion, they agreed that something was just not right and that Oprah springing it on her guests the next day should answer some questions.

Trish Alcort and Mayor Lopez were in make-up, preparing for their segment to be shown during the first time slot. The ABC affiliate in Miami was prepared for the feed to show Trish Alcort and Mayor Lopez finding the suitcases aboard the fast Intrepid boat at Trish's Miami home. Also, the ATF spokeswoman was standing by on a feed from Washington to confirm that the devices were indeed nuclear dirty bombs. Several members of the Intelligence Committee of Congress were arranged to discuss the possible connections of the bombs to al-Qaeda and Osama Bin Laden. Summer and Chip stayed in the control room until Trish and the mayor were escorted on stage. Once they were seated, Summer and Chip planned to stand just offstage as their overwhelming film was being shown.

The mayor and Trish were seated in two comfortable chairs in front of the Oprah logo on the set. Oprah sat in the other chair, ready to do the on-camera interview. The director gave Oprah the countdown bringing the show back from commercial break. The interview began.

"Today we have Mayor Lopez of Miami and Trish Alcort, the former Miss Rhode Island," Oprah said. "In a heroic turn of events, the two are credited with thwarting the most recent and deadliest terrorist plot yet. They discovered and took control of what the ATF has described as nuclear dirty bombs. These bombs are capable of blowing up literally city blocks. Good morning to you both, and thank you for being with us today."

"Pleasure to be here, Miss Winfrey," the mayor replied.

"Oprah, Mr. Mayor. Miss Winfrey sounds like my mother," Oprah teased.

"Okay, Oprah," the mayor corrected.

"We have some film showing the recovery that I would like to run before we talk. Could we roll it please? And you both can view it on the TV we have set up just over your shoulder. If you could tell us what you were thinking and doing during the film, it would help us to understand your feelings," Oprah instructed.

The film began to roll, and the mayor gave a description of the events as they were unfolding. He gave Trish credit for reporting the suspicious boat, and he acted as humble as his large ego would allow. Trish was taking full advantage of the camera and kept her beauty-queen smile going nonstop. Summer stood off-stage, just to the right of the main camera, and Chip was positioned behind with his hands on her shoulders.

The mayor suddenly stopped his dialogue, confused by the film footage now being played. He saw Trish on a boat helping a man hold a young woman just over the side. Suddenly it hit him what he was witnessing. Trish noticed the horrid look on Oprah's face and relinquished her camera time to look at the monitor behind her. She could see that it was a complete video of her and Curtis killing Yasmina. The gasps from the stagehands and audience were picked up on every microphone.

Trish Alcort rose to her feet and scanned the stage area looking for an escape. Suddenly her eyes met Summer's, and she knew immediately who had supplied this horrible film to discredit her success. Trish reached into the pocket of her tailored blazer and quickly produced the chrome revolver.

Bang. Bang.

The crew hit the floor as the mayor instinctively jumped up and grabbed Trish's hand holding the gun. He wrestled the gun from her and restrained her in her seat. Oprah gathered her composure as other stagehands came to help the mayor hold Trish down.

"Let's go to break, and when we come back, I hope we have things settled down," Oprah said, catching her breath.

In all the excitement, no one noticed the young man heaped on top of Summer, sobbing. Chip was holding Summer, and in overwhelming emotion he could not yell out for help. Oprah suddenly realized that the young blond girl had been shot. She had the presence of mind to call out for any doctor that happened to be in the audience. A female medical student from the third row ran to Summer.

The medical student could tell the wound was critical and hollered to have someone call 9-1-1. Chip was separated from Summer as the young woman began placing compresses to Summer's chest, attempting to stop the massive bleeding. Oprah helped supply the clean towels she was using and asked, "How is she doing?"

"She's bleeding out," the young woman said with a grim expression. "I am barely getting a pulse, and I think her chest is filling with blood causing her lungs to collapse and be unable to breath. I'll be honest, I don't think she will make it to the hospital."

CHAPTER 33

▼

The two men used their familiar meeting place. Much had happened since they had last met in their secret hiding place in Kabul. Curtis Harrison had been lying low, keeping himself a step ahead of Interpol. On the other hand, his business partner was enjoying tremendous admiration and success. Mayor Lopez entered the room, and they embraced as normal.

"Well, Mr. Mayor, you have become a national hero in the United States," Curtis began.

"Yes, and it is all thanks to you and your plan," the mayor replied.

"It has been a great plan. The country is enthralled with your bravery and insight in saving them from nuclear attack. And grabbing the gun from Trish Alcort on national TV could not have been staged any better. Not only are you perceived as a hero, but you were able to show it to the whole world. Our plans for your advancement in the political arena are under way. We have used the wisdom of the young lion, and everything is falling into place," Curtis bragged.

"I am still concerned considering all our success," the mayor said. "Will Trish Alcort talk and bring us down?

"I had a conversation with Trish before she entered the mental ward at the hospital. I advised her that she should act insane if she wanted to ever get out. I also promised that the money would be waiting for her upon her release. She agreed and ever since has been prancing around the hallways of the hospital with a towel over her shoulders, pretending she is Miss America. I am sure they bought it because of her background," Curtis described.

"My friend, you seem sad or distracted when you talk about Miss Alcort. Is there a problem?" the mayor asked in a concerned voice.

"I am certain I can trust you with the information I am about to divulge. I must ask for the strictest confidence. If this information were to be heard by others, it would devastate me," Curtis said in a worried tone.

"What could possibly take the glee from this happy occasion, my friend?"

"When I returned home to Kabul, I had my servants remove Trish Alcort's belongings from her room to be boxed and stored. They came to me, and I rummaged through her things to make sure there was not anything of a confidential nature. Upon my review, I came across some shocking materials," Curtis described grimly.

"What did you find? Some evidence of espionage?"

"No, worse than spying. I found a medical report for Trish, indicating that she is in the advanced stages of the dreadful AIDS disease. I confirmed it by finding a multitude of prescriptions used to treat the disease with her name on the bottles," Curtis said, holding his head low.

"Poor soul. She will die incarcerated with that terrible affliction," The mayor said in sympathy.

"You don't understand. I have not been able to sleep, eat, or function since the discovery. You see, my friend, we were intimate on many occasions and without protection," Curtis relayed sadly.

"Have you been tested? Are you infected?"

"I have been tested, and although I am negative now, the doctor told me it could be as much as ten years before the test would confirm any exposure. I don't know if I can live with this horrible thing hanging over my head," Curtis stated and bowed his head.

"Think positive. They are finding cures every day. I know you will be alright," the mayor stated positively.

"I agree, my friend. I can only hope for the best."

"Now it is on to my future and the future of our business. I know Osama and Fidel are very pleased. We have great things ahead of us, my friend," the mayor concluded.

As the two parted ways, Curtis Harrison could tell that his long-time friend and associate was hesitant to embrace as they had always done. Curtis thought to himself that being publicly exposed as having the terrible AIDS affliction would be a fate worse than death. He would become a modern-day leper.

Trish Alcort sat in the activities room located in the mental-health wing of the hospital. She looked blankly at the TV screen as she adjusted the towel draped around her shoulders. The act of convincing her keepers that she was insane was taking its toll. When staff was in the area, she would prance about, humming the Miss America tune.

The TV announcer began the daily news.

"The FBI has reopened the investigation into the purported suicide of James Alcort at the Colonnade Hotel in Boston last month. After reexamining the autopsy report, officials agreed that the bullet removed from his skull, not falling fourteen floors, was the primary cause of death. Ballistics experts compared the bullet from him to the one removed from Summer Tolly's chest in the bizarre shooting filmed live on the Oprah Winfrey Show. They have determined that the bullets were fired from the same gun. Trish Alcort, daughter of slain James Alcort, has been held in a criminal mental facility in Chicago since firing the shot on the popular talk program. The FBI now suspects she was responsible for both shootings.

"In a related story, Summer Tolly continues in a coma at Northwestern Memorial Hospital after being shot during the Oprah Winfrey program. It was reported that she lost nearly sixty percent of her blood due to the injury. Doctors sadly stated that if she is fortunate enough to recover from her injuries, she would remain in a vegetative state."

Trish's fear of being connected to her father's death turned to a broad smile when she heard of Summer's demise.

"That bitch deserved what she got. Now I just have to hang in there, and Curtis Harrison will get me out. The money he is holding for me will assure that I am set for life," Trish mumbled to herself.

The rain drizzled down as the young man knelt in the muddy sod with his hand on the tombstone. His fingers clenched the cold stone as his emotions overtook his body. Chip Murphy was not dealing with his recent losses too well, and he spent numerous hours talking to the person buried six feet below. His tears mixed with the rain and slowly fell off his cheeks.

Chip heard a sound behind him and hesitated turning until he could wipe the embarrassing tears from his eyes. He glanced over his shoulder, shielding his face from the intruder. The young woman struggled to steady the wheelchair as she rose to her feet.

"Chip, I knew you would be here at Jimmy's grave."

Chip looked up and saw Summer standing above him as if in a dream. He wiped his eyes hard, thinking he must be hallucinating. He extended his hand toward her, and she grasped it firmly.

"Chip, I am okay. I woke up, and I was told you have been by my side day and night," Summer said, pulling Chip toward her.

The two kissed and embraced. Tears flowed freely from both their eyes. Chip continued to thank God profusely for his fortune of having Summer back. Summer separated from him while still holding on to his arms for support.

"We have so much to do. There are still three bombs missing, Curtis Harrison and Bin Laden to find, and the pictures of the abuse at the prison in Kabul need be revealed," Summer rattled off.

Chip took his finger and softly put it over her mouth. "Now is not the time for this," he said. "You need to get well and stronger before you save the world."

Summer pulled an airline ticket jacket from her pocket and handed it to him. Chip took the envelope and began to speak. "I am telling you, Summer, you are not going to chase around the world till you are better. You know that…"

"Shut up, Mr. Murphy, and read the tickets," she teased.

"Tickets to Chicago and Washington DC?" Chip asked, perplexed.

"I need to confront Trish directly, or I will never have peace again. The final stop in Washington DC, is because the president has asked me to accept a new position, Special Investigator of Intelligence Agencies. He called me this morning. Finally, I think someone is listening," Summer explained.

"I am so happy for you, Summer. Your tenacity has made the difference. You are not the shy little girl I remember from South Boston. You are now a world leader," Chip congratulated.

Summer entered the criminal mental facility where Trish was being held. The memories of her confinement in institutions flooded back to her. She was happy to see her new friend from the FBI waiting for her at the entrance. Agent Angie Williams was placed in charge of reopening the investigation into James Alcort's murder.

The female agent carefully pinned the listening device to Summer's bra and made sure it was totally camouflaged. The agent then handed Summer a folder to use when meeting with Trish Alcort.

"I will be behind the two-way glass," the agent said. "If anything happens, just scream, and I will be on top of her in two seconds. Remember, Summer, I need to get her on tape confessing to her father's murder. The other crimes are out of my jurisdiction."

Summer entered the small room and could see Trish's back as she sat at a small table. Trish had a towel wrapped around her shoulders and was rocking in her seat while humming some tune. Summer walked around the end of the table and sat directly in front of Trish. Trish mouthed the words so no one else could hear, "You rotten bitch."

"Well, I see you remember me, Trish. It is so nice of you, and thanks for the warm welcome. Of course last time we met, you shot me, so I guess this is a bit more pleasant."

Trish did not answer and used her eyes to tell the story. The hate from her green eyes reminded Summer of the child in the movie *The Exorcist.*

"If you don't want to talk, you don't have to. I am here to show you that I am fine and to ask you a couple of questions for old time's sake. I want to talk about how you killed your father."

The agent behind the glass began wringing her hands. She felt Summer was being too direct and that Trish would not open up at all.

"I know you killed your father. The FBI knows because they have matched the bullets from my chest and your father's head," Summer said.

"They can't tie me to the gun in my father's case. Anyone could have been in that hotel room and shot him. I ended up with the gun that shot you, and it proves nothing. By the way, I am sorry I missed your pretty little head. The FBI has nothing other than an attempted murder case on me for shooting you. I am insane, so I will be out in a year," Trish stated in a sarcastic tone.

Summer reached into the envelope the FBI agent had provided her and pulled out some pictures. "Look at the picture I have of the pair of shoes. They are custom designed Franco Sarto shoes," Summer detailed.

"Yes, I like them, and I can tell they are not yours because they are way too classy for white trash. Why are you showing me these shoes? Are you going shopping for me, Summer?"

"Recognize them? They were found in the suite at the hotel where your father was killed. Since your father did not wear women's shoes, it had to be a female. They are your size, Trish," Summer taunted.

"I am sure there are a million women my size. If this is what the FBI has on me, then I will be out in six months," Trish bragged.

Summer carefully thumbed through the other photos and found one she placed on top. It was a close-up of the insole of the shoes showing a nine-digit number.

"Here we go. See, the shoes have numbers on the inside here. The thing you may not know is that any custom shoes made by Franco Sarto have a serial number. The FBI checked, and guess who these shoes, found at your father's murder, belong to," Summer asked precisely.

Trish was silent, trying to register everything she was hearing in her mind.

"Well, since the cat's got your tongue, I'll help you. They were custom made for a Miss Trish Alcort. Gee, I think we have a winner. You just won a one-way ticket to life in prison."

Trish jumped to her feet and lunged across the table at Summer while yelling, "I did kill the old bastard, and you are next."

The door burst open, and Agent Williams was on top of Trish within seconds, as promised. She handcuffed Trish and pulled her struggling to her feet as she read the Miranda rights to her.

"Trish Alcort, you are under arrest for the murder of your father, James Alcort. You will be transferred to the women's prison in Framingham, Massachusetts," Agent Williams explained.

Trish looked toward Summer as she was being escorted out of the room.

"You think you have won. I have connections guaranteed to get me off the hook. Then I will come for you if it is the last thing I do," Trish spewed at Summer.

"Trish, I feel sorry for you. The hate you have in your heart will eat you alive. I will see you again, but only to testify against you at your trial. When you are convicted, I will close this chapter of my life and forget you forever."

"You bitch, how dare you feel sorry for me? I have important friends that are certain to come rescue me," Trish yelled.

"By the way, the president has appointed me Special Investigator of Intelligence Agencies. In my new role, I will be focusing on getting your so-called friends behind bars with you. You have no one, and you are nothing but a hateful, empty young woman who will grow old in prison," Summer concluded.

Agent Williams pulled and prodded Trish to the waiting vehicle for her trip back east. Summer looked at her nemesis and was startled by the contrast between Trish on the runway at Atlantic City and her now, being dragged to her final demise.

CHAPTER 34

▼

The Rose Garden ceremony began exactly at ten in the morning. Chip was seated in the front row next to the first lady. Summer was positioned behind the podium next to several Secret Service agents. The marine band began to play "Pomp and Circumstance" as the president strolled in to begin his speech.

"Ladies and gentlemen. Today we are here to honor an American hero. Summer Tolly's heroic finding of the plot to smuggle nuclear bombs into the United States saved many lives. Summer has the strength of a warrior, the beauty of a delicate flower, and the persistence of the Washington press pool. Already we have been able to find and prosecute individuals responsible for heinous crimes as a direct result of her discoveries.

Today I am announcing the creation of a new cabinet-level position, Special Investigator of Intelligence Agencies. The role of the individual is to coordinate information exchange between our many agencies, and more importantly to keep me informed as to any difficulties. What better person to be in this position than Summer Tolly. Through her work she has uncovered numerous circumstances where communication and responsibilities between our intelligence people were less than desirable. I now want to bring Summer to the podium so I can congratulate her and make certain she will accept this important assignment."

Summer stepped up to the speaking stand and shook the president's hand in acceptance. The photojournalists asked for several pauses so they could get their ideal shot. Summer noticed the ceremony was about to end and leaned toward the microphone.

"Mr. President, can I say a few words?" Summer asked.

The president was surprised, and his aides began to whisper in his ear. Finally he made a gesture with his hand, showing it was fine to proceed.

"Thank you, Mr. President, for your confidence in choosing me for the position. I assure you I will do everything in my power to guarantee our intelligence operations are beyond reproach. In the coming weeks, I will expose the bureaucrats and politicians causing our people to be placed in jeopardy. I have seen firsthand the buck-passing ways of our agencies and the relentless activities to cover their own asses. The abuses I have witnessed and documented by our military in foreign prisons will be exposed. The corrupt politicians will be brought to justice. We know al-Qaeda and Osama Bin Laden are our enemies. What we need to learn is that our most fierce enemy could be the bureaucracy that allows zealots to exist. Some have implied that my appointment is a sham and a way to shut me up. The reality is that I have never been more committed to uncovering all of the abuses I have found or will discover. So, Mr. President, I accept the position with the clear understanding here today before the American people that I am not the weak little orphan girl from South Boston, but a mature woman dedicated to a cause bigger than any of us as individuals."

The president produced a weak smile wondering what he had gotten himself into, while Chip stood with the others gathered and gave Summer the standing ovation she so richly deserved.

0-595-33623-X

Printed in the United States
25901LVS00003B/42

9 780595 336234